Chris
Cou
aro ~ ~ Breathe it & Believe it!

THE 440 TRAIN
A NOVEL

Blessings!
Linda &

THE 440 TRAIN
A NOVEL

Linda Colucci

GODCHILDREN PUBLISHING
2011

Published by
Godchildren Publishing
"Where the Sage is free to play"
15021 Ventura Blvd. #551
Sherman Oaks, CA 91403

The 440 Train is a work of fiction. While, as in all fiction, the literary perceptions and insights are based on experience, all names, characters, places, and incidents are either products of the author's imagination or are used fictitiously. No reference to any real persons, living or dead, is intended or should be inferred.

Library of Congress Cataloging-in-Publication Data
Colucci, Linda.
    The 440 Train: a novel / by Linda Colucci — 1st ed.

ISBN-978-0-98377373-3

This book is dedicated to
CHAMP

who can read the map to my soul

ACKNOWLEDGMENTS

I thank you, love you, bless you, and am grateful for:

My Mom and Dad whose support, unconditional love and ancestral talents helped birth this novel.

Dennis, my husband, who has been a beacon of light welcoming and encouraging my creativity for twenty-seven years, and has always loved me just as I am.

Every beautiful woman in my life whose strengths, vulnerabilities, intuitiveness and powerful peaceful hearts inspired me to write a story that dances between fact and fiction. *Yes, I'm talking about you*!

My fantastic, fun family, both blood and through marriages.

My two handsome brothers whose respect and friendship go far beyond the bloodline. I love you, Bros!

All the men in my life who help balance the male and female energy we share.

The magical world of the 'Unseen' for without your guidance I wouldn't be who I am today.

The Animal Totems who help keep me grounded.

My God Children who entrust me as their spiritual mother. Wisely and humbly teaching me so much.

All my Four-Legged Children, whose physical touch in the "here and now" is rooted and pure.

And for those in Spirit whose illumination soothes me with eternal love.

With gratitude, admiration and humility, I thank:

Barbara Childs and Del Golden who cheered the birth of this book.

Sean McKenna and Mike Austin from X-site Media, whose friendly computer wiz talents permit me to write with ease (and updated software).

Danielle Hoon and Scott Pitters from Pulp Art Surfaces, for your eclectic marketing ideas.

All the people who have proofread versions of this book and honestly gave me their opinions, especially Valerie Riccardi, who continually encouraged me to dig deeper.

Phoebe Sharp, a.k.a 'Eagle Eyes,' an avid reader, subtle teacher and family friend for three decades.

Maria Crudele-Vietmeier who answered my prayer with your gift of insight and knowledge, causing a blessed domino effect on the finishing touches. Gracie Bella!

Barbara Schiffman, a skilled editor, gifted writer, and wise soul who edited this novel with a supportive and steadfast pen. As if like a crystal tumbler, she smoothed the rough edges and brought out the shine keeping the integrity of the original piece. Then guided me to Connie. Wow!

Connie Kudura for gently and professionally text/formatting the manuscript into a dazzlingly clean tangible form. And introducing me to Monte.

Monte Farris, whose graphic art expertise and perception highlight the book cover simply yet profoundly.

Kim McElroy for the outstanding book cover you painted. Your magical meditative connection and gifted hand brought 'Her' from the Invisible world to the Visible. Stunning!

Coming full circle to my Dad, whose heart-felt sketches complement and hold the energy of each chapter break and poem throughout the book. And Mom who showed me at a very young age that reading a book can open a door to self-discovery.

Mother/Father God. I Love You in all ways, Always.
Mother Earth, you are my Heart.

THE 440 TRAIN

A NOVEL

THE BOOK CLUB

IT WAS WEDNESDAY EVENING. The book club was to start soon. I was expecting eight women for the gathering. I gifted a copy of the book for each gal, placing it into an artsy, recycled gift bag.

In the late morning, several of them had called to say they couldn't make it. I was a tad disappointed but have learned over the years that "stuff happens." I believe what is supposed to be will be. *Acceptance* is one of my great "forty-something-year-old" revelations.

By late afternoon a few more women had phoned to say they couldn't make it either. The only ones who hadn't called by then were my newly found friends, Lucinda, Maddie, and Bea. It was a sign: *it was to be just the four of us.* The fact that they were the only ones coming now confirmed my suspicions about the interesting way we had met and bonded straight away.

After a long meditation I decided I would reveal my intuitive feelings about our unique connection and its association with the book we were about to begin reading. I was prepared for whatever would happen after making that revelation, knowing it would either make or break our novel new friendship. I had a feeling the night would be full of surprises and prove the Universe does indeed work in mysterious ways.

I could barely compose myself as I anticipated revealing my theory to them and seeing their reactions. I slipped into a pair of washed-out jeans and chose a black tee-shirt with "Peace on Earth" woven across the front. I ran my hands through my choppy-cut, medium length, brown hair, then put on a dash of eyeliner and mascara, making my brown eyes pop.

I set out light refreshments: red and white wine, crackers, shaved cheese, fruit, a salad topped off with toasted nuts, and chilled water from a stream near a volcano. The house was warm and inviting. I lit a few candles and chose harp music to play quietly in the background.

When the doorbell rang, my dogs barked frantically and rushed to the door, nearly taking me down in a race to greet the callers.

"Hi, howdy, hello!" sang Lucinda, Maddie and Bea.

"Hi! Welcome to our home, come in!" I replied while calming the dogs.

"Hello, babies," Maddie said, rubbing each dog's head. Her smooth, bronze, Filipino skin and cropped jet-black hair highlighted her million-dollar smile. She was petite like me, but looked and moved like a tomboy.

"Did you girls carpool?" I asked.

"We sure did," Bea said, gently shooing our male dog's snout from under her skirt which hugged her tiny waist and shapely bottom. Her hair was golden and wavy, her eyes hazel and flirty, and her voice soft-spoken with a Southern twang.

"Wonderful," I smiled. "I'm glad you're environmentally conscious and I'm so glad you're all here." I scooted the pooches to another room and showed the girls around the house.

"Is anyone else coming?" Lucinda wanted to know.

"Nope. Just us four."

Some might mistake Lucinda for the infamous "Barbie Doll" tall, slender, make-up perfectly applied, bright big blue eyes, caring smile and tiny tight buttocks. But underneath the pretty package I sensed her authenticity.

Everyone was hungry so we helped ourselves to refreshments, then crossed to the living room. Interestingly, we sat ourselves down in a circle like a beautiful human mandala.

For the first half hour we munched and unwound, getting to know each other a bit more. Sharing casual information about our careers and hobbies, it was as if we'd been friends for years. Just as I did on the day we recently met on the beach in Malibu, I thought; *we must have known each other in another lifetime!*

"I'd like to make a toast," Lucinda announced firmly. "To new friends. May we be blessed with good health and prosperity—to four, forty-something women!"

"To four, forty-something women!" we echoed.

As the words left my lips, my soul smiled. *Wait till they see the book*, I thought.

Maddie looked at the gift bags on the table. "Go ahead, take one. It's for you," I urged.

She reached into a bag and pulled out the book. "So this is the book we're reading?"

Bea took a sip of wine as she reached into her bag. "Thank you," she puckered, looking over the book. "Hmm, 'The Four-Forty Train'!"

I was getting excited; soon my theory would be revealed.

"Thanks, this is very generous of you. 'The Four-Forty Train'." Lucinda furrowed her brow, also looking at the cover.

"Uh-huh, 'The Four-Forty Train'," I said, crossing my legs Indian-style.

"The title sounds familiar." Bea shook her head. "I know I've seen this somewhere."

"I'm thinking the same thing," Maddie said, skimming through the pages.

Lucinda splashed more water into her glass. "I feel I have too."

"Wait! I know! You just toasted us as four, forty-something women!" Maddie noted.

"Oh, my gosh! That's an unexpected coincidence!" Lucinda nodded, looking at each of us.

My eyes were wide, watching their expressions. Be patient, I silently told myself. After all, the particular set of circumstances that brought each one of us here is a story within itself. We're four stories that deserve to be told, because it's all about the journey ... isn't it?

My Past

ONE LONELY AND DESPERATE NIGHT, I sat on the side of the tub in the bathroom and prayed for guidance. The pain I endured crept as slowly as a blue heron preying on its next meal. I was done digging. The hole was deep enough. I needed a miracle.

I'm not exactly sure how long I was locked in the room, praying and pleading, when I heard what sounded like God's voice: "Stand, Marlo. Look into the mirror. Look at yourself."

I did. I knew what was coming would be scary, but it was my prayer being answered. This had also happened a few earlier times in my life when I felt lost and prayed for help.

The room was dark except for a bluish beam of light shining through the window from the full moon. I looked into the mirror. For several minutes I looked at my face, then past it, deep into my being.

My face darkened. It moved up, down, to the left, and the right. I thought I saw someone else looking back. Blinking, I shook my head and began crying. I wiped the tears, then stared deeper into my eyes. I couldn't move.

Then my soul spoke to me. It told me to remember who I was and why I was here. It said I had gambled enough with my life. I was laying on the tracks, waiting to be run over. Now was the time to move, while I still could…

MALIBU, CA. – PRESENT DAY

GLANCING AT MY EYES in the visor-mirror, I suddenly shuddered, remembering that day when God told me to look in the mirror. I'm not sure why I had such a strong recall after all these years. Maybe the song playing on the radio triggered the feeling or perhaps it was simply a "thank you" coming from my soul for changing the path I had been traveling on. Whatever it was, I'm glad it passed. In fact, I'm glad it *was* my past and I'm truly grateful to be right where I am now.

As Thomas and I pulled into the Malibu Beach parking lot, the sun shone brightly on the Pacific Ocean. I rolled down the window. The force from the wind and sound of the waves were invigorating.

"Ummm … smells good." I took in the lingering scent of salt water and crisp air.

We got out of the car and stood looking at the ocean in appreciation. Behind designer sunglasses, my eyes adjusted to the glittering brightness of the shoreline where millions of tiny sun-beamed crystals danced on the water's surface.

"Do you see any of your friends?" I asked.

"Nope, not yet. We're the first ones here, and we will be for awhile," Thomas said, grinning.

"Why? What do ya mean?" I asked inquisitively.

He kissed me gently, then smiled. "I thought we could enjoy some time alone here."

"Sounds good to me—I'd actually like to do some more writing for the greeting card line while it's nice and quiet."

"See, don't I always know what my girl needs?"

"Yes you do, Thomas, you're a true romantic."

I watched my handsome, rock-n-roll-stylish man as he walked towards the water with the wind sweeping through his long, wavy, brown hair. His fair skin was already turning golden with an early summer tan. He was wearing a skin-tight, blue tee-shirt that defined his chiseled muscles above tattered denim shorts, which enhanced his manly body. After a decade together, we could still turn each other on in a heartbeat and make each other blush.

I stopped admiring the man I love and started to unload the car. He continued to scout a location for our set-up as a few people walking their dogs passed by. Fortunately, the beach wasn't crowded.

"Let's go over there, near those big rocks."

I looked to where he was pointing. "Oh, yeah, I love the rocks."

"It's pretty amazing to think they've been here for millions of years," he said.

"It sure is." My mind drifted to a faraway time when dinosaurs roamed the earth and whales inhabited the land as well as the sea. The squawk of a boisterous seagull snapped me back to the present moment.

"Marlo, please give a hand here!"

"You think we can take all this stuff in one trip?" I wondered.

"Heck yeah, you ate your fruit and grains today, didn't you?"

"Uh-huh." I made a muscle with my right arm. He nodded, impressed.

We loaded up and walked along the shoreline. It was a good hike. When we finally reached the rocks, I didn't waste a moment before dropping the heavy gear.

"I can't believe we've never been to this spot before," I said.

"It's a real treasure, isn't it?" he replied, pleased. I just smiled.

Thomas dug a deep hole in the sand for the umbrella while I spread out a blanket and unfolded a low beach chair. When I finished setting up camp, I stood in silence just watching the waves, feeling their mist, and inhaling the breeze. My breath slowed. I felt calmer, regenerated once again by Nature. It reminded me of my peaceful mountain days in Jersey and the journey that brought me to this day and this place…

"Connection"

*Now my hopes
and dreams
are closer than they seem
with you by my side.
Walk with me on the
journey of life.*

My Past

MY NAME IS MARLO. I'm five feet two inches tall on a windy day, but feel much taller. I smile a lot, love dogs and have a heartfelt kinship with all animals. I also have a soft spot for elders and children.

I'm close to my family and honor the bloodline theory. This makes me especially protective of the ones I love if someone crosses them. Our family gatherings are treasured times and our delicious home-cooked Italian meals are five-star with a dash of dirty four letter words.

I've always been in tune with the "little voice" inside me and rely on my gut instincts. I consider it a gift I cherish immensely. I'm also mesmerized by rainbows which trigger a "happy dance" in my spirit and my body. Rocks also intrigue me and I believe that their age and particular formations "speak," giving us important messages about the past, present and future.

I learned these things by aligning with Nature. When I'm calm in her company, words or feelings come into my being along with a sense of understanding and truth for "what is." Oneness is achieved by connecting to the God-like essence and beauty of all living things, the trees, flowers, grass, *you get my drift* and appreciating their sweetness.

Whenever I find a bird feather, I feel it's a blessing from a winged ancestor or friend who's flying "the good blue road." And when a group of pigeons or doves fly gracefully in sync, it tells me that Jesus is close, as if he's orchestrating their flight and saying, *"You are never alone, my child.*" Why else would they hang around telephone lines? To me, it's a sign of connection and communication.

I like to inspire people to see the "unseen" world where spirits flicker and their energy touches us on new levels of consciousness. The sadness from the loss of body contact can then be replaced by contentment as we reunite with the spirits of our loved-ones. This ability came to me as a young child, I would see and hear people who had passed away. In junior high I began relaying messages to my friends from their loved ones. Long story short, fearful adult reactions made me curb that gift and tuck it away until later in my life.

Now that gift is sought-after and I'm grateful for the divine guidance that stayed with me throughout my life. I'm also pleased with myself for listening to the signs and deeply grateful to my mom and dad for teaching me about discernment, intuition, the healing affects of journaling, and the peaceful power of expressing my true self. I feel as if I walk around with invisible angel wings tucked neatly in my shirt and am always available to help people who seek a deeper connection with their soul. You might say *I plant seeds!*

I'm also a strong believer in actions speaking louder than words though a well-written book with good intentions is lovely! Speaking of words, I have a fancy for lexigrams and can spend hours dissecting the secret meaning of a word.

Poetry is another fascination of mine which gave me the ability to ace my senior year English class by writing a book of poems. And last but not least, I stay young at heart by having fun, fun, fun and frequently playing elf-like practical jokes on my friends.

One more final thing—most importantly, I know we are all here for two reasons, to give love and to receive love.

If you thought I was only going to give you the good stuff, on the other side of the coin, I'm blunt to a fault and have a tad of a gutter-mouth (which I hope is balanced out by my sense of humor). I can't stand cigarette smoke and "evil-eye" anyone who smokes around me.

I can be hard on myself and also boldly competitive with myself. I'm slightly impatient with others and have an extremely low tolerance for negativity, repetitiveness and people who are whiners, self-absorbed or disrespectful of animals and Mother Earth.

By the way, I'm working hard on curbing my prejudices and judgments so I can reach a state of perpetual acceptance. You might say I'm a work in progress, learning to be at peace with things I can't change and roaring with courage to tackle the things I can.

In 1983, I lived on the top level of an old Victorian mansion in New Jersey that had been subdivided into three apartments. My place was the most unique and romantic, as well as the smallest—but it was ideal for me. The interior of my home was a mixed breed of antiques, Japanese and Native Indian items, family photos, books, hanging plants, and treasures from Nature. There was a vintage claw-legged bathtub and a hidden trap door leading to an attic that housed old furniture, glass bottles, and black-and-white photos of the original homeowners.

I had roommates—my handsome, white-and-orange, Himalayan cat, Patchouli, who was named after my favorite perfume oil, and two, colorful, chatty parakeets whose cage hung from an angled beam in the living room.

The coolest part of the place was a unique circular balcony off the kitchen. It was big enough for two chaise chairs and a large cobalt blue vase that I kept filled with seasonal flowers. A variety of wind chimes hung under the crown molding, serenading me on breezy days and nights. Patchouli loved to lie on the handcrafted railing and snooze in the sun. And I confess I did my share of nude tanning as well. Many nights I also rested there, staring at the constellations and admiring the vast open dark space.

The balcony overlooked the back yard where miles of ivy wrapped along the fences that outlined the property. Trellises, potted plants, and bushes were strategically aligned beside a brick path which led to a sitting area with a bistro table. When the weather was nice, this was where I would write, have tea and ponder.

I was proud of my home and loved having small parties or cooking for my friends. My favorite meal was homemade pizza with sautéed peppers, onions and garlic, accompanied by a crispy salad with my signature dressing; a blend of fresh lemon juice, rice vinegar and expensive, extra virgin olive oil.

I was blessed with many friends, but the only one I considered my best friend is Nina. We are more opposite than alike, from our looks to our personalities, but we've been best buds since age five. Nina married my baby brother, making us "*half-blooded.*" To this day, we share a bond that is unbreakable.

Career-wise, I always wanted to be a singer. I spent years in voice school and felt confident that singing was my niche. But after a funky experience with an agent who told me the only way a woman gets to the top is "by sucking a man's noodle," I decided to be my own agent. Ironically enough, it worked. In 1983, my singing career was progressing well and several times a month I ventured into New York to do background singing for original bands.

To pay the bills I worked as a cocktail waitress in a heart-thumping, hip disco. I made excellent tips, liked the nightly cash and enjoyed having my days off so I could venture to the mountains. My need to spend time outdoors with Nature and simply "be" was always in the forefront.

The fresh air and calming colors tamed my shadow-side—*you know the side I'm talking about … the one that wants to gossip, flaunt her power and cause some mischief.* Communing with Nature also helped keep my spirit peaceful, my body healthy and my emotions balanced. I'm still certain Mother Nature is the grandest healer on earth.

Overall, I was living the American dream, proudly driving around town in my bright yellow Volkswagen Beetle. *Beep, Beep!*

One particular day, I took a drive in the mountains to my favorite spot: the Watching Indian Reservation. It was only a half-hour from my apartment yet it felt like another world. First I stopped by a small ranch and fed a bag of carrots to some horses. They graciously nibbled on the treat as I stroked their soft noses and gazed into their soulful eyes.

Energized by their love, I continued on my journey. When I arrived, the reservation was quiet. I parked my Bug, grabbed the blanket I always travel with just in case the urge to picnic arises, and walked to a spot where tall pine trees flooded the area. It was magical.

As I waved the blanket in the air and spread it on the ground, thousands of pine needles scampered about. The sun's rays beamed through the trees. I felt as if God's hands were touching me. A telepathic conversation began with the nature elements, making me connected and at-one in the arms of Mother Earth. One of my favorite lexigrams is *Earth and Heart.*

I thanked God, my Spirit Guides, the Angels and all my loved ones for this life and all the beauty around me. I closed my eyes and allowed myself to fly. Pictures and events raced through my mind. It was unclear if I was in my past, present or future, but it was definitely a moment of peace. My breathing was slow and deep, putting me in a good place to receive information from my Higher Self. *Little did I know that these particular thoughts and visions would beckon a series of life-changing events.*

When I got home after spending hours in the mountains, I always felt tranquil, but on that particular night I later became restless. Something important seemed to be surfacing. Though I felt strong and happy, there was a quirky, unsettling, feeling in my stomach as well. I felt empty, and the emptiness created sadness.

It was frustrating to be having these feelings at a point in my life when all was going well. I was baffled, what could it possibly be? Was it a delayed "blue syndrome" from my recent break-up with a musician boyfriend after two years of dating?

My mind became my master but I didn't want to be its servant. It felt like I was mentally playing tennis and my body wasn't even on the court. After much back and forth contemplation, my gut told me that something I needed was about to enter my life.

I've read books about how we can feel restless, bored and agitated when our spirit is not in balance with our human actions. Was I out of balance? Was I working too much? Was I spending too much time alone? Did I need to meet up with Nina or some of the girls from work and do some female bonding?

I concluded that I needed to stop thinking. So I made a cup of herbal tea and cuddled with Patchouli on the bed while a soothing rainstorm pitter-pattered on the roof. I found an old 1947 black-and-white flick on television about an angel, 'The Bishop's Wife.' The warm tea relaxed me. I didn't want to miss the movie that was just starting, so I put a tape into the VCR and hit "record." Within minutes, my eyelids drooped and my head nodded.

I must have dozed off because I woke to the sound of an eerie whistle blowing in the distance. A low rumbling followed. At first I thought it was the TV. But after I muted the television, I realized it was a train from the next town over. When it rains the air gets dense, so a train whistle sounds louder and closer then it actually is.

An unsettling feeling came over me, the same queasy sensation I felt earlier. It made me think about the recurring dream I've had about a train. In it, I'm rushing down the aisle frantically looking for a certain passenger, but never find him or her. My Mom thinks it means I'm looking for some type of relationship which I unconsciously feel I'm missing. As accurate as this sounds, I haven't figured out who I'm actually looking for.

I suddenly felt detached and very far away from home. This was not the first time I had this feeling when hearing a train, but the sensation had an extra-eerie vibe this time. I closed my eyes and prayed.

Within moments I was in an altered state, what some people might call an out-of-body experience or astral traveling. For me it was quite normal, like being two places at once. I call it "dimensional drifting". It's a sense of connecting to the spirit world while staying rooted and sufficiently aware of my surroundings, like when I'm in the mountains and "drift off" as my body rests on the ground amongst the trees. Time seemed to stop.

When I opened my eyes, Patchouli was still cuddled next to me. Only a minute had passed according to the clock. The television was still muted and the whistle was still blowing.

I continued listening to the train pounding down the tracks, causing my psyche to ache as if it was coming to take me somewhere. Unlike times when I had purchased a train ticket and boarded a train, this felt like the train was boarding me. While my soul yearned to step up the steep metal stairs of a big black steam locomotive, my human self was scared.

The night following my bizarre train experience, I was working at the disco with five other waitresses. It was Saturday, couples night. We knew whoever got the back section with the booths was in trouble because it meant there'd be no good tips tonight.

I looked at the schedule posted in the break-room. *Fudge, it was my turn to get lovers lane.* The couples would sit, drink, smooch, talk and waste a perfectly good booth as they nursed the same drinks for hours. I used to imagine that under the tables their hands were doing things that should be done in hotel rooms or the backseat of a car—anywhere but my waitress section.

Four hours into the night, something life-changing happened when *he* walked into the club, time slowed down. The music, the voices, the bodies, they all faded. *All except him.*

He was beautifully handsome. At first glance, I knew he was there for me. He was meant to be mine; I was destined to be his.

Like a dog in heat, I could have tackled him on the spot. His long, wavy brown hair plus his funky-styled jacket, knee-high furry boots and skin-tight bell bottom jeans all turned me on. My eyes followed his every move. My body was numb yet vibrating.

It wasn't just his appearance that grabbed my attention, it was the way he walked, confident and proud, head held high. He was a leader, a humble leader, I sensed.

He seemed familiar, as if from a dream or another time when I dimensional-drifted. I continued to watch closely as he walked to the far end of the club. I felt he was my soulmate or rather, my soul remembered him. He was the "other-half" that people talk about, the one who makes you feel at home and safe.

I stood in the dark corner of my waitress station. *Get a grip, girl, you've seen cute guys before.* But as the words rolled off my tongue, I knew in my heart that this feeling was not completely of this world. I snapped out of it when a guy from one of the booths signaled for another round. It was their third and still no tip. I called the order out to the bartender while thinking, *get it yourself, you pain in the ass, don't you know my dream-man just walked in?*

I took a time-out from the dreamy bliss and cheerfully delivered the drinks. The disco dude paid with a $50 bill. I counted out his change, making sure to give him several $1 bills. Winking, he tossed two quarters onto my tray. I returned the wink, secretly knowing I'd given him the cheap vodka but charged him for the expensive stuff as I pocketed the difference.

Grinning, I skedaddled to my station feeling victorious. My eyes zeroed back in on the Mystery Man. One of my waitress friends came to my section and told me "the good-looking big tipper" was a Hollywood stuntman.

"A stuntman?" Geez, I had pegged him for a musician.

"What's the matter, Marlo?"

I lovingly shook her arms: "Hey! Can't you see I'm drooling over this guy?"

"His name is Thomas."

"Thomas?"

"Yeah, he's in town having fun while the Screen Actors Guild is on strike."

"Hmm … well, whyever he's here, I got first dibs." I thumbed my chest and grinned.

"You're too late. One of the other waitresses said she was going home with him."

"Who?"

"Who do you think?" She pointed to the classy-trashy waitress hanging all over Thomas. His grin made it seem as if he was enjoying her attention.

"Just look at her! We'll see about that. And to think I was going to ask all you girls to go clubbin' with me one night next week."

"I still want to go!" She smiled and scooted off to the break-room as

I studied the long-haired cutie-pie and his male friends who were sitting at a table by the dance floor.

I sensed Thomas was pretending to be a hotshot. In less than two hours, the stuntman had tipped all the waitresses $100 bills and invited them to his house for an after-hours party. I was the only waitress he hadn't met.

But I had a plan, so I asked my friend to cover my station. Then I put on some lipstick, fluffed my hair, slid the gum I was chewing to the side of my mouth, and waited for the right moment to make my move. Standing in front of him at last, I realized he was even more handsome and sexy than he'd seemed from across the room. His skin was naturally tan and fresh. His eyes were dark chocolate yet light from loving life. Inside I was screaming "hallelujah" while outside I remained cool as a cucumber. I looked him straight in the eye. He looked straight back at me. There was a connection, but he casually ignored it.

I said in a friendly, yet business-like tone as I shifted my eyes to the rest of the guys, "the club would like to buy you all a round of drinks."

Thomas laughed. "Look at all the drinks in front of us."

His friends agreed and also laughed. But I was quick on my toes: "Yeah, I can see you have many drinks. But these are free, on the house."

His friends laughed louder, almost heckling me. My tongue flicked my gum from its hiding spot and I began chewing as I shot a dirty look at them.

Thomas replied, "Free? Hmm, not many people are giving out free stuff. That's very kind of you." I smiled. "We accept," he said in response.

His friends went silent and raised their brows, riveted on our inter-action. Even though I was thinking not-so-nice stuff about his nosey friends, my smile stayed constant.

"Oh, wait a minute!" Thomas exclaimed. "You're here because you heard about the tip."

His friends repeated what he said and laughed again.

I was getting pissed. By now my jaw was chomping up and down on the gum. "Yep, I sure heard about the tip."

In raised octaves, his friends mimicked me. It took all my patience to keep from flipping them in the back of their heads with my angel wings. Thomas just watched me. Lord knows I was not interested in the tip. Well, not very interested, but it would make this a good night after the puny tips I'd gotten so far. You see, I wanted the whole package— Thomas and a tip.

I stood my ground, grabbed a few empty glasses and soiled napkins, then took a step away. "Have a good night, boys!" I chimed, acting as if I didn't have a care. I turned on my heel to go.

"Wait!" he said. I turned back. He continued: "What's your name?"

"Marlo," I tried to sound sexy without acting sexy.

"So, Marlo, do ya have another piece of gum?"

Gum-gum-gum, he wants gum. I always had gum in my purse, which was in my locker. So I replied nonchalantly, "I'll be right back."

"Wait! One more thing—if you find a piece of gum, I'll give ya $100 bucks."

I laughed. This guy really thought I just wanted the tip. Minutes later I was back at his table with bad news, "Believe it or not, I don't have a piece of gum."

His friends cackled. But Thomas just smiled and hopped off his bar stool to stand in front me. His presence forced me to lean back.

"How long have ya been chewing the piece in your mouth?" he wondered.

I answered without thinking, "Just a few minutes." It had really been a few hours.

"I'll take it," he said.

Oh crap, I thought, *I already beat the heck out of this piece. But if he wants it...*

"Okay." I reached into my mouth, pulled out the wet sticky gum and handed it to him.

His friends moaned. Thomas stuck it in his mouth, began chewing, and sat back down on his stool. I smiled so widely my cheeks hurt.

Grossed out, his friends wiggled on their chairs. Now I was the one laughing as I took a step away.

"Wait! Your tip." He reached into his pants pocket. "Uh-oh, I ran out of cash."

I snorted and grinned. He borrowed a $20 from one of the guys and slid it onto my tray. His friend glared at me as I winked and pranced away. I knew this was a good sign.

Back at my station, I bit my lip and shook off the magnetic energy from this encounter which was still jolting my petite body. There was some strong mo-jo brewing.

I took a few deep breaths and remembered the feeling I had the other night about something coming for me. *Was it him?*

At the end of the night he invited me to his house for the big party. I played it cool and said, "I might stop by." But inside I was jumping for joy.

Like a Hollywood superstar, he had two stretch limousines waiting in the parking lot. Thomas and the boys got into one as all the waitresses piled into the other. I decided to follow in my own car then I could leave when I wanted.

As I started the engine, I saw something on the windshield. I stepped half-out and reached for it. At first it looked like a bookmark, but I realized it was a train ticket. It read: "**The 440 Train—First Class seating to the next chapter of your life.**"

What the freak? A train ticket? The Four-Forty Train? It felt like something mystical was happening again. This was too weird,

The Limo Driver honked his horn, signaling me to follow. This snapped me back into the present. I tossed the ticket onto the passenger seat and accelerated.

On the drive, all I could think about was Divine Timing and the profound connection I felt with Thomas. Call it fate, destiny, karma, whatever you like but I was living it.

At the party I learned Thomas was also a musician. He had just written and recorded his first song. This made sense since I gravitated towards rockers and his look did not match my vision of a stuntman, which I thought of as a scruffy-looking guy with missing teeth who drank whiskey. I must have watched too many Westerns as a kid.

But this modern day stuntman was lovely, dahling, simply lovely! I was captivated by his gentle power, child-like innocence, strong independence, determination, and financial success. I came to this conclusion by observing his personality, energy and also the location and size of his big beautiful house.

One room was dedicated to his work. It was full of autographed movie scripts and souvenirs from television shows and films. I felt like I was walking through a trophy room in Hollywood. On the walls were photos of Thomas with movie stars, celebrities and women <u>lots of women</u>.

I noticed one photograph in particular, Thomas was wearing a pilot's uniform. He looked sexy in sunglasses and a captain's hat, his long dark hair hanging beneath it. His smile hinted that he had just achieved something or was just about to achieve something, maybe with the sexy, tall, black woman in a stewardess uniform standing close to him. His arm was around her shoulder and I couldn't help noticing how close his hand was to her breast, or was I seeing more than was really there? I felt a twinge of jealousy. *I really like this guy!*

While we girls were huddling in his living room over drinks, I made it clear to my friends that I felt a connection to Thomas and really wanted to get to know him. In a flash, they all but kicked me out of the way. One waitress had the audacity to offer to share him with me. *No thanks, I don't share my sweets, and I don't do rub-a-dub-dub three hynees in a tub.*

The other guys flirted with the girls but it was obvious that Thomas was the big fish everyone wanted to hook. Oddly enough, all of us girls went home alone that night. It seems he was more hell-bent on entertaining us then getting into our panties. *Darn, darn, darn!* He was not going to be an easy catch, but I honestly liked the challenge.

I decided to keep the train ticket from my windshield as a memento. I hid it in an old book that had belonged to my Grandmother. I had the feeling one day it would come in handy.

Later, I phoned Nina and told her about the magic man I'd just met. She was used to my gut-intuition stories and, though she teased me a bunch, she had a genuine respect for my opinion.

Over the following weeks my life continued as usual but Thomas stayed in my mind. Coincidence or not, we were constantly running into each other at convenience stores, diners, nightclubs and parties. At a few of the gatherings, we stood in eye-range and checked each other out. But he always had a group of guys and girls with him so it was hard to get too close. When we did look into each other's eyes, however, there was an intense feeling of recall and kinship that yearned to be explored even though he always got antsy and silly.

I was definitely experiencing something brand new. I wanted to be right about our strong connection and I also wanted to be intimate with him more intensely than any guy before. But something told me to proceed slowly. This knowing guided me to a new understanding. I wasn't used to surrendering, but a stronger force than me was at work here. So I gave permission to the Universe to steer me in the direction of my highest good. I truly believed that if it was meant to be, it would be.

Then it happened—as quickly as Thomas entered my life, my magical run-ins with him suddenly stopped. I heard through the grapevine that he was traveling back and forth from here to California. Yet he never reached out to me. I yearned to chase him but instead listened to my inner guidance. I was also bothered that my gut instincts were so far off about Thomas. It made me wonder if I was losing my touch as a woman along with my gift of insight.

I was continually playing mental tennis. But after one too many mind-boggling replays, I wrote in my journal to get some healing. Through this process, I literally wrote off our connection and accepted the fact that I was simply mistaken. *Some things are just that <u>simple</u> ... aren't they?*

I was relieved to learn from one of my waitress friends that Thomas was engaged to a stewardess who was African-American. I would never have guessed he was in a relationship, based on the way he acted with all of us women. Then I remembered the photo in his trophy room. I wondered whether his fiancé was the beautiful black woman. Maybe she wasn't a stuntwoman after all—*and I hadn't lost my touch*...

"Miss You"

Oceans away—
I look at your photo
and suddenly
I am there
Or should I say,
you are here.

MALIBU – PRESENT DAY

AFTER STANDING FOR SOME TIME, I sat on the blanket, and watched the seagulls chasing sand crabs. Thomas was still organizing a shaded spot under the umbrella while I was soaking in some rays. Watching what I thought of as "my feathered and crawling friends" reminded me of how my relationship with Thomas began. On some level he was the crab and I was the seagull. Or was he the seagull and I the crab?

My Past

TWO MONTHS LATER, THOMAS AND I ran into each other at a mutual friend's party. As much as I had thought I'd written off our connection, I obviously hadn't. I became anxious, my heart raced, the butterflies in my stomach fluttered. I took a nice deep breath to get centered.

He looked quite healthy and fit with his golden tan, white teeth, shiny long hair, bright sparkling eyes, and a body that exuded strength and agility. I was pleasantly surprised to see him, and his re-action indicated he felt the same about me. We smiled and did that flirty thing again with our eyes. I looked cute that night in a black fedora hat, a sexy low-cut black blouse, a muslin ankle-length skirt and lace-up black boots.

He was with the usual suspects and I was with two waitress-girlfriends. There was no way I was going to let this opportunity slip away. So I ditched my friends to at last confront the man I couldn't stop thinking or writing about.

"Psst, Thomas," I gestured. "Come 'ere."

His entourage watched as he followed me into a bedroom. I quickly shut the door.

"What's the story with you?" I half-smiled.

"What?" He blushed and walked to one of the windows.

"When you look at me that way."

"What way!" He turned towards me and did it again.

"That way—you know what way," I twanged in my street-girl voice as I approached him.

"You're cute, that's all." He looked back out the window.

"Thank you. You're cute too." Suddenly, I flashed back to kindergarten, I was five years old and had just kissed a boy for the first time.

He turned to me again. "I like your hat."

I smiled. "I like your jacket." I paused. "One of my friends tells me you're engaged to a California girl." I paused again.

He didn't answer and moved towards the door.

"So ... are you?" I asked.

"Not technically."

"Technically?"

"Ya know, I really don't like to gossip," he said.

"We're not gossiping, we're having a conversation."

"I'll just say we were close friends for years, but then she wanted to be more." He reached for the doorknob.

"Wait! So it's only a rumor? You're not engaged?" I walked towards him.

"I'd rather not get into this."

"Okay, okay. Well then, are you available?"

Again, he didn't answer. I was getting frustrated. "I have another question. I don't know the prim and proper way to ask this so I'll just say it—do you prefer black women?"

"Gee, Marlo, you're sure blunt!"

"What! It's a legitimate question. I was just wondering if you only like a certain type of woman." Even I couldn't believe my line of questioning, but frankly I wanted to know. "Some guys like blondes, some brunettes, others redheads; some like petite gals, some like long legs, a lot like busty women, some prefer cushy booties, you get my drift." I sighed.

"She's African-American."

"Oh, African American, of course. So ... do you only like...?"

"I refuse to answer. So I'll keep you guessing. How's that?"

"Well ... just in case I don't see you for awhile, and before you go off and get married..." I rushed up to him and stood on my tiptoes. "Here's a kiss from a Jersey Girl!"

He looked surprised. I gently grabbed his head and leaned in to kiss him. At first he resisted, but he quickly sank into it.

After a few moments, I took a step away and sighed with pleasure. He looked dizzy. Our eyes remained locked.

His lips were the softest I had ever kissed. My body throbbed with excitement. He stood frozen, looking shy. I wanted to throw him onto the bed, but my mission was now complete.

So I straightened my shirt, fluffed my hair and spoke ever so lightly as I quickly left, "Have a fun night. And congratulations if you *are* engaged..."

My plan to get Thomas to want me more clearly didn't turn out as I had hoped. My short and sweet tantalizing taste of him was just that—a taste. After that night I didn't see or hear from him. So I told my waitress friend not mention him anymore. It was better that way.

I was happy being single, fully enjoying coming and going as I pleased and not checking in with anyone. I had great suppers and gatherings with my family and Nina. I spent quality time playing with my young nieces and nephews.

On the music front, several New York studio managers called me regularly to lay down background vocals on albums. I appreciated the gift of music and loved being in the soundproof room singing into the microphone. Hearing my voice on playback was exciting, although that took some time to get used to. But the quest to improve and also accept things in my life remained in the forefront.

Since my income bumped-up immensely from the studio work, I no longer had a need to be a cocktail waitress. It was perfect timing. The stench of cigarette smoke and the drunken butt-holes who grappled me night after night had worn paper-thin. The icing on the cake was the night a jock yanked my strapless uniform down, revealing my bra-covered breasts while I was carrying a tray full of drinks over my head. I quickly pulled up my dress with my left hand and kicked him in the shin with my right foot, instantly breaking the skin and drawing blood.

Minutes later I was summoned to my boss's office and reprimanded with a warning of termination. I smiled as I responded, "Let's make it simple! I quit!"

I went back to teaching calisthenics at a local gym. It was a win-win. I had fun and kept in shape while instructing others to do the same *and* I got paid for it. My favorite exercise was the 'fire hydrant' where you kneel on all fours to imitate a dog peeing. After two hundred of those on each side, you're grateful to stand up again, but your bootie is two inches higher. It doesn't stay like that for long before going south again, however, so the daily exercise was a bonus for me.

But as the saying goes, "all work and no play make Jane *(or Marlo)* a dull girl." I missed my girlfriends, Nina, and the waitresses from the club. So I finally picked up the phone to schedule a girl's night out. Everyone seemed to have other plans, *dates*, to be exact, except, for Nina. We agreed to meet at a quaint Italian restaurant where I had worked years ago for a very brief time. It was one of many businesses along Route 22 in New Jersey where I'd worked. My dad always said I worked more jobs in my early years then he worked in his whole life.

I sat at the charming bar, sipping brandy with a soda back, a sophisticated cocktail that needs to be savored slowly and with purpose. I looked at my sterling silver and onyx watch. Nina was late. It was unlike her.

"Hey, Marlo!"

I turned around. "Thomas! Wow, what a surprise to see you. What are you doing here?"

"I'm friends with the owner's son, Tony."

"You're kidding? Me too. You know, I used to work here!"

"Really? Small world."

"It sure is," I agreed, taking a sip of the refined mouthwash. I wanted to ask Thomas many questions but I just held the pretty snifter and smiled casually while checking out his duds. *Cool-cool-cool. This California cat was nice.*

He became antsy. "I … I'm here 'cause I'm going to invest in a pizza parlor with Tony, here in Jersey."

"Great! Sounds like fun." I could hear myself talking on autopilot. But what kept running though my mind was how handsome he was.

"Forget about it!"

Did I miss something? "Okay," I frowned as I sipped my drink again, wondering if he'd heard my thoughts. Remembering the power of our kiss at the party ignited my urge to kiss him again.

"Forget about it." *Geez! He is a freakin' mind reader.*

I was getting ticked off. "Alrighty, I will."

Oh my word, this guy definitely has ESP. I was getting a buzz so I put down the drink and grabbed the water.

"Marlo, 'Forget About It' is the name of the Pizza Parlor."

"Oh – *fungool!* Funny, very funny." I laughed at myself for misunderstanding.

Then we looked at each other in that 'I feel like I've known you a long time' way.

He finally said, "I've thought about you a lot."

"Me too you," I quickly admitted, then glanced away. I wanted to scream **so why didn't you call?** but I didn't.

"You married?" I asked, looking at his left hand.

"Nope."

"Ah, are you here with anyone? I don't see your groupies tonight."

"Now you're being funny. I'm here solo."

Tony suddenly shouted for Thomas, who excused himself and crossed to the back room.

My head dropped, I couldn't believe we ran into each other. I was blown away but tried not to over-think this unexpected meeting. Yet I couldn't help wondering: *Was it fate? Did I make the right choice by surrendering to the Universe after all?*

An hour later, Nina still hadn't shown up. I had a hunch she had hooked up with my younger brother. They had just started dating so things were hot and heavy. At this point, it was best for me to go home. When Thomas came back, I didn't want to be sitting alone, looking deserted. And if he left without saying good-bye again, it would hurt way too much. *Maybe, just maybe this time, my departure would make him want me more!*

I paid my bar tab, left a fat tip and was just about to walk out the door when I heard my name. Minutes later, I was happily anxious as Thomas followed me back to my place. He drove a spiffy little sports car with a personalized license plate. DOGOOD.

As we climbed the three flights of stairs to my apartment, it was obvious by our body language that we were both a bit nervous.

I opened the door and said, "Make yourself at home. I'll be right back." I slipped into the bedroom to change into a tight pair of jeans and a relaxed yet sexy tee-shirt. As I went through all the right motions, it felt as if I was in a romance movie playing both the lead and the audience.

I soon headed to the kitchen, followed by Thomas: "What can I get you to drink?"

"Do you have hot chocolate and whipped cream?"

"As a matter of fact, I do." I opened the door to the balcony and in blew a cool peaceful breeze along with delicate music from the chimes.

"You look nice," he said, fumbling with knick-knacks on the table. "You looked nice before too. Why'd you change?"

"Uh, I'm not sure. I guess I'm nervous," I admitted with a smile as I measured two heaping spoonfuls of chocolate into a mug.

We moved to the living room with our steaming drinks, green tea for me. We chatted small talk about each other's careers and what we'd been up to. I still wanted to kiss him, but this time I refused to make the first move.

He must have read my mind again. "You know, you drove me crazy that night at the party," he said. I grinned, pink with satisfaction.

"I'd like to get to know you better," he added.

"I'd like to get to know you better too," I said with restraint. *Finally,* I thought.

"I'm not like most of the guys you're probably used to."

"How so?" I wondered. I already knew he was a rare bird.

"I believe that being intimate is a very precious thing, something that should be undertaken slowly and respectfully."

I didn't know how to respond. So I just looked at him, jaw hanging open, eyebrows raised.

"Did that make you speechless?"

"N-no, I guess that's an honorable way to be." *Darn! We weren't going to have sex!*

Since we were talking openly and honestly, now I wanted to ask if he got the same feeling about us knowing each other in another lifetime that I did. But I couldn't get the words out. I was still playing it safe.

While all these thoughts rambled in my mind, he sat there petting Patchouli. *I wished he were petting me!* This man completely captivated me. But I felt ungrounded in his presence. On another level I felt the way I do when I'm in the pine forest, vulnerable, open, ready to receive.

Out of the blue he asked: "Do you want to come to California with me and write and record songs?"

I gagged on my tea. "Wh-aat?"

"Do you want to come and live with me in California and we can record songs?"

"Funny—that's a good one. You had me there."

"I'm serious."

"Are you for real? I'm stumped, Thomas. We barely know each other and you want me to move to the West Coast with you and record songs?"

"Why not? We *do* know each other. We've been running into each other for some time."

"Yeahhh, but we've rarely talked, and I don't know much about you!"

"What would you like to know?'

"So many things, I don't know where to start."

He smiled as if proving his point: "Ask me anything."

"Okay, well, for one thing we've never had sss…" I couldn't say it. So he did: "Sex?"

"Yup. That."

"Marlo, that's not a question, it's a statement."

I snorted. "What are you, a grammar scholar? You know what I mean."

"I'm well aware that we haven't made love and I just told you how I feel about sex."

We haven't made love? "Okay, okay, well, does this mean you want me to come to California as your friend and live together as roommates?"

"Sure."

"That's not an answer," I heckled. "**Just** roommates?" I was clearly fishing.

"Yes."

"Okay, wait a minute—I need something stronger than a cup of tea for this conversation." I poured a cordial. "You want one?"

"No, don't you remember, I don't drink booze. I like a clear mind—it keeps me focused on my goals so I have no excuses for my choices."

Is this guy too good to be true? "Oh yes, I remember, you drink diet cola with whipped cream."

"See, we do know each other."

I couldn't help but laugh. He flipped his hair, proud that he'd made me laugh. But his seriousness and sincerity were scaring the crap out of me while his sexiness was driving me bonkers.

"What about your fiancé in California?"

"I don't have a fiancé."

"Then what about your girlfriend?"

"I don't have a girlfriend."

"Oh, Well, I've got to ask, do you like me as more than a friend?" I was screaming inside.

"I like you a little but love you a lot."

"Hmmmm," my street-girl voice came out now. "You what!"

"It's an expression, Marlo. You're a great girl, I'd like you to come live with my dogs and me in California and record music. Whatever happens from there happens."

"You make it sound so easy. But I have a life here in New Jersey and all my family is here."

"I understand. I used to live here too. I know about family and leaving your hometown."

"But, Thomas, you had a dream and a goal and you went after it."

"Don't you have dreams and goals?"

"Yeah! Of course I do." I was getting defensive. "And I'm living them!"

"All of them?" He stood and looked around my home, then looked at me. He seemed so mature and wise. "Aren't you the girl that can see people in Heaven and sense people's past lives?"

"Umm, sometimes." I was flabbergasted. *How did he know?*

"Sometimes? I thought you've been doing this for a long time."

"On and off. Here and there."

"You never noticed me watching you?"

"No."

"You helped one of my friends by encouraging him to be more creative and share his talents with others."

"Oh, I did?"

"Yeah, why are you acting so nonchalant?"

"I just pass on messages. But I'm always grateful to assist someone. I feel blessed that I can be of service."

"I've seen you at the parties, helping people talk to their loved-ones. You really seem comfortable in your skin."

"I am now. It wasn't easy though. As a kid I had to hide the gift at times. Eventually I stopped feeling scared of it. Then a few years ago it re-birthed to a new level."

"Well, what you do is wonderful, you give people hope."

I was flattered, humbled and happily surprised that he was paying attention to me. But my head was spinning from this intimate level of observation. *And to think I was holding back on the woo-hoo magic stuff to keep from scaring him off!*

"Well then, let me ask you a question … do you feel we have met before in another lifetime?" I said at last.

"Anything's possible. I prefer to be the observer rather than the observee."

I cackled, *how appropriate.* "So let's get back to your heavy radical invite!"

"Heavy is your perception."

I sighed again. *My perception, huh?* "Okay-okay. Here's one, smarty-pants, what if we hadn't run into each other tonight? Would you have looked for me to ask me this, or is this a spontaneous offer?"

"Does it matter if it was planned or not?" A subtle smiled appeared on Thomas's handsome face. I opened my mouth, but nothing came out. "Marlo, why do you need to know why something is happening?"

That was a good question but I wasn't going to tell him. I was lost for words, which was definitely not typical.

He gazed at me. "You and me, Marlo, we're here now in the present."

I waited for more but he just sat there, looking at me.

"Aaand?" I leaned in, opening my hands.

"Just think about it, or better yet, don't think about it just go with your gut."

Ah, the gut thing now he had me reeling. "I will, Thomas, and thank you for the offer. It's a lot to consider. But why did you bring up the stuff I can do?"

"Only you know the answer to that question."

"Mirror back at you that's not an answer, Thomas."

"No, it's not." He stood and came towards me, making me even more nervous.

Then Thomas bent down and kissed me on the lips, quick but still soft and sexy. He abruptly said goodnight and headed out the door, leaving me hanging.

Wrestling with my thoughts, I was disoriented. I locked the door, catching a glimpse of his car headlights as he backed out of the drive-way.

At that split second, I heard a train whistle and dimensionally drifted. I wasn't in the mountains this time, by the trees with sunrays beaming down on me. I was in my own house, knowing in my heart what I had to do…

Two weeks later, I told my family I was moving to California with Thomas. Rumors travel fast in small towns so they had already heard about the infamous Hollywood stuntman who was buying a pizza parlor in his hometown. My Dad thought it was great to meet a guy who stunt-doubled for some of his favorite television heroes. But the Hollywood glamour didn't stop my Dad from laying down ground-rules when it came to his daughter.

I felt especially sad to leave my Mom. She and I were dear friends, and my being her only daughter strengthened our bond. I'm blessed that my parents have always been supportive. Whether I was telling them about an intense dream, seeing ghosts or talking with spirits, they genuinely listened and shared similar experiences so I wouldn't feel like a triangle peg trying to fit into a square hole. Though they haven't always agreed with my life choices, their love always flows, which keeps the door open. Their support of my decision was a perfect example.

My older brother, who's a detective, had Thomas's background checked. Later that night at supper, he warned Thomas that he had friends who were connected and he wouldn't hesitate to call in a favor if my heart got broken. I felt warm and fuzzy that my big-bro was so protective of me, but I did feel a tad bad over Thomas getting an interrogation from him.

My younger brother was also leery of my hasty decision. But he hugged me and whispered words of love anyway. I think Nina's being there, supporting my decision helped. He told me loudly and firmly that if I ever needed him he'd be on a plane bound for California in a heartbeat.

Despite all the masculine threats, my California travel companion charmed my parents and re-assured my siblings that I was in good hands. Emotionally it was hard to leave them, but my soul was focused on my new journey.

I got my things in order fast. I informed the studio and the gym that I was moving. I ended my apartment rental agreement. A neighbor adopted my parakeets and plants. I sold most of my antiques back to the shop where I'd purchased them and said good-bye to my beautiful Victorian home.

A few days later, a limousine dropped Thomas, Patchouli and me at the airport. My family and I agreed to say our so-longs at home rather than having a dramatic good-bye scene at the airport. It was my second time on a plane, but my first time traveling with a cat as well as traveling first class. When the engines started up, the plane shook and I breathed deeply, closing my eyes and saying a prayer for my family and me. Tears welled in my eyes, but I looked at Thomas and he smiled. "It's okay. You'll be fine." He held my knee for a moment.

His touch relaxed me. As horny as I had been in his presence before, this particular moment brought no throbbing sensations. The plane roared along the runway and up into the clouds as I clenched my fists and prayed again. Thomas settled into the big leather seat, pushed it back as far as it would go, and closed his eyes.

When the plane finally leveled off, I took Patchouli out of the cage and sat him on my lap. He was sleepy from the homeopathic tablets I had given him for the ride. I opened a spiritual book my Mom had given me about archetypes and dreams. I read the pages but couldn't tell you what they said. My mind raced as I thought about who and what I was leaving, then it jumped to where I was heading.

To shift my focus, I squeezed some drops of a calming homeopathic flower essence under my tongue and shut my eyes. I imagined being in the pine forest with the trees, birds and the smell of Mother Earth. Patchouli's warmth and soothing purr serenaded me until I dozed off.

"Wake up, we're here," Thomas said suddenly, shaking me.

I looked out the window and had trouble seeing the ground. It was hidden by smog. As we continued our descent, I could see patches of blue down below. "What are those?" I asked.

"Swimming pools," Thomas said, stretching his arms above his head.

"Wow! I can't believe I'm really in California." It felt surreal.

As we exited the plane, I thanked the stewards and captains for a safe and smooth flight. My mind flashed back to the photo of Thomas portraying a pilot with his arm around his ex-fiancé!

The realization that I was now stepping into new territory scared the beejeebers out of me. But as I hustled along the corridor in a wave of people who had also been on the plane, I only had one choice—to suck up and go with it.

Around me, LAX hummed with activity. It was more colorful and animated than Newark Airport, and the thrust of Hollywood glitz was electrifying.

As we approached the baggage claim, a well-dressed man held a small sign with Thomas's last name on it. He took our carry-on bags and escorted us to the luggage carousel. I liked the personal attention. Within minutes he retrieved our luggage and we headed outside.

The electronic doors opened to a rush of sounds and activity outside. I was glad we had to walk a bit so I could release my pent-up energy with fast strides.

At his town car, the driver opened my door and nodded for me to enter. I gratefully stepped into the fresh-smelling interior and sank into the luxurious dark seat. It suddenly dawned on me that my life would never be the same. It may sound silly that a fancy car would have this kind of impact, but the town car was just the tangible form of the shift. What was unseen had even more impact, and the total feeling was overwhelming.

Thomas smiled at me and patted my head. "It's okay, Marlo. You'll get used to it."

I returned the smile and slid my hand into Patchouli's cage to rub his warm fur. I needed to feel something familiar or I was going to cry from the surge of emotions flooding my body.

As the car slowly made its way through the heavy LAX traffic, I tuned into the classical station on the radio and looked out the window. The palm trees were fascinating they looked as unreal as they did on television. I was in awe of how many there were, standing perfectly streamlined and swaying ever so slightly in the breeze. The freeway was clean and wide, much different from any highway I had traveled before.

What a strange feeling to be in California! Yes, this was my new home. I had just arrived, figuratively and literally.

Thomas's San Fernando Valley home was a comfortable house on a quiet street. It had several bedrooms, a swimming pool, and a bouncy waterbed. It didn't feel as homey as his house in New Jersey, nor was it my style. But since I was the "roommate", I surrendered to settling in among what already existed.

The décor was modern with lots of mirrors, chrome, and framed photos of Thomas doing stunts. I couldn't help but look around for photos of him and his ex-fiancé. I was pleasantly surprised to not find any.

Thomas's three greyhounds were tended by his pet-sitter who took care of their needs when their daddy was traveling or working in town. The two-year old mother-dog and her one-year old pups were rescues. At first lick, they won my heart. They were so gentle and graceful that being around them gave me a sense of family right way.

Patchouli, on the other hand, was apprehensive and swiftly found shelter under the bed. After a little sweet-talking and coaxing with treats, all the four-leggeds realized they were going to be roommates. One by one and sniff by sniff they learned to accept each other.

Thomas and I never talked again about our conversation in my apartment. We simply shifted into our new arrangement as easily as he shifted gears in his fast, sleek, black convertible Porsche in which we drove around town to acquaint me with my new surroundings. In New Jersey, it would have turned lots of heads, here in Hollywood it wasn't such a big deal.

It was exciting to shop at food stores where well-known celebrities shopped and so many people seemed to be health conscious, which I loved. The vibe was alive with energy and just as intense with the *unseen*. I could sense and sometimes see spirits guiding people, many of whom were animal totems. I knew my gift was evolving and I continually prayed for guidance and direction. *I guess it's true what they say about Los Angeles being "The City of Angels."*

For many months we kept to ourselves. We loved hanging home with Momma, Sister and Brother dog and Patchouli. I thought the dogs' names were cute and appropriate. I also pondered how the word 'Dog' is 'God' reversed.

I got hooked on eating Mexican food, especially avocados and fresh salsa with lots of cilantro, an herb that was not common in New Jersey.

We spent hours writing songs, playing guitar, and singing by the poolside while working on our tans. The leisure life was grand and guess what! The other thing that kept our creative juices flowing was SEX yeah, sex and did I say sex!

I bet you're curious about the juicy details of our first encounter. I mean, come on—almost two years of celibacy between two young active people who were physically attracted to each other must have ended with fireworks, or at least sparklers, right?

Okay, you forced it out of me. It was a warm evening. The sun was just setting. The sky was streaked with pink and purple. We were on our way home from a game of tennis when we decided to stop at a traveling carnival, one of those with spinning rides and a Ferris wheel. We munched on popcorn and strolled through the action-packed carnival.

Thomas loves playing games, winning stuffed toys, and eating cotton candy. He played a game where he threw softballs into a basket and won a big stuffed bear for me on the first try. As it got dark, the air was perfectly peaceful and mesmerizing.

"Let's ride the Ferris wheel," Thomas excitedly suggested.

"Really? I'm not good with heights."

"I'll protect you, little girl." He hugged me close.

I put my armful of toys down by the ride operator, then stepped into the cage. It wobbled back and forth. Thomas quickly stepped back out and whispered something into the machine operator's ear.

"I hope you told him not too keep us in here too long," I said hopefully as he joined me in the cage.

Thomas just smiled. The Ferris wheel suddenly started moving. As we climbed higher, he thought it would be funny to sway the cage.

"Don't rock the freakin' cage," I declared firmly.

The wheel went around a few times. Slowly, I began to relax. The view was beautiful, the stars, the lights on the rides, the laughter of the people below, and the sweet smell of fun.

Just as suddenly as it had started, the Ferris wheel stopped. We were smack on top.

"Shit! What happened?"

"Relax, Marlo, relax. Come here—sit on my lap. I'll hold you."

"I don't wanna sit on your lap, 'cause I'll be higher in the seat, closer to the edge!"

I was wearing a short tennis skirt with built-in panties. Thomas casually slipped his hand between my legs. "Whadya doing?"

"Make love to me, Marlo."

"Here! Are you nuts?" My heart raced. I don't know if it was from the height, the wobbly cart or because Thomas's hand was still fondling me. "Did you pay the guy to stop this thing?"

I was getting warm all over. Thomas kissed me with a passion I had never experienced before. I lost all sense of time and surroundings. All that mattered was just us, here and now.

When the ride was over, we stumbled out of the cage, grinning from our guilty pleasure. I have to admit it wasn't how I had envisioned our first time would be, *but it was worth the wait, and we were now officially boyfriend 'n' girlfriend!*

For the next year and a half, we stayed true to our goal and created some great songs. We laid them down on Thomas' eight-track recorder until we were able to get into the studio.

Life on the West Coast was grand. I was happy and felt a strong connection to the land, as if I was exactly where I was supposed to be. Without warning, the train switched tracks. I didn't see it coming. Thomas and I approached a tunnel. Lots of strange, radical people started hanging around. Suddenly I was moving too fast and my feet weren't touching the ground.

As the train picked up speed, its rocking motion made me sick though it was probably from the cocaine I ingested. I wasn't new to drugs, but they had never taken a strong hold on me before. *Famous last words!*

Thomas was a drug scene virgin until one dreadful night at a Hollywood Hills party. He was at the right place to meet with some music contacts but it was the wrong time for anything good to occur. Everyone seemed to be having such fun. *Note the verb "seemed."*

When the black glass plate with the pile of white powder got passed to him, Thomas fell hook, line and sinker. After that, all he wanted to do was *'to party.'* Our music career went on hold. *Darn, I thought we were going to be the next Sonny and Cher.*

I was still head over heels for Thomas and trusted we would be okay. *This will be a short phase,* I told myself. So I sold my independence, values and morals for love. But the tunnel was dark and cold. Together we spun out of control. And the money my boyfriend had worked so hard to earn quickly blew away like a punk-weed in gusty Santa Ana winds.

The train picked up more speed and moved even faster. I found it hard to know day from night. It was the eighties and this fluffy-horned drug had no prejudice. People from all walks of life were hanging around, helping Thomas burn his money. The doctors, lawyers, nine-to-fivers, fathers, and mothers were all looking for something outside of themselves. But none of us could help each other. We were "misery acquaintances," caught up in the illusion that this drug would make the pain go away. *A lexigram of illusion: so-ill-is-on-us.*

During my sober moments, I knew I was kidding myself. I was aware that I was on a mission of self-destruction. Yet, I continued to ignore my gut instincts and rather than fleeing to the light, I took refuge in more gloom. My morbid emotions wanted more morbidity so I made a choice and sank even deeper into it. *You might ask how could she sink any deeper? But we all hold the shovels!*

My mind continued to trick me into believing I needed to suffer. So I began reliving past deeds that I wasn't proud of. Now, however, I not only needed to deal with the present situation but also to confront things I had thought were done deals. It was a vicious circle. Until I healed the fragment of my core, which accepted all my choices, I wouldn't be able to move forward. Even more vital, I wouldn't be completely whole again.

Thomas was meanwhile dealing with his own demons. Coming from a family of divorce messed with his sense of security. On top of that, those tricky little coca leaves kept his head spinning with paranoid scenarios about everyone and everything. Even the friendly little boy who delivered the daily newspapers had an agenda, or so he thought.

We weren't much help to each other in those days, beyond keeping our dirty little mutual secret from our families and hiding from the outside world in the safe haven of Thomas's house. We covered each other's backs many times when our families phoned. We came up with every excuse in the book for why we couldn't have visitors or do the visiting. Living that lie made the pain hurt even more. We walked around with our heads down.

I desperately needed a girlfriend to talk with. Strangely enough, I forgot just how important it was to have friends of the same sex. Another funny little thing love can sometimes make us forget is that we still need a life outside our intimate relationship. I needed a friend—someone who would not judge me but could comfort and guide me through the muck, someone who would be a sounding board for my situation.

The verdict was finally in. I was in big trouble. My cute round face had become thin and my eyes exuded insecurity. My great curly perm had become dry and stringy. My perky solid body was skinny and weak, and my angel wings felt ruffled and broken.

But as nasty as those physical appearances looked, the worst part was my *inner reflection,* how I felt about me. It was sad, but the Marlo I had been no longer existed. I was responsible for my condition and no one was going to get me out of the tunnel except me, and my faith.

Thomas and I continued creating surmountable lessons to overcome individually and also as a couple. Quite frankly, the odds were against us, big-time!

One lonely and desperate night, I found myself sitting on the side of the tub in the bathroom, praying for guidance. I pleaded as I prayed, in fact, I needed a miracle.

I'm not sure how long I stayed locked in that room when I suddenly heard God's voice: "Stand up, Marlo. Look into the mirror. Look at yourself."

I did. I knew what was coming. It would be scary, but it was my prayer being answered. This revelation happened a few times in my life when I was lost and I prayed for help. I looked into the mirror. The room was dark except for a bluish beam of light, peering through the window from the full moon.

For several minutes, I looked at my face, then past it—deep into my being. My face darkened. It moved up, down, to the left and right. I thought I saw someone else looking back. I blinked, shook my head, and began crying. I wiped the tears, then stared deeper into my eyes. I couldn't move. It was time. My soul spoke to me. It told me to remember who I was and why I was here.

After my intense awakening, I felt my connection to God, my family and Mother Earth coming alive again. I wept loudly.

Thomas banged on the bathroom door: "What's going on in there? Are you alright?"

"I'm alive!" I cried, "I'm alive."

As I looked out the window, for the first time in a long time I noticed the large trees standing tall and powerful. In the sky, the stars twinkled as Grandmother Moon's glow felt like it was passing through me.

The angels were definitely with me that night, as I stopped doing cocaine. They consoled me as I stopped punishing myself. They embraced me as I remembered I loved me. They unfurled their wings as I declared, "I forgive me."

I sat down on the side of the tub, my body trembling. Shutting my eyes with gratitude and faith, it felt like I had emerged from the dark tunnel.

One week later, Thomas stopped partying as quickly as he'd started. Though it wasn't easy, the two of us grumpy, tired, hungry and processing. Through the grace of God, we became healthier each day, remarkably surviving the runaway train. *Amen*!

The following weeks, we processed many emotions. As tough as the decision was, we knew we had to make pivotal changes as individuals and also as a couple. We chose to put our music career on hold. Thomas focused on what he knew best—being a stuntman and I re-connected with my love for writing poetry.

Not long after that, I finally made a new girlfriend. You're not going to believe this…she was Thomas's California mystery girl! Yes, I became friends with his ex-fiancé, Jada. She had been helping him with his sobriety, which actually made me a bit jealous. But he seemed to need a friend so I set aside my petty ego and humbled myself for his well-being.

Jada was everything I had imagined; pretty, flawless dark skin, a great figure, and tall. She was also cunningly smart. I relied on my uniqueness to get me through this stage as I still wasn't feeling as confident as in the past.

When Thomas insisted we gals would have fun together, I was leery at first. My gut told me Jada still had feelings for my boyfriend, while my boyfriend insisted I was just having paranoid drug withdrawal symptoms. I knew the truth, but I also needed a woman friend. So I changed how I viewed the situation and we started spending time together.

Repeatedly, Jada told me she was involved with another man, so I had nothing to fear. But I remained cautious, keeping our conversations light and not too personal. She talked a lot about her job as a stewardess and had great stories about traveling to Europe. She was a classy woman who had seen a lot of the world. I could see why Thomas was attracted to her.

She turned me on to swap meets, which were like the flea markets I used to frequent on the East Coast. While I looked for antique furniture and jewelry, Jada was busy at the costume jewelry counters. This baffled me as I thought of her as a classy woman. *Maybe she had another side after all.* Her taste in music was also different than mine, she liked country-western whereas I loved Motown.

It only took a few months for us both to realize our friendship was created by a man we both loved, not a real connection as women. Instinctively, we parted ways. Meanwhile, she and Thomas slowly drifted apart as well. Though he never admitted why, in my heart I knew that he knew she was not 100% over him and staying friends wasn't good for either of them.

A few months after the derailment, Thomas and I consolidated the assets we had left. He sold his house in New Jersey and put his California house on the market. It was my job to find an affordable new place for us to live, one without old memories. I would also stay home and pamper our four-leggeds, including a new rescued cat named Sirius who found Thomas while he was hustling work in Los Angeles. Sirius was scruffy-looking when he came to live with us. But after a few baths, his long soft grey hair shone handsomely.

Thomas's California house sold to the first interested buyer. I moved fast and sixty days later we were living in a clean modest rental house in Universal City. Thomas's ego of once owning a larger home did not surface, even though some of his business associates reminded us of what we had thrown away. Fortunately, their words slid in one ear and out the other, failing to pierce us consciously or unconsciously. I followed Jesus' advice, "Forgive them, for they know not what they do."

Our family members took turns visiting now. It was fun touring the homes of the stars, movie studios and amusement parks with them. Taking them to Wolfgang Puck's restaurant was fun because they got star-struck over "old time classic" actors who were also dining there. When Mom bumped into Sidney Poitier on the way to the restroom, it was the icing on the cake.

Benihana's was also exciting as they watched the chef flip his knife and toss seafood under his hat. The East Coasters weren't at first receptive to dining at a table with "strangers." But by the end of the meal they were all chatting up a storm and passing around their Polaroid souvenirs to our table-mates. I later traveled back to the East Coast twice a year, and Thomas did his best to see his two families every so often as well.

Besides writing, I got back into cooking. We loved entertaining small groups and I was soon whipping up four course meals that would make Julia Child smile. But my dishes were Italian not French, with olive oil instead of butter. Thomas loved my salads with toasted pine nuts and especially my signature dressing. I made softball-sized meatballs (and meatless-balls) drenched in marinara sauce and sprinkled with the finest blend of grated cheeses. Alongside the sauce was always a heaping plate of pasta.

As we regained the weight we had lost doing drugs, we both dove into workout routines. Long walks and yoga helped balance my intake of food, clear my frame of mind and tone my muscles. Thomas hired a personal trainer and quickly got back into prime shape with weight training, running, and high protein meals. No more pasta for awhile.

Inside and out, we started a new chapter in our lives and with these changes came gifts. Thomas landed a television series, his first since his long drug-influenced break from the business. It was an action-fantasy series in which a young NBA basketball player time-travels to one of his many past lives as he sleeps. I thought about my "gift" and how far I had gotten from relaying spiritual messages. I really missed that, but I didn't have many opportunities now. So I said a prayer to open me up to being a messenger once more. If that was still part of my purpose, time would tell.

On several occasions, I went to the TV series set. The Jersey girl in me kept me from getting too star-struck, but it was riveting and also surreal. The process of filming was exciting but took a lot of patience. I gained an appreciation for filmmakers and also my boyfriend's extreme talents.

On the set I also met some strong and independent stuntwomen. I got on with a few and we became friends. Again, I kept our chats on the lighter side since they worked with Thomas, careful not to jeopardize their business relationship. I'd also heard one too many Hollywood stories about backstabbing and jealous motives. But my new girlfriends were thrilling and energetic. I had fun horseback riding, learning trapeze, and kickboxing with them and just hanging out in afternoon coffee-chats.

With this new experience of female bonding, I felt whole again. It amazed me to think that along the way, along the speedy train ride of love, so much of me got left behind without being necessary. No woman or man should give up vital fragments of their essence in the name of love. Oddly enough, we don't usually become aware of this until our train switches tracks or completely derails. Then, like a lightning bolt, we remember what got left behind, given up or compromised.

Most days when Thomas was busy at the studio, I would take one of the dogs to a nearby park for a walk. We'd sit under a big old tree where I loved listening to the sparrows chirp and crows caw as they would

"*Flowers Blossoming*"

Princes and queens,
not tread on your dreams
for you are
the king of thyself.

spring up and down on their agile legs, showing off. Fairies disguised as gnats also floated around me, glistening in the sunlight.

Nature's language inspired me to write even more poetry. I realized I had missed writing as my words came to life on the page again. Writing was my sanctuary. Following a gut instinct, I submitted a pile of poems to several greeting card lines. I had no expectations and left the results in the hands of the Universe though, being human, I still had high hopes.

One day I was having a cup of tea, when the doorbell rang. The barking dogs raced to the front door where the mail carrier had a certified letter. I signed for it and thanked her.

Sitting at the kitchen table, I noticed the return address: **Emily Dickinson, Castlemark Greeting Cards.** I was nervous as I ripped open the seal.

The letter inside read, *"Dear Marlo, we have received your poems. I typically do not read unsolicited poetry but yours somehow slipped through the cracks to my desk. I like your style of writing so I have decided to make an exception. Castlemark would like to purchase all the poems you sent and retain you on an independent writer's contract with our new spiritual line. If you are interested, please call immediately."*

I danced! I shouted and danced! I called Thomas and left a message, then called Mom and Dad. *Oh my Goddess, my writing would be read on greeting cards with the intention to inspire!*

On the Castlemark contract, I opted for credit by name mention, in exchange for less money. I thought the credentials would help me launch my first book which I'd recently started writing. It was titled "Invisible Flowers."

That evening I took my handsome man out to dinner to celebrate. We gave thanks for our second chance at a healthy life. Our meal was delicious, but I insisted we go home for "dessert."

I put on a tight black negligee, fishnet stockings, fingerless gloves, black high heels, and a hat with a long feather that would serve its purpose later. I also put on a Motown song and did a dirty dance. I rubbed my hand up and around my cleavage, then slapped my boy-toy's face. He blushed and wiggled a bit as I flopped on a soft cushy rug in front of a roaring fire and smashed chocolate-covered cherries over intimate parts of my body. I ran my finger along the sweetness and took a taste. *Dessert is served, dahling!*

That night I sprang awake, heart racing. I kicked the covers off my legs. I was sweating. I looked at the clock—it was 2:22 a.m.

I continued to lay awake. As hours passed, I tried meditating, praying, reading, counting sheep, but nothing worked. My mind was overstimulated.

As I finally got out of bed, I quietly checked on Thomas, Patchouli, Sirius and Momma Dog. They looked so cute cuddled on the couch. By daybreak my hard-working man had to be on the movie set, so I tiptoed back to the bedroom and wormed my way between Sister and Brother Dog who were sprawled on the king-sized bed. Their warmth made me feel like the cream in the middle of a two-wafer cookie.

I must have fallen back to sleep because I had barely opened my eyes to say good morning to Thomas when he kissed me good-bye. His toothpaste breath and soft lips made me relax into an even deeper slumber until I got a phone call at ten in the morning. It was Thomas's ex-fiancé. She wanted to meet for lunch.

At the restaurant Jada suggested, we both pulled into the parking lot at the same time. As she got out of the car I noticed she was pregnant. She put her arms out to hug me. I returned the hug with a tentative "Congratulations!" before leading us inside. As we crossed through the restaurant, many scenarios played through my mind. It had been a long time since we last talked.

After an uncomfortable moment of silence, we chatted small talk, mostly about Thomas. She finally cut to the chase, her reason for asking to meet me. She said she was moving to England with her baby's father and now understands what true love really is. After lunch, we wished each other well and said a sincere good-bye. But I thought it was strange for her to tell me, and not Thomas, that she was leaving LA. I finally realized she wanted me to tell Thomas her news. When I did, he was genuinely happy.

Several years later and after much discussion, the time had arrived for my man and me to dive into a bigger commitment. First comes love, then comes marriage. But we didn't want a big shindig, we wanted low-key and simple.

With the help of my Mom and Nina, our quaint and delightful wedding occurred on a New Jersey ranch where we promised to love, honor, and definitely <u>not</u> obey each other until we leave this earth. It was the ranch in the mountains near the Indian Reservation where I used to feed the horses. On this beautiful spring day, the sky was a brilliant blue, and the clouds floated dreamily in an ever-so-slight breeze. Being surrounded by nature, birds, deer, rabbits, and horses grazing in the distance, was my wedding dream come true.

My two sisters-in-law stood next to me at the altar. Nina was my maid of honor and my older brother's wife was a bridesmaid. Thomas's brother was his best man and his uncle was a groomsman. Nine of our nieces, nephews, and godchildren were flower children. And we were blessed to have several of our grandparents with us as well. The whole family looked stunningly beautiful, and any animosity between my groom's divorced parents was well-hidden for our sake.

The love and gratitude shining on everyone's faces was the greatest gift of all. I hope every woman feels like I did that day as I gazed into Thomas's eyes and we exchanged vows.

Our color scheme was black and white so we had the photographer shoot many photos on black and white film for our album. Our musician was a Native American flutist, which harmonized with the wedding theme. The inside of the ranch house was spacious and warm, like a log cabin, as our guests sat and mingled. Thomas's business partner, Tony, from the pizza parlor, provided the food—Italian, of course! Lasagna, linguini, grilled veggies, stuffed clams, and mushrooms, garlic bread, Caesar salad, and pizza filled our bellies and made our hearts content.

The cake was an edible art-piece. Fresh bananas, strawberries, and custard were stuffed into a moist yellow cake under a rich dark chocolate frosting. For the kids, we had fresh fruit cut into flower shapes, as well as a soft-serve ice cream and frozen yogurt dispenser.

We skipped an exotic honeymoon location and chose to invest in a piece of property, which was our next big commitment. But we agreed that on our first wedding anniversary we'd have a huge kick-butt California party and on our fifth we'd take a trip to Umbria, Italy.

Once we got back to the West Coast, a real estate agent and I worked diligently to find us a house. I actually liked the hunt, especially since exploring the wide range of houses in Southern California was more fun than combing New Jersey's split-levels and Cape Cods.

For months we looked at houses in a thirty-mile radius. A few were close to what we wanted but there were no bell-ringers until we looked in Pasadena. There we found a beautifully restored Victorian house on a tree-lined street. A bold wrap-around porch echoed the house's unique personality.

"This reminds me of the New Jersey mansion I lived in."

"It does have that feel to it," Thomas agreed.

We told the agent we would call her soon, then we stopped at a local restaurant for a bite while we discussed our options.

"This would be a dream come true to live in a classic house with updated rooms and shiny new appliances."

"It is nice. Nothing like I imagined I would live in, but I do really like it. And the area is quiet and beautiful."

I was excited. My heart was beating with enthusiasm as I thought about how I would decorate the house and the great meals I could whip up in the huge gourmet kitchen. The backyard was a garden-heaven. When I thought about writing and meditating outside, I got goose-bumps.

We drove around the city to get a feel for the overall neighborhood vibe. Pasadena's old world charm and trendy quaint shops had a way of intermixing beautifully with the current style. When I spotted one of the oldest train stations in California, a confirmation rang loud and clear in my mind that this is where we needed to be. In that moment I knew we were moving to Pasadena.

By the end of the day, we had made an offer and in less than two hours the sellers accepted. It was great to be entering this new phase of my life with the man I loved, a blossoming writing career, and love and support from both our families.

The following day, we anxiously waited for the inspection to go through. Although the house looked to be in top mint condition, we needed to be sure the internals were just as pretty. A house is like a body, though it may look good on the outside, we need to keep tabs on the inside for a full, fun experience.

I was unsurprised, and ecstatically happy, when the house was approved with flying colors. Straightaway I sent pictures to our families in New Jersey so they could also experience our journey. Thirty days later we moved in. A group of stunt friends were hired to help us. In one day, one long, butt-breaking, hard-working, but well-worth-it day we moved into our first home as a married couple.

It was June so we had sunlight until 8:30. As we thanked the stunt moving crew and watched them wearily drive off just as the sun set, we happily sighed in exhaustion and excitement. It was now safe to let the dogs out to run freely. They loved the large fenced-in backyard and had no trouble marking all the trees.

Patchouli didn't want anything to do with the outside. He nestled on a windowsill in the kitchen. Sirius, on the other hand, liked hanging outdoors. I grinned as he crawled low to the ground, curiously sniffing the new territory. Once his paws landed on a mosaic-tiled path, he started hopping up and down like a bunny. He followed the path that ran along the middle of the yard through a variety of fruit trees, colorful bushes, and aromatic flowers. Zen wind chimes, bird feeders, and the smell of Mother Earth all resonated around the perimeter of our new home.

Thomas gave a loving shout as he wrangled our four-leggeds inside and locked up the house. I dimmed the lights in the kitchen. Simultaneously we relaxed. We'd been pushing so hard for the past few months that it was refreshing to decompress as the tension of our physical work fell gently off our bones.

Slowly, I ran my hands over the shiny, tumbled, granite countertop. The colors and coolness of the natural stone were calming as I gently traced a quartz crystal vein running through the malachite base. It was organic "medicine," the same as I used to experience in the pine forest.

The living room opened to the kitchen with a side adjoining-room, a quaint greenhouse already filled with plants. I decided this would be where I would keep many of the crystals I'd accumulated over the years. The large geodes would be placed throughout the rest of the house. We were truly blessed to be able to bring these nature friends inside. Our new home was a dream come true, as if the previous owners had designed it especially for us. *Or could our thoughts and prayers have possibly manifested this home?*

I watched Thomas stand in the doorway admiring his new office. There was ample space in it for all his photos and memorabilia. My new creative room was across the hall. I promised myself to keep it light, spacious, and organized. The master bedroom was also downstairs on the opposite side of the house. Our king-sized bed seemed small in the spectacularly large room. I wasn't used to such a grand space to sleep in but something in my gut told me I would get used to it quickly. My gut was right, as usual.

Because this house was so much larger than our last one, we had to buy new furniture to mix with what we had brought. The décor became a harmony of bold woods and soft chenille, mellow brown, and green earth tones alongside sparkling blue air tones, a union of male and female energies. The floors were tiled with porcelain that looked and felt like suede. We placed luxurious area rugs throughout so the dogs wouldn't slip and slide too much. It also gave the house a cozier feel. Upstairs were two guest bedrooms, each with their own bathroom and private balcony. These were great places to sunbathe in the nude.

Over the following two weeks, we worked like beavers, getting the house decorated. The resulting ambiance and overall balance of our new home confirmed that we were exactly where we were supposed to be.

"It's time to take a break," Thomas said one night during supper.

I agreed completely. After our meal, our whole family plopped on the square-shaped sectional couch and got comfy. "Ahhh, this is what it's all about, being together and sharing the love." Thomas grinned, turning on the television.

Thomas and I sat on the opposite ends of the big sofa. I liked the lounge chair section that had a long wood table leaning against its back. On the table sat my writing materials and an amber swing-arm lamp that illuminated the area.

I reached for my notebook and pen, already thinking about poems to work on for my greeting card assignment this month. After a brief but deep meditation, I chose a water elements theme, natural things that directly connected to water. I felt it was time for messages of inspiration related to our deep emotions. I imagined a creek set in a scene with lots of grass, river rocks, and a copper penny-colored horse gazing over the water. I paused and closed my eyes.

The woman Castlemark hired to do the artwork for this particular line of cards was profoundly talented. Since we lived in different states, we communicated via mail and inspired each other with our creative ideas. My mind's eye traveled to her hand and paintbrush, as I clearly envisioned how beautiful this piece of work could be. I prayed for confirmation that I was being guided to share something about the healing powers of water.

As Thomas flicked through the television channels, I tried to shut out the distraction. Suddenly he got off the couch and headed into the kitchen. *Perfect timing.* Then the phone rang. I wanted to let the answering machine pick up but something told me to get it. I'm glad I did, it was my Mom.

"Hey, Marlo, how are you guys doing in the new house?"

"Great! I can't wait for you and Dad to visit." I filled her in on the latest details.

Minutes into the conversation she asked, "Have you had the dream about being in a train and looking for someone lately?"

"No! Not in awhile," I realized.

We share the gift of having similar vivid dreams and spend hours interpreting each other's.

"Have you been dreaming about trains, Mom?" I wondered.

"Yes. Last night I dreamed I was on a train. It was raining and there was a beautiful river running along the countryside."

"Oh my gosh! Are you looking for a certain passenger too?"

"No, sweetheart. That one is yours. I'm still working on mine. Have you been having any similar dreams?"

"Not recently, Mom. But I was just praying for a confirmation that I should be writing about water elements for the card line."

"Wooow, Marlo! I wonder what your brothers would say about this one?"

"As always, they'd wanna know what we were smoking." We laughed.

"So you're going to write about water!"

"Yes, about its connection with our emotions. You're my confirmation! Thank you."

"You're welcome, daughter. Anything I can do to help. And let's not forget that dreams about water are a sign that something in our psyche needs to be healed."

"I love that! Then it seems you're interested in traveling soon but you're heart says one thing and your mind says another."

"Hmmm, sounds accurate. Thanks for the feedback," she replied.

"It's nothing. I was taught by the best."

"Who's that?"

"You! Like I've been telling you for years."

"I don't know about that, Marlo."

"You're what I call a <u>quiet</u> teacher, Mom, both Dad and you. Sometimes we learn the most from the quiet humble ones."

"Well, thank you very much!"

"Ah, there's more, the thing about trains? Yesterday I went to the bookstore and did my 'please guide me, Spirit Guides' prayer to find the book I'm supposed to read. You won't believe which one I was drawn to and it's also the book we'll be reading at my book club."

"A book club! That's wonderful, Marlo. What book will you be reading?"

I was about to answer when our conversation was interrupted. Dad picked up the other receiver, "Marlo, your mother is getting more psychic in her old age."

"That's great. Dad. What about you, any insights for today?"

"Yeah, tonight the sun will set at 8:18 and the moon will be full."

"Remarkable, Amazing Kreskin," Mom mocked.

I chatted with Dad about the new house and the summer equinox before he signed off. Then Mom and I talked more about how water, trains, and traveling dominated our dream space.

"Marlo, you never said what book you bought at the bookstore."

"It's a novel called 'The Four-Forty Train.'"

"More trains?"

"Yeah, and how the book came into fruition is a unique story itself."

"I'd love to hear more but can you write it in an e-mail? Our favorite television show is about to start."

"Sure." I smiled at her honesty.

"One more thing, sweetheart, do you still get that funny feeling when you hear a train whistle?"

"Yes, I do. But now that you mention it, it's been a while—even though there's a train station not far from here. Hmm, I wonder why?"

"That is yet to be revealed," she replied secretively.

"Very mysterious. I like it!"

"Take your own advice, Marlo, everything happens when it's supposed to if it's in alignment with your soul's purpose."

"Wow, Mom! You really socked it to me with that one."

"Well, I have a good teacher."

I sighed with a smile. "Well, enjoy your show."

"I love you. See you soon, Marlo."

"I love you, Mom."

As we prepared to hang up the telephone, we agreed to make a cup of tea and be with each other in spirit until late autumn when I could visit my family. I took a yellow and blue porcelain teacup and saucer from the cupboard. With a cup of steaming chamomile on the table next to me, I picked up my pen and began writing a "miss you" card.

"Miss You"

Last night I walked
in the rain with
intentions to hide my tears.
Thoughts of you
flooded my eyes—
then a surge of
Calmness warmed my
heart as I realized the
Angels in Heaven
Were crying with me—
No longer was I alone.

Several hours passed as I "gave birth" to my monthly quota of poems for Castlemark. My hand and eyes were tired from writing.

"I'm going to bed, babe," I told Thomas as I lazily walked to his side of the couch.

"Alright, sleep tight. Hey! Don't forget, this weekend we're going to the beach to meet some friends," Thomas said as I bent over to kiss him.

"Oh yeah, I remember. I sure can use some sun on my face."

"There will be some girls for you to meet, too."

"Oh, great." I laughed loudly.

"What?"

"By chance are any of them your old girlfriends?" I lovingly bit his ear.

"Ha-ha! No," he squirmed.

I went on, "Hey, wasn't it kind of strange that one of our first pieces of mail in the new house was a photo-card of your ex and her family?"

"Yeah! But you have to admit she looks happy. The European lifestyle definitely suits her."

"And her child and hubby are cute."

"What did you do with the photo, Marlo?"

"I stuck it on the chalkboard in the kitchen as a reminder to send one of my greeting cards to them."

"That's nice. I'd like to write something too," he said. "Anyway, are you excited about meeting some new girlfriends tomorrow?"

"Sure. Who knows—maybe one of the gals will turn out to be the friend I've been needing out here, like Nina."

"Maybe one? What about all of them?" He patted my butt.

I took a step away. "Let's not push it. I have no expectations."

"I'm surprised to hear you talk like that. You're usually more positive." He reached for my hand.

"You're right, I'm just tired from the move. I have faith, and if I get a bunch of new friends in one shot, it'll be a blessing."

"That's my girl." He tugged me towards him and kissed me.

Thomas was right, I needed some tribal bonding. It had been way too long and no one's fault but my own. Though I was friendly with several stuntwomen, I was obviously still a bit guarded from mixing Thomas's business with my pleasure. Nina suggested I start a book club as a way to meet the neighbors and drop my guard with the stuntwomen. She was usually right about things like this so I was game.

I was just about to doze off when I heard a train whistle. The wind must have been blowing just right for the sound to travel into the house. I smiled and wiggled around the covers as I listened intently. The depth of the whistle's hum made me think about whales and how their song also cuts right through me. I had an "ah-ha" moment realizing that train whistles and whales have a sound frequency that takes me to a place of deep remembrance. Something in their resonance feels like a call from the depths of my soul.

MALIBU – PRESENT DAY

THOMAS AND I WERE SO CAPTIVATED with the area that we didn't see his friends until they were right upon us. "Hey Thomas, what's up?" a broad-shouldered pretty boy said as he and a tall blonde beauty dropped their things. It was Ricky, a real wise-guy with a 'tude from what I could recall.

"Hey, Ricky, good to see you," Thomas smiled, putting his hand out. "It's been way too long."

"For sure, man." Ricky pushed Thomas's hand away and hugged him tightly instead. "Let's not let so much time go by."

"We just saw each other on the set," Thomas teased.

"But it's not the same, man. This is the real deal," Ricky grinned at me over Thomas's shoulder.

I straightened up. "That's so nice. Boy bonding."

"Sorry I couldn't help you move a few weeks ago. My father was visiting from New Jersey and I had to take him sightseeing," Ricky continued.

"No problem, man. We had plenty of help."

The blonde, 'a tall glass of water', and I had been eyeing each other. She looked familiar. I was instinctively comparing her to Nina whose friendship was simple, honest, and balanced in give-and-take. Lucinda smiled as it dawned on me that I had seen her before at a stunt softball league game where she seemed like Ricky's flavor of the month. Obviously she was more.

LUCINDA'S PAST

LUCINDA WAS A LONG-LEGGED, striking blonde, sexy and single in Austin, Texas. It was the nineties and she worked as a hairstylist and make-up artist in an upscale salon. A fun-loving person, she had a pig-like snorting laugh and high I.Q. score which killed the "tall, dumb, and blonde" stereotype.

Lucinda's soft voice, gentle spirit, and ability to listen enabled her salon clients to share their dramas while sipping champagne and nibbling dark chocolates as their transformations took place. They sensed her ability to live in the moment and appreciate all of life's situations. Despite the heartache and tribulations she encountered, her compassion and willingness to help others gave her inner beauty.

When she was a child, Lucinda's big brother Carl died while playing hide-and-seek with her. She was devastated. Questions about why this happened haunted her. Her father's strict religious beliefs forced her to be strong through prayer and weekly church services. His faith and guidance bonded the family with his powerful voice and scriptural quotes.

Years later, Lucinda's faith was tested on Christmas Day when the family's home burned to the ground, destroying most of their personal effects. Again, her father kept the family together literally and physically. He rebuilt their home with his own two hands while delivering the words of the Lord's Prayer which penetrated deep into her psyche. Most girls her age were playing with other girls but she stayed close to her family and their cat.

At sixteen, Lucinda's faith was her salvation yet again, when her father was diagnosed with cancer. This challenge quieted his intense demeanor. His aggressive fight to keep moving onward was replaced with vulnerability as he was forced to let himself be cared for. Instinctively, Lucinda stepped into the role of primary caretaker for two tough years. But this ended one morning when she found him passed away in his bed, the Bible in his hands.

To maintain the momentum of daily life for the sake of her mother and younger sister, Lucinda put her grief on hold and buried her feelings. At the time she thought it was the stronger and wiser thing to do. To deal with her new responsibilities and pressures, she made a new friend, booze. Alcohol numbed the pain of losing her father and brother by dimming the reality of all her misfortunes. To earn income for the household, she worked after school at the town's beauty parlor. But by

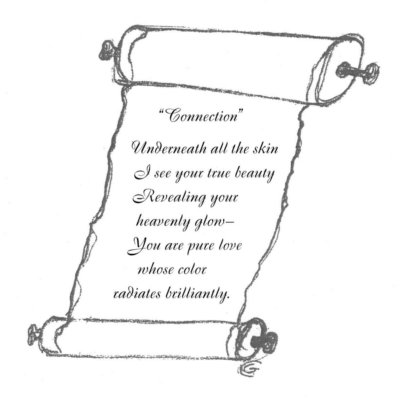

"*Connection*"

Underneath all the skin
I see your true beauty
Revealing your
heavenly glow—
You are pure love
whose color
radiates brilliantly.

mid-evening, she was always home preparing dinner for her mom and sister, and by late evening she was hanging out with more new friends, the local hoodlums.

Playing three very different roles was easier than she would have imagined. In fact, performing to suit the situation and please others became a game to Lucinda. But as months passed, her over-worked and reckless behavior turned dangerous. One night after too many drinks she got behind the wheel of her car and woke up the following morning in the middle of a ditch. With a throbbing head, disheartened spirit, and banged-up car, she sat in the muck and reflected on her actions. Then she heard her father, like an angel, speaking to her. He insisted she clean up her act and turn to her faith. Unbeknownst to her mother, she followed her father's heavenly advice and quietly sought out moral support from a local pastor. This shifted her trust back to the Lord.

Back to the nineties: At the end of a long day at the salon, Lucinda would hop into her sports car and race through the streets of Austin. As she entered her sacred space, a seductive red walled, leopard upholstered adorned house, three show-cut Shih Tzus would greet her.

For the most part, Lucinda was always a loner. She did most of her socializing at work. Being with her pets was her ideal way to spend an evening. This particular night, the four retreated to the living room after dinner and settled on their favorite spot, a cozy down feathered sectional sofa. Outside, a rainstorm cooled the house and created a relaxing drum-beat on the roof. Lucinda flipped on the gas fireplace switch and turned on the television set to watch her favorite hospital drama. She tossed a satin blanket over her legs, sipped from a glass of white wine, and sank into the sofa.

Halfway through the show, she got sidetracked, reflecting on the day and then on her whole life. The shrink who helped her move through her buried grief had called this *The Emotional Food Snake.* She would say, "Lucinda, sometimes it's unhealthy thoughts, other times it's junk-food. But either way, once you put it into your body or your mind, you must process it or it will sliver its way through your psyche and tear you apart."

Lucinda had worked hard on dealing with her emotions. So she wanted to tackle the 'EFS' once and for all. But where should she start, when it wasn't tangible?

Lucinda rubbed her tired eyes and said out-loud: "Heavenly Father, why am I doing this? I already made peace with these things. My faith in you is unwavering. I give to you my burdens."

Her thoughts and prayers invoked a series of life changes, unbeknownst to her. Moments later she was sleeping. In her dreams, she relived one of the final arguments she'd had with her ex-husband prior to her divorce a year earlier. They were in the kitchen and she was crying: "I want to help you. Together we can beat your drug addiction."

He resented her implications. So he grabbed the dishes drying on the drain-board and slammed them onto the floor, violently shattering the ceramic.

"I don't need your damn help. Leave me alone," he shouted, stomping out of the house.

The dream shifted. Suddenly she was running down a long country road. Lucinda could feel someone behind her. But when she stopped and looked no one was there, just the land and its energy. After miles of running, she came upon an old rusty watering can and flipped it over; it was empty. She was tired and thirsty. The feeling someone was catching up to her became unbearable. She tossed the can to the side and tried to run faster. But her legs became heavier. Her body moved in slow-motion as her mind raced with fear.

Finally, she came upon a thick cornfield. Lucinda cut into the field and collapsed, lying amongst the vines feeling like something was coming for her. The nightmare shifted yet again, she was sitting at a high-stakes poker table with four people, chips neatly lined up in front of her. Lucinda held an Ace and a Queen. Stone-faced, she placed a high bet. Her opponents placed high bets too. The flop was flipped, an Ace and Queen. Showing no emotion, she placed another bet. Two of the four players matched it. The turn comes, all low cards.

Lucinda doodled with her chips, then confidently bet again. One opponent stayed in, matching her. Now comes the river, more low cards.

It was her bet. She slid all of her chips in. The other player matched her again. She flipped her cards. *Ye-ha, cowgirl! You won. No-no, wait a minute, you tied with the other player who also held an Ace and Queen!*

Lucinda split the pot and walked away with a few bucks. She craved more, wanting the whole pot, a new watering can full of cold refreshing water. She knew in her heart she deserved it all.

A loud sound suddenly woke her from the dream. Lucinda turned over. "What's that noise?" she asked, looking at the doggies nestled between her legs.

The three tilted their heads and raised their ears. The sound got louder.

"It's coming from the bedroom," she mumbled, getting up. The dogs waddled along like ducklings following their momma.

It's a train's whistle. Lucinda froze. *Now it's coming from the front of the house*! She ran back into the living room, the doggies racing after her. Panic-stricken, she slid a red velvet curtain to the side and looked out the window. There was nothing but the reflection from the streetlights shimmering on wet pavement.

Moments later, Lucinda flopped back onto the sofa, unable to shake the haunting feeling that something was coming for her, just like in her dream.

Malibu – Present Day

"HEY, MARLO, GOOD TO SEE YOU AGAIN—it's been a long time." Ricky bent down to kiss my cheek, then quickly adjusted his hair back into place. He was a handsome specimen and he knew it. I had met him several times on the movie set and heard many stories about his extra-curricular romantic activities.

"Good to see you too."

"Thomas, Marlo, this is my girlfriend Lucinda. You met at one of the softball games."

We shook our heads and smiled wider. "Hi," we said in unison.

"I remember that game cause it's the only one I've been to," I admitted.

"Me too," Lucinda said.

"You two are already yackin' away. Good. I knew you would get along," Ricky boasted.

We laughed. He reminded me of the disco guys I used to serve at the bar. It dawned on me that I probably did serve drinks to Ricky—the more I watched and listened to him, the more sure I was. Then it hit me—*could he have been the lousy tipper in the booth with the girl the night I met Thomas? Hmmm.*

"Well, it's sure nice to see you both." Lucinda turned to Thomas, "Ricky has told me so much about you."

"Don't believe everything, but it was me who ran for the eighty-yard touchdown in senior year," Thomas said.

"No way, Tommy," Ricky protested. "You can stop there. I already warned her you might say that."

I raised my brows. I wasn't use to hearing someone call my Thomas "Tommy." It was cute, the heckling between the boys. I sensed a true friendship and even some healthy competition between them.

Lucinda and I glanced at each other and shrugged. "Looks like New Jersey breeds them well," she commented.

"Yeah—and who would've guessed that we would be the lucky ones to find them?"

LUCINDA'S PAST

LUCINDA WAS TIRED AND OFF-BALANCE from the restless night with train whistles and weird dreams. Over her morning coffee, she concluded it wasn't so strange to hear the whistle of a train since the station was just a few miles away. It was her awareness of this that was new.

She looked at the clock, downed the last of her coffee, and hustled into gear. She didn't want to be late for her acting class. Her true passion was acting. She felt confident that with dedication and hard work she could land a role on a television series. When the most popular psychic in Texas had vowed she would be a big-time movie star, it confirmed her desire and made her want it all the more. For over two years, once a week she attended acting classes where the role-playing she did as a teenager seemed to come in handy.

"Aspiring ones, remember the demo reel you made a few months ago?" her acting teacher dramatically asked one day.

"Yes," the students replied with curiosity.

"Well, I sent it to my friend, the casting agent and, no surprise to me, one of you has been chosen to play a small part in the Martin Scorsese film that's coming to town!"

The class froze in their seats, anxious to hear who had landed the role.

"First, I'd like to say that all of you are truly gifted actors. But for this particular scene they have chosen Lucinda. Congratulations! This is the chance of a lifetime, dear, to work on a big budget feature with top actors. You'll be in the opening scene with one of the leads."

Lucinda was stunned. "Thank you so much for this opportunity! I won't let you down." She jumped up from her chair and hugged her teacher.

For the next few weeks at the salon, the main gossip over the shampoo bowl was about her upcoming part with one of Hollywood's sexiest men. In her waking and sleeping hours, Lucinda recited her dialogue backwards and forwards.

One month later, she was on the movie set for the first day of filming, which was nerve-wracking. But she loved every amazing minute as the cast and crew worked hard to get into the flow of the film. She would soon be face-to-face with one of her favorite actors. It was truly a dream come true.

Scorsese wanted a wide master shot with only one camera, no cuts. So each of the 33 people in the scene had to know their part and position perfectly. Over and over, she listened to instructions from the Assistant Director guiding her on where to bump into the lead actor, detain him for a few seconds, then blend in with a group on a crowded sidewalk. After twenty rehearsals, the Director was finally ready for a run-through with the leads.

As the stand-in stepped out, in walked the lead actor. He was taller, slimmer and even more handsome than on film. Lucinda tried not to stare as he casually headed towards her.

"Hi, I'm George."

"Hello I'm Lu."

"QUIET!" shouted the Assistant Director.

Not a peep was heard from the crowd, but Lucinda heard her heart pounding under her blouse and she swore George could too. They did a few rehearsals that were spot on. Then it was time for the real deal. "AND ROLLING," the Director called out.

As adrenaline rushed through her body, Lucinda took her cue, then moved towards George. Playing like she was chatting on her cell phone, she bumped into him.

"Oops, sorry, hey, don't I know you from somewhere?" She said her line seductively, looking into his eyes.

"Uh, I don't think so. I would remember you," he grinned.

"Oh, maybe it's not you after all." She said her final line with a ditzy 'tude and casually returned to talking on the phone as she disappeared into the crowd. George shrugged, then continued on his way. Knees weak from excitement, Lucinda continued to her final mark. On the way she spotted a dark haired, good-looking man watching her closely.

He kind of looks like the actor, she thought. His eyes didn't leave her. Not paying attention to where she was going, she tripped on the curb and quickly caught herself before she could fall flat on her face. Embarrassed, she kept her head down and blended in with the people scurrying along the sidewalk.

"Cut, cut!" the Director shouted, breaking the moment. Everyone froze. "It's a print—it's a print. And it's a beauty, man!"

The energy was riveting. Everyone clapped and cheered. The A.D. quieted everyone again while Scorsese viewed the piece on the play-back video monitor. Not so much star-struck as struck by Cupid's arrow, Lucinda peeked between two people, trying to find the mystery man who resembled George. She finally spotted him scanning the area. "Is he looking for me?" she wondered hopefully.

Strangely enough, her thoughts flew back to last month: the train whistle, the weird dreams and the haunting feeling that someone was chasing her.

"Ouch," she gasped, reaching into her back skirt pocket. "What the heck's sticking me? Wardrobe should've removed this tag." She pulled it out.

A blink later, the mystery man stood before her, "Hi, I'm Ricky."

Lucinda was frazzled. Her throat became dry.

Without skipping a beat, Ricky continued, "I'm the stunt double for George Clooney." His voice was deep, with a heavy East Coast accent. He was definitely Italian too.

Lucinda tried to answer but could only smile. Ricky thrust his right hand out to shake hers.

I know she can talk. She had dialogue, he thought as he waited for her to respond.

She finally reached out her left hand, dropping the tag she was holding to the ground. He picked it up. "What's this?"

"It's from wardrobe."

"It looks like a train ticket."

Lucinda snatched the paper from him. "A train ticket?" She looked at it closely as her eyes popped wide. "It's a train ticket!"

"Where ya going?" he wanted to know.

"Um...I'm not sure!"

"Well, what's the ticket say?"

She read it aloud: *The 440 Train—First Class Seating to the next chapter of your life.*

"Hmmm," she mumbled, as puzzled as Ricky.

"I think someone's playing a gag," she said, concealing the 'butterflies' flying wildly in her tummy from his presence.

"With this cast and crew, it wouldn't surprise me."

"But everyone's so nice and happy."

"It's movies like this that make the downtime less awful."

"I can imagine. But this is my first union job."

"Wow! Did you luck out! You did really well."

"Thank you—but inside I was trembling."

"It didn't show."

She blushed. "So, how long have you been a stuntman?"

"Almost fifteen years."

"Wow!"

A long pause as the two just smiled at each other like embarrassed children.

"Well, I better get these clothes back to wardrobe and sign out with the Unit Manager."

"Will I see you again?" Ricky asked hopefully.

"I'm wrapped—but I guess I can swing by the set later if you want me to."

"Yeah, yeah, I'd like to talk more with you."

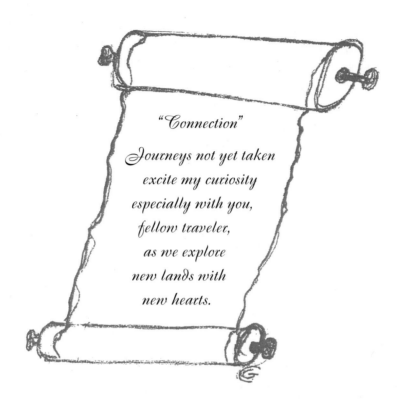

"Connection"

Journeys not yet taken
excite my curiosity
especially with you,
fellow traveler,
as we explore
new lands with
new hearts.

"Then I guess I'll see you soon." Lucinda smiled.

"Alright then. See you soon," he chuckled, starting to walk away. Then he stopped. "Wait! What's your name?"

"Oh, my gosh! Lucinda, it's Lucinda."

"Well, it's been very nice to meet you, Lucinda."

Now they both turned away, still grinning. Lucinda nearly tripped on her own two feet, but quickly turned to see if Ricky was watching. He wasn't. He had disappeared into the crowd.

At the dressing room trailer, Lucinda ripped the masking tape with her name on it off the trailer door as a keepsake and used it to stick the train ticket on today's page in her day planner.

Then she jotted some notes in her day planner: *"I'm taking this as a good sign. What a blessed day. Thank You, Heavenly Father. Wait a minute, a train ticket? Last time I heard a train I had a feeling something was coming for me. Is this some type of joke? Or is it serendipity? Holy Horsehair, what was that stuntman all about? Oh my, I think I'm in love. No-no, I'm not in love, not love, just love-struck. Yes, there's a big differ-ence—isn't there?"* she sighed and closed the book.

MALIBU – PRESENT DAY

MY CURIOSITY GOT THE BEST OF ME. I had to know if Ricky was the guy in the booth, the lousy tipper: "Did you ever go to the High Amp Disco on Route 22 in Jersey?"

"Yeah! Many times. I was the one who turned Thomas on to the club."

"Really?"

"Yeah. The night you two met, I was there."

"You were?"

"I was with a date, though—I wasn't with the guys."

"Oh my gosh!" I laughed.

"What? You remember me from that night?" he blushed.

"I think so…"

"A date, huh?" Lucinda chimed in, mock-jealous.

"It was before you and me, babe!"

"I'm sure, I'm sure," she joked.

"You know you're the only one for me." He hushpuppy-eyed her. She returned a Cheshire cat smile.

I interrupted their flirty gaze. "I'm pretty sure I served you and your date drinks that night."

"You sure it was me?" Ricky shrugged.

"I think so. I kind of remember an interesting money exchange?"

"Really?" he said defensively.

"Oh, that!" Lucinda teased, pinching him.

"Now, now girls," he glared.

I could tell he was becoming more uncomfortable with this line of questioning so I switched gears. "Uh, maybe it wasn't you."

"The sun sure feels nice." Thomas put his arm around my shoulders, letting me know is was time to move on.

"Yes it does," Ricky happily agreed. "Babe, let's get hooked up here so we can catch some rays," he directed as East Coast as they come.

"Okay, okay," Lucinda grumbled, while winking at me. I got the message that she knew her man had been a cheapskate.

LUCINDA'S PAST

LUCINDA CAME AROUND THE SET several times through-out the month to watch the filming and give her heated attraction with the sexy stuntman a chance to evolve. He always seemed glad to see her, but there were always lots of women around him. She couldn't help thinking, *I know he's stunt-doubling for one of the sexiest men in Holly-wood, but does he take it literally?*

"Hey, Lucinda, good to see you," Ricky shouted, heading her way as the group of women he had been entertaining stared at Lucinda with curiosity. "I thought we could go out for a drink after I finish tonight." He kissed her high on the cheekbone.

The kiss threw her off. "Um, sorry, I'd love to but I'm working on an infomercial."

"Good for you, another gig. Whadya' doing?"

She sighed. "It's not an acting role. I'm doing the make-up and hair for an actress who's plugging an electric toothbrush."

"Oh, cool, you got lots of talents up your sleeve actor, make-up art-ist, hair stylist."

"Thanks," she said, blushing.

It suddenly dawned on him that he just got shot down. His jaw tightened and his head tilted as he said, "You know, I'm getting mixed vibes here," in his East Coast accent.

"What do you mean?" Her brows came together in concern.

"Well, you've come by a few times and it seems like—well it seems like we got some chemistry, but you always have something going on so we can't go out."

"Oh. Sorry, it's just a busy time for me right now."

"Hey, no harm. But I'm leaving town soon and I…"

"You are!" she interrupted in surprise.

"Yeah, we're heading to L.A. for the rest of the filming."

"Los Angeles, hey?"

"Yeah, home field advantage."

"Oh right, you live in California."

"Yep, I love L.A."

"Really?" she remarked in a low tone.

"Really. Well at least I'll get to see you Friday night, right?" he said hopefully.

"Yes, Friday night, I'll see you," she replied, feeling out of sorts.

The Stunt Coordinator needed Ricky in the next shot. As he scooted off, she hesitantly waved good-bye, thinking, *I hope I didn't move too slowly.*

On Friday, the Texas Wrap Party was underway at a five-star hotel. As soon as she arrived, Lucinda spotted Ricky talking to a group of beautiful women near a majestic marble fountain. There he is with his usual entourage, she thought as the women flirted with him. They hung on his words, tossed their hair, and touched his shoulders a lot.

Lucinda took a deep breath, thinking *This is my last chance to make an impression,* and entered the room exuding confidence. Ricky spotted her immediately. He continued talking to the girls as his gaze fixed on the hot blonde in the tight low-cut red dress that just about covered her girlie-hood assets. Five minutes later they were outside in a private dark corner.

Ricky stood against a wall. Lucinda stood in front of him. "I'd really like to get to know you better," she whispered sincerely.

"I'd like to get to know you more to Lucy," Ricky said, pulling her against him.

"Please call me Lucinda," she requested with bated breath.

"Okay Lucinda," he agreed, twirling her long hair.

"I wish you weren't leaving already. I wanted to slowly get to know you better," she admitted.

"So, because I'm leaving tomorrow you aren't going to take it slow?" He gently tugged on her hair. She stepped back a bit, "No such luck," she smirked.

"This is about as slow as I can go. You know, with me being a man, you being WO-man."

"Great." She pulled away. "You're into cave man theories."

"No, not at all. I'm hip."

"You probably believe women should always be pregnant or in the kitchen cooking."

"Well, not always pregnant you gotta keep your girlish figures. But cooking yes."

"WHAT!"

"Kidding, just kidding, I'm a modern guy. I believe in equality, but I'm leaving town tomorrow and you're beautiful and smell so good," he said, forgetting his primitive comment.

"Uh-huh. Thank you, Mr. Smooth Talker." She glared into his hazel eyes.

Ricky gently grabbed Lucinda's face and pressed his lips tenderly into hers. She surrendered to the moment. His skin was soft and warm. His hands were large and cushy, like fluffy down pillows. Lucinda suddenly sensed something new and it scared her.

"Wait!" She snapped back her head.

"What? Do I have bad breath?"

"No not at all. You taste sweet like peppermints."

"Oh, good," he said with a devilish grin, moving back in for another kiss.

Lucinda put her hand over his mouth. "I want to play it safe."

"Oh I get it. No problem, I brought protection," he mumbled, his tongue moving between her fingers.

"You're impossible," she chuckled, dropping her hand.

Ricky looked deeply into her eyes, then kissed her long and passionately.

"Is this safe enough?" he moaned, still kissing her.

"Umm-hmmm," she responded, her lips sealed against his.

Slowly, his hands moved to her butt. She interrupted the kiss and stepped away, looking at Ricky with concerned hound-dog eyes. "Maybe we should go back into the party," she suggested.

"Well, wait I need to cool off a minute." He tugged his shirttails.

She blushed and looked away. Lucinda was being a cautious Virgo —she wanted to understand the exact purpose of this man in her life before saddling up the Italian Stallion.

Lucinda excused herself and headed to the ladies room to reapply her lipstick. Looking into the mirror, she had an epiphany, she knew in her heart that Ricky would be in her future. But how it would all play out was the part that scared her. She was scared of herself and scared that the Emotional Food Snake would slither its way into her logical thinking rather than letting her pursue her heartfelt desires. *Okay, I'm just going to trust what I feel and not get too caught up with expectations*, she affirmed to her reflection.

For the rest of the night, Ricky and Lucinda mingled at the party making small talk with people about the movie. But in their thoughts they both kept replaying their magical kissing scene. After an hour, she invited him to her house for coffee and crumb cake. She knew he liked the sweet cake from watching him nibble it on the craft service table at the set.

After only a few minutes of Lucinda's chattering about her interest in the movie business—which felt like hours to both of them it became obvious she was not going to offer him anything beyond food. Though the late night snack was satisfying, Ricky had hoped for more. *Geez, how much can a guy take,* he thought as she crossed and uncrossed her long lean legs. Finally, he rose from the couch.

"As much as I like you, and your house and the dogs, I should get going. My plane leaves in a few hours." Sporting a sweat, he tugged on his stretched-out shirttails.

"Oh, okay. Well, I had a great time getting to know you more and I'd love to keep in touch," she said, walking him politely to the door.

"And thanks for honoring my wishes about taking it slowly."

"Yeah-yeah, sure, you're welcome. We'll keep in touch, that sounds great. And if you ever decide to give Hollywood a try, let me know." He kissed her lightly on the cheek and ran to his rental car.

"I will." She smiled while slowly shutting the door, then rested against it for a moment, thinking: *He was actually listening.*

Minutes later she was cuddled up with her pooches, content with how the night had gone. But as she replayed their couch scene, she felt more insecure. *Oh gosh! Maybe he wasn't listening as much as I thought. Should I have given in to a one-night stand? Or did I play my cards right?*

Lucinda flopped her head down on a pillow and sighed. Then she sighed harder as she caught the scent of his cologne on her neck. *Uh-oh I think the Emotional Food Snake just reared its head again!* And let's not forget poor little Ricky, who flew *stiffly* back to Los Angeles.

"Miss You"
If I were to surrender
my love to you
Where would that leave me?
If I were to shelter you
from the storms
Would you feel safe?
If I only touched
your heart once,
Would you
remember me?

MALIBU – PRESENT DAY

"WELL, THEN LET'S ALL ENJOY THE SUN," I reiterated seeing that Ricky felt put on the spot by the walk down memory lane.

"I will. I brought the baby oil to fry me," he said seeming more relaxed now.

"And I brought the sunscreen," Lucinda added as they continued with their beach set-up.

"I'll catch you kids later. I'm going to look for sea-glass while it's low tide." Thomas kissed me on the lips. "Do you want to come along, Marlo?"

"No thanks. I'm having a terrific time just melting into the calmness of the beach mood." As Thomas walked towards the water, I smoothed the sand out from under my butt and positioned myself into a comfy spot. I was pretty jazzed about meeting such a neat woman as Lucinda and had a feeling we would become good friends.

Suddenly I felt Lucinda coming up behind me. "Hey, Marlo. I hope I didn't make you uncomfortable with the comment I made to Ricky— I was just teasing him."

"No-no, I felt he was getting embarrassed so I thought it was better to leave the past in the past. You know, just in case he is *still* a lousy tipper."

Lucinda snorted, then laughed. I laughed at her laughter.

"Oh my gosh." She turned red then snorted again.

"It's okay, I just farted."

"You didn't!" She raised her brows over large leopard-framed sun-glass.

"Kidding!"

It was refreshing to meet someone so warm and funny. It seemed like I had known her for years. I felt a bit guilty for telling Nina about the long-legged beauty with gigolo Ricky the first time I saw her. But at the time I thought she was just another one of his pretty trophies. My instincts now sensed that her real beauty resides inside, so I couldn't wait to call Nina and tell her the juicy revelation. I imagined Nina doing her eerie 'Bette Davis' imitation, said of course with love and laughter: *"Rotten, dahling, stinkin' rotten, pretty girl and she's nice! What shall we do with her?"*

Lucinda looked at me with curious eyes. "What?"

"Nothing, just thinking about something. It's a good thing."

"If you say so." Her one brow rose. "There are more people coming today, right?"

"Yeah. Two more guys with their girls."

As Ricky fumbled with their blanket and folding lounge chairs, Lucinda got distracted. "Great. Well, I better help Ricky with the chairs, so I'll talk to you in a few."

"Sounds good." I shifted my focus to Thomas moseying along the beach and thought about how imperative the shoreline is to the Earth. It's the meeting place of land and water, water and land. Thomas was ankle-deep in the ocean, chasing sea glass and shells, filling his blue bucket with Nature's gifts. He was always so happy at the beach, free as a child with no responsibilities.

Ricky and Lucinda had settled into their spot on the sand and looked ideally matched as couples go. Both were tall, well-groomed "Type-A" personalities, she the blonde playful palomino, he the dark assertive stallion. But sensing beyond their physical looks I could tell they really loved each other. More importantly, they seemed to really like each other.

LUCINDA'S PAST

AS PROMISED, LUCINDA AND RICKY kept in touch straightaway by e-mails, phone calls and an occasional greeting card in the mail. They joked, talked about their past, including former romantic relationships. They shared their dreams and chatted about current events. They were friends, not lovers, although a penetrating cold shower or a self-inflicted massage may have taken place in private after the telephone receivers were hung up.

One night before falling asleep, the Texan goddess thought long and hard about Ricky. She recalled the unusual occurrences prior to and during their meeting, including the bizarre train ticket stuck in her skirt.

She remembered the even stranger message the ticket contained and wondered, *Is this kismet? I do feel we'll be together and it seems obvious that this is the next chapter of my life.* She shut the ringer off her phones and dozed off with fantasy scenarios playing in her mind.

The following morning, Lucinda woke up cheery, optimistic and happy. Her life seemed to have some type of magical order. It was a feeling she had yearned for. What she didn't expect, however, was that the day would bring an unexpected turn of events making her re-think her early optimism.

While her morning coffee was brewing, Lucinda checked her answering machine. It blinked, showing two messages.

"Hi, Lucinda, it's me Randal. I want to let you know I'm well, very well. I've done a lot of work on myself and I'd love to see you. I miss our chats and I have some spectacular news I'd like to share."

My ex! Lucinda paced the floor, heart racing. She twiddled with her hair, then flopped on a chair as the next message came on.

"Hi, babe, it's me Ricky. I'm coming back to Texas tomorrow. The company is sending a skeleton crew to do some pick-up shots on a fight scene. I'll only be in town for two nights. I hope we can hook up. Ciao, baby."

By now, Lucinda's hair was knotted in a ponytail. A couple of finger nails were chewed and sharp. *What the heck is going on!* she grumbled.

The alarm signaling the brew was completed rang on the coffee maker, startling her. Walking like a zombie, she crossed to the kitchen and poured coffee into a mug. The dogs watched, patiently waiting for their breakfast by the dog dishes.

The rest of Lucinda's morning ritual was a blur. After arriving at the salon, she was able to think more clearly. Looking into the mirror and seeing her reflection gave her a sense of steadiness and composure, an opportunity to stay in the present moment.

"Well, well, well. Lookie here, flowers for Miss Lucinda." A co-worker handed her a vase of lilacs, freesia and tuberoses.

"Oh my goodness, they smell heavenly!" She breathed in the fragrant blooms, placing the vase on the counter of her workstation. "How did he know these are my favorite?" she mumbled, unclipping the small greeting card: *Please meet me at our old favorite place at seven, Randal.*

Lucinda plopped onto the chair and twirled around several times before facing center again. *This can't be happening. Why now? All those times I wanted to talk and he wasn't available now he's available and I'm... well, I'm into someone else.*

Her cell phone rang. The caller ID showed it was Ricky. It rang a second time, third, forth. She finally picked up: "Hi."

"Hey, babe, did you get my message last night?"

"Uh, yes. How great that you're coming to town."

"I don't have to work till tomorrow night so we can hook-up later if you'd like?"

"Sure—that sounds great."

"You okay? You sound funny."

"No. I mean yes, I'm okay just some news."

"You want to share?"

"Um—no. I mean it's nothing just something silly I have to work through."

"Okay, well, if it's a bad time to get together, I can see you another time."

"Yes. I mean no, it's not a bad time, I'd like to see you tonight."

"You're funny."

"How about we meet at my place at eight-thirty?"

"Eight-thirty it is. I look forward to seeing you."

"I look forward to seeing you too, Ran…Ricky" *Holy Horsehair! I almost called him Randal!*

Lucinda's client soon walked in and turned her troubled thoughts into a three-hour creative make-over project. The rest of the day was busy and loud, full of chit-chat and drama—just what she needed to get Ricky *and* Randal off her mind.

When she got home, Lucinda poured herself a glass of white wine and relaxed on the couch. She rubbed her tired feet as she sank back into her comfy sofa. *What am I going to do about Randal?* she whined to her dogs. *I should just tell him it's not a good idea to meet and that I'm involved with someone else.*

She took a few more sips of the sweet grapes and reached for her cell phone. It was not in her purse. From her landline, she dialed her cell number as she listened carefully, hoping to hear it ring from under a pillow, under a table, in the car. But no phone. It suddenly dawned on her that she'd left it on her workstation. Still holding the landline, she dialed Randal's number, recalling it by heart.

"Cheerio!"

"Hi, Randal it's Lucinda."

"Lucinda, oh how lovely I was wondering if you were going to call after receiving the flowers and my request."

"Uh—Randal, about tonight."

"Flowers Blossoming"
You have changed
immensely and intensely.
A flutter of your wings—
A redirecting
of your eyes
A train rolled in
and your new life
arrived.

"Yes, Lucinda, I'd like too see you, there's so many things I'd like to say and I don't feel the telephone will do. We need to be face to face," he pleaded.

"It's just that so much time has gone by and I'm not sure that seeing each other is a good idea."

"I understand your trepidation, but I have some news and I'd like you to hear it from me rather than someone else."

"Oh, oh, my gosh! I misunderstood your reason to meet," she laughed, finishing the wine.

"Oh dear! Well that could be my fault, my message possibly gave you the wrong idea, and then the flowers. Oh I see what you mean, Love, so sorry!"

"It's okay," she sighed. "But I'm glad we got that out of the way."

"Yes, phew! Well, now that we know it's not about <u>that</u> we can carry on, yes?"

"Yes, we can carry on."

"So tonight at seven at our old favorite spot?"

"Sure, but I only have an hour."

"Splendid. I appreciate you making the time for me."

Lucinda took a long look at the living room, pleased with her swift ambience setting for Ricky's arrival. Tall candles stood decoratively on all the tables. A bottle of champagne chilled in an ice bucket. Freshly-cleaned throw blankets were casually laid over the arms of the couch. A platter with meats and cheeses would be put out when she came home.

As she approached the restaurant an hour later to meet Randal, however, she became nervous. It had been over a year since she had last seen him and even longer since they had an intelligent conversation. But in her heart she knew this was a good thing—possibly an ending to her occasional nightmares.

When she opened the door to the steak house, Randal was standing next to the hostess, chatting, looking debonair and handsome as ever.

"Lucinda, love, you look smashing. Thanks for meeting me." He hugged her.

"Hi. Glad to see you looking so well too."

The cute hostess escorted them to a table—their old favorite by a window in the far corner.

"Would you like a glass of red? Or maybe white this evening?" he asked.

"Just water with lemon for me. What about you?"

"I'll be having a bubbly water with lime—that's my new cocktail."

"Well, whatever you're doing, it looks good on you."

"Flattery will get you everywhere, darling. I'm so happy you agreed to meet me tonight. I have some exciting news, actually two pieces of news."

"Really? I'm very curious."

The waiter placed the soft drinks down, along with the check, and told Randal to flag him if he needed anything else.

"You told him we needed *priv*-acy didn't you?" she asked, putting an emphasis on the British pronunciation of the word.

"Yes I did, you tease. I know you have plans after this and I'm too excited to eat."

"That's fine. So, Randal tell me what in heaven's name brought you to call me after all this time."

He explained in animated length his painful route to sobriety. Then he handed her a cashier's check.

"What the heck is this for?" she asked, staring at the paper.

"It's the money I would have spent on drugs and booze—if it wasn't for you saving me."

"What!" She shook her head in disbelief.

"It's true, Lucinda. This is what was left from my father's wedding gift to us. I want you to have it. I deprived you of so much the last two years of our marriage and this money was supposed to be for our future. I figured I blew the other half so you should have this, to do with what you please."

"I-I don't know what to say. It feels odd to accept this."

"It's yours. Please enjoy it freely."

Lucinda stared out the window, barely seeing her reflection in the glass.

"Oh, I know what you're thinking," he said.

"What?" she dared.

"You feel like it's a pay off or some kind of redemption act."

"Actually yes. Is it?"

"No, not it the least. It's yours. My father would have wanted it this way. It's the gentlemanly thing to do."

"I can hear your father now … *Randal, my son*." Lucinda delivered her best English accent and soon had her ex laughing so loudly that all heads turned in their direction.

"Now, the second part of my good news—I've met someone. We've known each other for some time now. I'm moving back to England and she is coming with me to be my bride."

"Oh my gosh! Wow! You're really shocking me tonight. All good news, of course, but I'm shocked nonetheless."

Randal nodded and smiled. "It's big news, I know. But I'm so happy and she's such a wonderful lady."

"Congratulations." Lucinda grabbed his hands and held them. "God bless you, Randal."

For the remaining time, she told him what she had been up to, including the new love in her life.

On the way home Lucinda laughed aloud and did a sitting jig as she thought about the hefty check in her purse and how truly funny life is. As soon as she got home, she lit the candles and put her favorite mellow country CD into the player. Ricky would be arriving any minute.

As she passed the telephone, she noticed she had a message. It also dawned on her that she never picked-up her cell phone from work after meeting Randal.

She hit the play button. First message: *"Babe, you're not going to believe this—I was on my way to the airport and they've changed our location to Philly! It seems there was a major problem with the street permits there. I'm so sorry I wish I were talking to you in person. I'll call you once I'm settled into my hotel room."*

Lucinda replayed the message to make sure she heard correctly. *Oh rats!*

One by one she blew out the candles, watching the smoke dance until it disappeared. Once all the candles were diffused, the living room was filled with a misty cloud of wax residue and quiet emptiness.

Lucinda put the champagne back in the refrigerator and stood at the open door grazing on the meat and cheese platter. She must have lost track of time because when the telephone rang, startling her out of her food trance, a quarter of the platter was already gone. She rubbed her belly and ran to answer the phone.

"Hi, babe. Man, am I sorry about the travel mix-up," Ricky said quickly.

"I understand, but I sure was looking forward to seeing you."

"Me too you—for sure! So tell me, what's new and exciting?"

"Funny you should ask," she took a long breath.

MALIBU – PRESENT DAY

THE BEACH WAS ALIVE AND INSPIRING. Nature's music was feeding my creativity. I was bombarded with ideas. I pulled out a new antique-style hardbound notebook, put a pen to paper and began writing.

Thomas returned from his walk and dumped his bucket full of sea treasures onto the sand. Tiny fragments of green and white sea glass and assorted shells were his prized findings. While he inspected each piece, I continued with my writing.

A few pages later the sound of laughter caught my attention. It was Lucinda and Ricky playing paddleball. Watching them play, heckle, compete and smile at each other made me think about how relationships actually start. And then about how they evolve to a middle place with hopes to comfortably hover there for the duration of their love. But when it doesn't work out, the end of a story can be so catastrophic to the body, mind, spirit and emotions of one's being. Relationships are a genuine mystery to us humans.

I shook off the drama rattling through my imagination and thought about Thomas and me, and our love story. After years of togetherness, we are quite content in the hovering mode. But hovering can take a lot of energy, and it's the energy of working together that either makes or breaks a relationship.

I wasn't sure why I was so fixed on the topic of relationships, but the thoughts were strong and real. I concluded that I wasn't the only one thinking these random thoughts—they must be coming from the Cosmic Whole and I am simply feeling the feelings of many. Let's face it, more and more we're discovering that we're all connected. Even if we're thousands of miles away from each other, we are linked in some way, shape or form.

While I was thinking about love and partnerships, I continued on with my poems. It made for some good writing and heart-felt greeting cards. Meanwhile, Thomas was simply enjoying being at the beach, his oasis, while Lucinda and Ricky continued running and playing in the sand.

"Harmony"

Our connection is pure
—wrapped in a
cosmic blanket
that only you and I can
feel —others can see.
I'm blessed to have
met you and am
grateful to the Stars
for lining us up.

LUCINDA'S PAST

SIX MONTHS LATER, LUCINDA was still fixed on the higher purpose of meeting Ricky. Meanwhile the telephone bills were racking up and she wasn't the least bit attracted to any other man. It was also getting harder for her to say good-night to him long-distance. She wondered if he was missing her as much as she was missing him, and if he was also having trouble connecting to the opposite sex since their meeting.

One day while taking a break between hair clients, she thought *If Ricky is going to be part of my future then I better get off my high horse. I need to stop playing it so safe and ride in on Faith's horse so I can make moves in a new direction.*

She guided herself with a new conviction. Two weeks later, Lucinda's salon and acting class friends came together to throw her a going-away party. Juicy steaks, finger-lickin' drippy ribs and pounds of creamy white potato salad were featured with endless shots of the finest whiskey.

With her make-up kit, doggies, some of her favorite furniture and clothes in tow, Lucinda drove cross-country with a trailer hitched to her Mustang, destined for California. Faith and determination were her closest friends and she kept them at the forefront of her mission at all times. She had planned her move like a true Virgo—with the help of a friend in the real estate business, she had been pre-approved for a month-to month lease in a luxurious animal friendly apartment in the

San Fernando Valley. The money that Randal gave her allotted her some time to get her house in order, literally and physically.

When she arrived at her new building just off Ventura Boulevard, Lucinda hired a couple of guys from a street corner who were looking for work to help her with the heavy furniture. In a matter of hours, she was sitting on an old chair in her new home with the dogs snuggled in their cushy bed. Her landline phone wouldn't be connected until tomorrow so she used her cell phone to make the highly anticipated call.

"Hi Ricky! How are you?"

"Hey, Lucinda! I'm good, I'm good. Just on my way to meet the guys and watch the NBA playoffs."

"Sounds like fun."

"Whadya doing?" he asked.

"Well, you may not believe this, but I'm in California."

"What!"

"Yes, I moved here with my dogs," she said, clenching her jaw.

"You've got to be kidding! Why didn't you tell me?"

"I wanted to surprise you."

"Holy Toledo, you sure did."

A pause. Lucinda bit her lip and waited. "So what do you think?"

"It's a great surprise, I'm just shocked. I know you talked about moving to Hollywood, but I had no idea you'd really do it."

"Yup, I have faith. When I really want something, I do it," she said fast, with one leg bouncing up and down.

"You go, girl!" he replied, laughing.

Relaxing at last, she fell back onto the chair. Her leg stopped shaking.

"Where are you now? I'm coming over," he said.

"Really?" She sprung up.

"Yeah, I mean if it's okay."

"Yes, it's great! I'd love to see you. "

She gave him the address, then quickly hopped into the shower.

Giddie-up, welcome to Hollywood Texan.

Lucinda had her reasons for not letting Ricky know he was the main motivation for her move to California. It only took a few dates for her to see that this native New Jersey stud was living the Hollywood dream. Without a doubt, this man put the "B" in Bachelor and she didn't want to be just another notch in his bedpost—she wanted to be the only one. She had assumed the harem hanging around him on the movie set was just a fluke and never realized this was his true nature. *Ah, hello, red flag!*

She thought back to a few of their conversations. Looking at it from a fresh perspective, she realized there had always been hints of Ricky's Don Juan syndrome. So she played it safe again and stayed committed to only having romantic dinners, sweaty workouts at the gym, and long chats at coffee shops with him. Ricky didn't approach her sexually after what he had gone through in Texas. In fact, he seemed to be enjoying their platonic friendship. The idea of no sex was a turn-on challenge in his eyes. For Lucinda the hopeful romantic, it was about integrity and a sustainable future with a man she was deeply in love with.

They played cat and mouse for a few more weeks until one heated moment when she couldn't take it anymore. The bell rang it was time for her to bravely face her fears.

It happened at her place: A few glasses of wine, soft music and subtle lighting made for the ideal romantic atmosphere. While sitting on the couch, she leaned into Ricky and placed her lips on his. He melted like soft-serve ice cream on a hot summer's day. Her root chakra throbbed with desire, pulsating like a drum to the beat of her heart. The folds of her flesh tingled.

She pushed him down and crawled over his firm, muscular body. He happily surrendered to her. From all the anticipation, the first round was short-lived. But within minutes he got back up for the Texan. This left her speaking in tongues and feeling as free as a wild horse running through an open field. Making love to Ricky was everything she had imagined and more.

For weeks they satisfied each other's needs emotionally as friends but now with the bonus package of steamy tantalizing sex. Lucinda was pleased. There was no doubt she had played her cards right with the flirtatious stuntman.

Shortly after, however, he did a complete about-face the Italian Stallion suddenly became unavailable, leaving Lucinda to re-evaluate her big move. "I know he's afraid. We're getting so close, that's why he pulled away," she told her four-leggeds, "it's okay, I know how to work this I'm going to give him some space to deal with his feelings, then he'll come back to me."

"*Rruff!*" One barked playfully, seemingly to reassure her.

She hooked a leash to the dogs' collars and took them for a walk. *It's the perfect opportunity to forge ahead with my two other reasons for moving to California*, she thought, waking down a tree-lined street.

The following morning, Lucinda drove to the Screen Actors Guild office in Hollywood and picked up a current list of talent agents. Then she spent days sending out hundreds of introduction letters, photos and resumes.

Meanwhile her savings account was shrinking. California was much more costly then Texas. She decided to take a breather from the acting plan and set her sights on finding a paying job. She thumbed through the classifieds for a beauty salon that was renting out space. But that didn't go as well as expected—shop owners weren't convinced a stylist from Texas was worthy of working in an L.A. salon.

What a bunch of ego maniacs, Lucinda grumbled, walking out of the third shop in frustration.

She found herself in the thick of the waiting game—waiting for Ricky to phone—waiting for an agent to call—waiting for a job and waiting wasn't one of her strong suits.

MALIBU – PRESENT DAY

FOR THE TIME BEING, I was done writing. Thomas sat beside me fumbling with seashells. Lucinda and Ricky wore themselves out with paddleball and retreated to their blanket.

A wave of emotions came over me as I suddenly felt as if I were waiting for something. "Thomas, when are the four of us going to start socializing?" I blurted.

"What do you mean?"

"Well, didn't we come here to meet up with your friends and social-*ize,*" I twanged.

"Yeah, so what's the problem?"

"The problem! Well, don't you think we should be sitting with them?" I nodded toward Lucinda and Ricky.

"We're all just doing our thing. Relax, Marlo."

I swore it was like dreaming a bizarre dream. Did I miss something?

Here I was waiting for my husband to take the lead while I had all the capabilities of starting the social chatter. It reminded me of other times I waited for my man to do something and it didn't go according to my schedule.

I thought about years ago, waiting for Thomas to call, to ask me out and to make love to me although that was worth the wait. But other times I just patiently waited and waited. Waiting at the post office, the bank, the market, the gas station, or even waiting for a train to pull into a station is one thing. But waiting for someone else to make the first move *or any move* is down-right infuriating!

I was having a huge shift in awareness. Typically I would become resentful or frustrated at the person causing me problems. Then it hit my like a brick *I was really upset with myself.*

I jolted out of my awakening and stood up. "I'm done waiting! I'm in my forties and I'm simply done waiting. Look out, handsome, 'cause I have only myself to be responsible for and waiting for anyone else is not on my calendar."

"Wh-what are you moaning about?" Thomas asked, dumbfounded. "Is it your hormones?" he wondered with a look of fright.

I bit my lip, then smiled at his obvious concern. "Maybe. Or maybe it's just the new Marlo." I kissed him, then walked confidently towards Lucinda and Ricky.

"Wait! Wait! I'm coming." Thomas shouted as he ran to catch up with me.

LUCINDA'S PAST

IT WAS EARLY MORNING. The sun had just come up. Lucinda was still on East Coast time so she used these early awakenings for reflection and prayer.

She sat up in bed. *Ahh, what a difference a day makes*, she thought as she stretched her arms over her head. *I refuse to look back. I'm here and I'm staying. I have faith this is where I'm supposed to be.*

She sat in silence and prayed for a sign. When her mind wondered too much, she recited a prayer. After an hour she felt regenerated, so she got out of bed and crossed to the living room.

On the fireplace mantle was a photo of her brother. She lit a candle in honor of Carl's birthday, which was today and thought about what age he would be and what he'd be doing. She took a few deep breaths, then went into the kitchen and prepared a pot of coffee.

While it was brewing, she removed a fireproof lock box from the hall closet and rummaged through its contents. Inside were keepsakes belonging to her brother. A smile broke across her face as a magical feeling resonated from the memorabilia. It was the energy of Love.

As she looked at some old photographs, a hand-sized card fell onto her lap: "Red Railroad, worth 200.00 dollars," she read aloud. *Funny, I remember he always bought the railroads in Monopoly.* She put the card back into the box, then locked it.

In the kitchen, Lucinda splashed some coffee into a cup while thinking about how often she used to play the board game with her sister and brother. *Those were good times.* She drifted momentarily, then took a sip of her coffee. *But what the heck is it with the all the train messages I've been getting over the past months?*

Lucinda topped off her coffee, then picked up the telephone and dialed a Michigan exchange, "Hey, Mom, how are you and Sis doing?"

As the day progressed, Lucinda knew what she had to do to change her chances of getting a job so she could keep moving forward. Her time in silence revealed this strategy. Suddenly the presence of her father surrounded her. The feeling of never walking alone encompassed her spirit. *Thank You, Father, for that confirmation.*

She stepped into a pair of shorts and put on a tee-shirt, then walked to a local Korean nail salon and indulged in a manicure and pedicure. *One of the few things that are less expensive on the West Coast,* she thought.

Back at home, she dug through an unpacked box of clothes and took out a leopard shirt and matching skin-tight spandex skirt that hugged her bootie to the max. She squeezed into the slinky outfit and looked in the mirror.

Nope something is still missing for this Hollywood vibe. She pulled a black bra out of a drawer. *Ah-ha! This is a deal maker!*

Lucinda snapped the bra and maneuvered its water-filled cups a little to the left, a little to the right like she was playing with water balloons. *Ha, ha,* she laughed, *now they're even.*

She applied her make-up heavier than usual and chose a darker shade of lipstick than she usually wore. She canned her usual leather cowboy boots and slipped on a pair of plastic high-heeled sandals instead.

Before getting to her final destination, she ran into a drugstore and purchased a mock pair of designer sunglasses. Minutes later she was walking into one of the hottest salons in the Valley, one known for their artsy work on celebrities. Eight hours later she walked out of the salon with cash in her pocket and a full-time job.

It was perfect timing. The salon owner, a native Texan, fell in love with Lucinda's independent attitude and years of hair dressing experience. It didn't hurt that they both used to frequent the same steakhouse back home.

On the way to home, Lucinda checked her cell for messages. "Hi, Lucinda. It's me, Ricky. Sorry I've been a bonehead lately. I miss you can I see you tonight?"

As hard as it was, she decided not to call him straightaway. She waited until the following afternoon and invited him to her house for a home-cooked meal. He happily agreed.

Lucinda took her time planning an evening to remember. The kitchen table was set with colorful Fiestaware. In the center was a round leopard-designed tray with seven white candles. The mood was calm and romantic. She prepared filet mignon with baked potato and steamed broccoli.

At exactly seven o'clock, the doorbell rang. Ricky was on time. This impressed her. She took another quick look in the mirror and gave a tug here, a flip there and a shimmy everywhere.

When she opened the door, she was awestruck by his stance, his smile, his joyful expression. He stepped into the room, lightly kissed her cheek and handed her a single pink rose. While she placed the rose into a bud vase, he moseyed around.

"Before we sit down to eat, can we talk?" he requested, placing a large gift bag on the floor.

"Yeah, sure." She admired how handsome he was in a button down coral-colored shirt, pleated blue jeans and classy white-and-black 'pimp' shoes. They sat on the oversized velvet loveseat that she had brought from Texas.

"Can I have some wine?" he asked, wiping his forehead.

She could see he was nervous. "Sure."

She popped the cork and poured the wine. He took a long sip, then sighed.

"Lucinda, I really like you," he said, holding tightly onto his glass. "I haven't had a solid relationship in years. I've gotten used to being wide open to dating."

She sat silently, listening to his words, and watching his body language.

"But I'm ready for a change. I would like to be your man if you would like to be my WO-man." He stood. "Remember Me man, You WO-man—from the party?"

"I remember." She put her head down and doodled with her fingernails.

With great anticipation, he waited for her answer.

She finally raised her head. "I would like that very much, Ricky, to be a couple."

"You would! Great! Phew! Okay, so it's safe to say that we're officially dating?"

"Yes." She smiled.

"Geez, it sure was easier when we were in high school," he said.

"Good observation, I agree. Maybe it's because we weren't so aware of the commitment."

"Commitment," he echoed softly, then smiled.

She stood, taking the glass from his hand and placed her arms around his waist. He held her head, leaning it on his breastbone. He gently stroked her soft hair. Gradually, she peeked over his shoulder.

"Hey, what's in the bag?" she asked with an innocent grin of a five-year-old.

"Open it it's for you."

"For me? You shouldn't have."

"I shouldn't have?"

"Well, I'm glad you did." She lifted a long box out of the bag. "Monopoly! Oh my goodness, what made you bring this?"

"I thought we could dirty up the game a bit with real money and sex barters."

"Sounds like fun. But why this game?" she asked wide-eyed.

"I don't know. I had a strong urge to play it with you, so I went to the store and bought it."

"This is too coincidental." She took a sip of her wine. "I came across something of my brother's that has to do with this very game."

"Hmm. Well, now that you mention it, it is kinda weird that I would buy this game 'cause I haven't played it since the Sixties."

"Really?"

"Yeah, the idea just popped into my head."

"Or maybe someone put it there. *Do do do do*," she sang eerily."

"R'you trying to get a rise out of me?"

"Sounds enticing."

He grinned and reached for her hips.

"Down, boy."

"Alright, alright. I just don't like to be spooked."

"Really? A big boy like you is afraid of divine intervention? With all the telephone conversations we had, I thought you believed in synchronicity."

"I do. It's just that well, maybe I don't have the faith that you have quite yet, especially regarding the world of our loved-ones who've passed away."

They looked into each other's eyes. Suddenly the kitchen lights flickered.

"Whoa—what's that?" he asked, startled.

"Probably just a bulb that needs changing."

"You sure?" He looked up. "Now you have my attention."

They headed into the kitchen. The light bulb popped, leaving the room flickering with shadows created by the candles.

"Come on now, tell me that you planned all this?" With wide eyes, he looked around

"No I promise you I did not. But it is nice, isn't it?"

"Yeah, if you're sure we're alone."

"We're never alone."

"There's a lot more to you than meets the eye and I think I like it."

"Glad you do. Now, are you ready for a juicy piece of meat?" She licked her lips.

"Oh yeah!" He reached out for her.

"Down, boy, I mean steak!"

Looks like the 440 Train has a new destination.

All bets were off. Lucinda's clear and precise Virgo mentality was definitely love-struck. The arrow that pierced her on the movie set was still lodged in her heart and moving in deeper. It only took three months for her to give up her apartment and move in with Ricky.

It was a process, adapting to a highly testosterone-influenced home, but she loved every quixotic minute. Statues of naked Greek gods in mythology lined the interior of the house as if protecting its owner. White furry throw rugs were placed romantically near a fireplace. An array of "T&A" videos lined a bookshelf. A wet bar sporting a variety of cordials adorned the kitchen which overlooked a waterfall that flowed into a pool and hot tub. The ambience was bold, sexy and riveting. The invisible vibe was that of men being fed grapes by pretty subservient women. But even with all the masculine décor there was something warm, loving and compassionate about Ricky's home. This sweeter presence is what Lucinda held onto as she grew into her new space.

Now let's talk about the other things going on in the house such as telephone calls and unannounced visits by Ricky's ex-girlfriends. These were not subtle or joyful experiences for the blonde Texan. It was one thing for her to learn Ricky was still friendly with his ex-lovers. But it was another to deal with his frequent e-mails to them or his small talk at the gym with skimpy-dressed buxom ladies. But thirdly, and definitely a strike-out, was to have these women show up at their front door acting all noteworthy. This was not part of the live-in arrangement she had signed up for.

One incident in particular brought her to a new realization that something had to change and quickly. It was late morning. Lucinda had slept in and she looked that way. The doorbell rang. A bleached-blonde hot tamale stood on the steps sporting a designer suit. She had Beverly Hills plastic surgery written all over her.

"Can I help you?" Lucinda asked, placing a hand on her hip.

"Is Ricky baby home?" the woman asked, puckering her poochy lips.

"Whom may I say is calling?" Lucinda put emphasis on the word "calling."

"You the house cleaner?" The babe removed her sunglasses and glared.

"The house cleaner!"

"That's what I said!"

"Well, I oughta." Lucinda clenched her fists and stepped forward. Ricky shot in between them, quickly shoeing the blonde to her car. Two minutes later he was back in the house and sweating.

"Who the heck was that chick?" Lucinda demanded to know.

"A friend, just a friend," he replied quickly as beads of perspiration slid down his temples.

"I'm fed up with girls coming out of your closet!" Lucinda sassed. "This type of relationship was not what I envisioned or committed to."

"I didn't know she was coming over. She's a real estate broker."

"There was nothing *real* about her and if she comes here again with that attitude, then the only thing she be-*broken* is her 90210 nose."

"That's funny."

"I'm not being funny."

"Oh!"

"I'm only gonna ask once—please respect me in and out of the house." Lucinda side-tilted her head. "If you can't curb the ties from your past, then I'll need to reconsider living here with you."

She strutted out of the room, leaving Ricky speechless. This request would be a hard nut to crack since her man was sentimental; he didn't like change and had strong links to his past. Oddly enough, Ricky took offense at her ultimatum and became aloof as well as cocky. He was still adjusting to a live-in girlfriend, three needy pooches and a lot of blonde hair floating around his imported tile floors.

Frustration was getting the best of Lucinda, however. She tried to stay in the present moment but it was increasingly difficult. The Emotional Food Snake reared its head and slithered around. Lucinda's feelings of being abandoned and disappointed were coming on strong.

She put on her workout clothes to run around the block, trying to erase the memories of her past. But it was too late. The 'EFS' made a deposit, no paper receipt—just a direct drop in her heart chakra.

MALIBU – PRESENT DAY

BEFORE I COULD GET TO Lucinda and Ricky's blanket, Thomas tackled me into the sand. Then he kissed me.

"I'll follow you anywhere," he teased. "Just wait for me. Please wait!" A large feather was stuck in the sand next to me. I brushed it across his face and laughed.

As we got up and brushed ourselves off, a petite tanned woman and a tall-distinguished man made their way down the beach. He was a few feet in front of her. She about-faced and headed back toward the parking lot. Unaware she wasn't behind him any longer, he kept walking toward us. I found it rather strange that he didn't look back or notice she wasn't following him.

"Thomas, do you know him?" I pointed.

"Yeah, it's."

"Heyyyy, Ricky!" the guy suddenly shouted.

Before answering, Ricky enthusiastically jumped up and greeted his friend.

"Howie, you ole stud, you look good. It's great to see you. Where's your wife?"

"She ran back to the car to get something."

I looked away, feeling nosey and presumptuous.

"How are those magic hands?" Ricky praised his friend.

"Good, they're good you should come in for a treatment, it's been awhile."

"You know, man, I'll definitely do that. Hey, Tommy, you remember Howie from the old days at the gym?"

"Of course I do. Good to see you." Thomas shook Howie's hand.

"Good to see you too. Hey, that show you're running is really hot. I love the sci-fi stuff."

"Thanks, I'm having a good time. I feel very blessed."

"Good for you, man. It's funny how things have worked out for us," Howie recollected. "Some of my greatest memories are working out with you stunt-dudes at the gym."

"You knew what you were doing. Ninety percent of the guys became your patients. Nice marketing plan," Ricky teased.

"Ah come on, that was never my intention. I liked the vigorous workouts." Howie raised a leg and attempted to belly-kick Ricky in his mid-section. The seasoned stuntman caught and twisted his friend's foot, tossing him over to the side before Howie made final contact.

Thomas cheered, egging on his two friends. It was cute watching them interact with each other as I slipped away to Lucinda's blanket.

"Well, now that the guys are catching up, I thought it would be nice if we got to know each other."

"Sounds good to me," Lucinda smiled.

The boys continued kickboxing with each other until they were both winded. Laughing, they slapped each other's butts and starting chatting like busy bees producing honey.

"What do you think they're talking about?" Lucinda asked, crossing her arms.

"Recipes, the latest Hollywood scandal, hormones and sex." I replied with a straight face.

"You had me until you mentioned sex," she said, smirking. I smiled at her quick comeback.

"Say, Marlo, do you know him?" she asked, indicating Howie.

"Nope. Do you?"

"No."

The petite woman quietly joined the boys now and stood close to her husband. In sync, Lucinda and I glanced at each other with raised brows.

MADDIE'S PAST

IN 1981, MADALINE HAD JUST GRADUATED at the top of her class in college. Known by her friends and Filipino family as Maddie, she was single, petite, cute, and a tad shy. Her most recent residences ranged from her mom and dad's small Filipino village home to a modern condominium shared with her cousin in Manila.

Maddie set her standards high and worked diligently on conquering her goals, both for business and pleasure. When she was in the city, she usually competed in marathons and was always challenging herself to improve on her best running time. After a vigorous run, she would celebrate by treating her friends to a round of beer and singing American billboard songs at a karaoke bar.

Then she was off to work at her part-time managerial job at one of Manila's hottest restaurants. The locals always felt welcome there, knowing they would not only get a good meal but also good service when Maddie was at the helm. Her deep sexy voice and bi-lingual accent charmed the tourists while her calm, yet demanding leadership, kept the restaurant running smoothly. For these reasons, the restaurant owner paid her handsomely but she always gave back. One way she shared her wealth was by treating the village kids to sodas and lollipops.

Maddie was popular and loved by many. Her wacky sense of humor charmed young and old folks alike—but it was Maddie's natural beauty and casual boyish attire that attracted both men and women. She was the talk of the town because only a few knew her sexual preferences for sure. She made it quite clear to village nosey-bodies that what was her business was <u>her</u> business, but this didn't stop the perverted gossipers from fantasying about this tantalizing mystery.

As far as Maddie was concerned, she lived by the Las Vegas motto, 'what happens in the Philippines stays in the Philippines'. Better yet, what happens in the bedroom stays in the bedroom. Since the villagers liked being invited to her wild parties with an unlimited amount of food and alcohol, they kept their distorted thoughts well hidden. Plus she was always *packin'* which was another reason people didn't confront her with their trivial suspicions. No one ever suspected that this friendly young woman could load a gun as quickly as she could pop open a bottle of beer and hit the target between two balloons. She got her gun training at a young age from her father who would always say, "Be humble and strong, daughter that is how you earn the people's respect." He also got her involved with the Filipino military where she became highly ranked.

Maddie stayed involved with her family's farm, from hands-on planting of the rice to financial dealings with buyers. At political gatherings, she was also known to deal with the dignitaries to protect the village's welfare.

Maddie was on the move and always multi-tasking even before the word was coined. Yet as tough and educated as she was, her spiritual side was soft and vulnerable. Quietly faithful to Catholicism, she prayed to the saints and beloved spirits. But she was also easily shaken by anything that goes bump in the night.

Beneath all of Maddie's layers, her family served as her life force and she assisted them with dignity, love and financial support. She was the thread that weaved the bond between her brothers, sister and parents, and kept it strong.

One particular day, worn out from running around town, Maddie retreated to her condo for some rest. The place was in disarray so she put her nap on hold to straighten up. While cleaning like a busy beaver, her mind raced with concerns about her family, the restaurant, chores, her personal life, and especially the future. She had tried to focus on her dream of becoming an architect but couldn't resist dabbling in the family business. This usually ended up requiring her full attention *and* her monthly earnings, however.

When things got really hectic, Maddie became even busier. Dismissing her needs, she'd grab "the child within" and laugh away the sage voice desperately trying to come through. The ability to nurture herself and not feel guilty about it was a lesson she was always dancing with and since she only liked ballroom and salsa dancing, this brain-chatter was quite an annoyance. Maddie was in need of something more, more for her soul and more as a woman.

Hours later, Maddie's orange peel scented condo sparkled. Lastly, she organized a messy pile of papers on the dining room table. Exhausted mentally and physically she collapsed on the carpeted floor and stretched out her achy body in a yoga pose. Pressing her thumb and pointer fingers together to keep the energy flowing. Eyelids closed, Maddie focused on her heart, connecting to its rhythmic beats. Fifteen, thirty, then forty seconds passed.

She almost fell asleep before the loud voice in her mind stepped in. Her breath quickened as her eyes opened. She prayed to Saint Peregrine who had asked God to heal him but only if God was pleased to do so. Maddie now asked the saint for less business affairs and more fun, much more sleep and also something new and exciting in her life.

She climbed onto the couch and got comfy. A warm feeling surrounded her. The mind chatter quieted. She began a mantra: *Maddie, it's okay to relax Maddie it's okay to relax.*

Thoughts transmuted into nothingness. In minutes Maddie was in a deep sleep. The invisible forces at work helped her relax. The energies within her being and those she called Spirit amplified her prayer. These stirrings in the air began spinning a web of life-changing situations.

MALIBU – PRESENT DAY

LUCINDA AND I JOINED THE GUYS as Howie introduced them to the petite woman.

"Ricky, this is my wife Maddie."

"Damn, wife, girlfriends, kids it's been way too long," Ricky replied.

"Hi," Maddie said softly.

Ricky then introduced the rest of us. "Hello," we tweeted.

"Hi," Maddie replied, then looked down at the sand, avoiding our eyes.

Howie jumped in on the hellos and thrust his hand out. When I shook it, I felt a surge of heat. "You sure got some strong mojo," I responded to his handgrip.

Howie laughed, then looked at me oddly. Thomas gave me the 'come on, Marlo leave the woo-woo stuff alone look'. I pursed my lips and backed off.

"Do you need help setting up your blanket?" I offered Maddie.

"No thank you."

Thomas smiled at me. I nodded my head like a good little girl, but it didn't last long. My radar sensed a weird vibe between Howie and Maddie that was heavy and hard to ignore. *Crap.* I mumbled under my breath. *This couple's got troubles at home.*

Howie kept looking at me, almost reading me. I looked at Maddie, then back at him. He knew I sensed something. We both knew that we knew.

Lucinda broke in, "So this sure is great meeting here today."

"Yes, it is," Howie and I said in unison. I casually stepped a few feet away from him.

Lucinda shimmied over to me. "What the heck was that about?" she whispered.

I broke into song: "It was just my imagination … running away with me."

"Hey! You have a good voice. Did you ever think about singing?"

"Once or twice," I teased.

MADDIE'S PAST

MADDIE WAS STILL SLEEPING on the couch. She wore a pair of black boxer underwear and a white sports bra. It was one of many nights when she didn't make it to the bedroom. Since it was Saturday she could sleep in and not worry about the day's responsibilities.

The afternoon sun broke through the shades. She tossed a few times, repositioning but quickly falling back into a deep sleep.

"Get up!" her cousin demanded abruptly, shaking her awake, "You're needed at the restaurant!"

By the time Maddie opened her eyes, her cousin was out the door. The telephone rang and she yanked up the receiver. "Hello! What? I didn't hear the phone ring. How many times did you call? I must have been really tired—but it's my day off. Okay-okay."

She slammed down the receiver, put both feet on the floor, and stretched. Maddie stood on her tiptoes, then flopped over like a rag doll. Then she ran in place for five minutes, followed by one hundred jumping jacks.

Suddenly a heavy gust of wind ripped through the open window, bringing with it a high-pitched scream. The clean and shiny vertical blinds clanked side to side. Startled, Maddie put on her eyeglasses and listened intently, thinking, *I'm not having a good feeling. Is that you Aunt Etana? Mom told me you'd visit one day.*

No response then a moment later she laughed. But just as she calmed, the scream started again. She listened harder. *Awe, shhh-i-it's just a train whistle.*

Suddenly she felt the presence of someone lurking outside the condo. "Cousin, is that you? Did you forget something?" she yelled, her stomach queasy. No one answered.

Paranoid, Maddie retrieved a handgun from under the couch and cautiously pulled open the front door. No one was there. The whistle grew louder. *Why is that train bothering me so much today?*

She slammed the door, put the gun back under the couch and sat down, looking around the room. *Someone is in my house—I feel you.* She rubbed her tummy. *Aunt Etana, please—is that you?*

Another gust of wind blew through the window, scattering a neat pile of papers from the dinning room table onto the floor. *Come on, you're freaking me out.* Maddie made the sign of the cross while praying to Saint Sabas.

As she closed the window, a warm feeling surrounded her. She believed this to be the energy of Sabas' calm and peaceful presence. The condo got quiet, no more breeze, only stillness. *Thank you, thank you,* she sighed.

Although she was more relaxed, Maddie couldn't shake a feeling that something was about to happen. In fifteen minutes, she was dressed and out the door, but the haunting feeling followed her to the restaurant. She knew she was not alone, but she also knew she couldn't tell anyone at work that she was afraid, or that someone or something not of this world was following her. In Maddie's mind, revealing her fears and vulnerability to her peers was scarier than facing the spirit world.

The next morning, Maddie felt rested despite yesterday's haunting experience. She realized fatigue had gotten the best of her and was playing tricks with her mind. She laughed aloud as she did her morning stretches, thinking about her reaction to the sound of the train, the wind blowing, and the sense of being followed by her deceased aunt, which had quickly dissolved once she got busy with work.

Today was a new day, Sunday. It was a day where she would be enjoying the New Delhi Asian games in Manila. She took a long hot shower and dressed in a sporty red-striped black tank top and shorts.

They showed off her body which was fit and firm, her legs smooth and muscular.

When Maddie arrived at the center, hundreds of people were buzzing around as athletes warmed-up for their sport. In the middle of the excitement, she spotted an American man. His six-foot-three stance and wavy blonde hair popped out among the crowd. She watched from the shadows as the fair skinned man worked on the track athletes.

She soon approached an armed guard she knew and asked, "Who's the American?"

"He's a hands-on healer and hypnotist."

"Really!"

"Yeah, he does some new kind of energy healings."

"Interesting." She raised her brows.

"He was hired to keep the athletes focused and healthy."

"Very interesting," Maddie said, keeping her eyes on the man.

From fifteen feet away, she watched as he rubbed a runner's neck and shoulders. His eyes were closed while he laid on the healing touch. He was handsome, like a movie star. She had an unusual urge to touch the American, to feel his skin, to run her hands up and down his body. Her stare must have sent out some powerful mojo because his eyes opened and fixed on hers. Like a deer facing headlights, she froze.

Maddie got anxious and scooted in the opposite direction. She found a secluded spot where she composed herself. She closed her eyes, focused on her breathing and calmed down.

"Whatcha doing here?" a beautiful long-haired Filipino woman wondered.

"Sonya! You scared the heck out of me. I'm just chilling out from the crowd."

"You know, I can help you chill out even more."

"Uh, not now."

"I can massage your back. It will relax you. Maddie, you seem so tense today."

"No, no massage."

"What's wrong?" Sonya asked.

"Nothing's wrong."

"But I miss you, I miss us."

"Sonya, don't…" Maddie pleaded.

"Why don't you call me anymore?"

"I'm focusing on my goals and don't need distractions."

"Is there someone new?"

"We don't have any commitments to one another!"

"I thought we were good as lovers."

Maddie cut Sonya off, "I don't have time for this conversation."

She made a beeline back towards the activity and spotted the American. He also spotted her. They gazed at one another. Again, Maddie broke the stare and looked away. She tried to shake off the tingly feeling in her stomach. It was the same feeling as the other night, fear of the unknown.

Swiftly, she moved to the far end of the crowd.

"Dear Mother Teresa, please help me get ahold of these feelings. I've never felt this feeling towards a man. I'm really confused again."

From behind, someone tapped on her shoulder. She turned. It was the American.

"Hi. I'm Howie."

"Helloooooo, Howieeee," she said, staring up at him.

He was really tall. Nervous, she quickly looked for something to doodle with. She reached into a pocket on her denim vest. The hypnotist smiled as she fumbled and pulled out a small pad, a pen, a miniature flashlight, and a silver cross, then shoved them back into her vest. The cross got stuck between her fingers and dangled.

"Do you think you'll need to use that?" He raised a brow and grinned.

She looked up. "Wh-what?"

"The cross. Will you need to use it on me?"

"I don't think so unless you're warning me." She chortled and stuffed it in her pocket.

He hissed, then smiled.

"I keep the cross as a good luck piece, not to fight off vampires."

They laughed, but an athlete who needed some reassurance about an old ankle injury interrupted them. "Please excuse me," Howie said. "I'll be right back. By the way, what's your name?"

"Mm-maddie," she stuttered, relieved for this opportunity to regain her composure.

With the athlete at his side, Howie walked off into the crowd.

Man, he's tall. She rubbed her neck. *Why does he want to talk with me? I'm not even girlish.*

She took a deep breath and pulled something else out of her pocket: a train ticket. She read aloud: "**The 440 Train—First class seating to the next chapter of your life.**"

What's this and how did it get in here? I don't know what it means, but if it's a sign, then I will trust it, she thought. *Hold on, the train whistle last night, now a ticket today? Oh, Saint somebody, what's going on here? Is this some kind of karmic blast?*

Maddie looked to the north where Howie was standing and began laughing hysterically.

"Sorry for that interruption," he said, walking towards her.

"It's okay." She quickly pulled herself together and slipped the ticket back into her pocket.

"Maddie, you a runner?" he said, eyeing her legs.

"Ah! Just for fun and a few marathons here and there."

"Don't be modest. I've heard through the grapevine you're an avid runner, and fast at that."

She blushed.

"You have a beautiful body, Maddie, and it shines in good health."

"Thanks. I don't know what you see." She turned away.

"What I see is a woman that I'd love to take to dinner." He touched her arm and leaned into her, looking directly into her dark soulful eyes.

"Okay," she answered without hesitating.

"Do you have a favorite restaurant?"

"Uh, the one I work at has really good food."

"Which one is that?"

"Belvidere's. They have great fish and chips."

"That doesn't sound like Filipino food."

"It's owned by a Englishman who used to be the chef for the Four Seasons Hotel in Santa Barbara, California.

"Really?"

"Yes. Really."

"Belvidere's it is then. Shall I pick you up at eight?"

"Let's meet there."

"Ah, independent. I like that."

"Do you?" she flirted.

They parted, smiling as wide as their lips could stretch.

Even with no lipstick or perfume, something inside Maddie was reminding her she was all woman. *Oh my gosh! He's something else. Did he hypnotize me or what?*

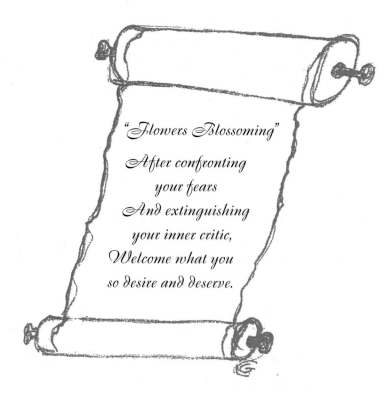

"*Flowers Blossoming*"

*After confronting
your fears
And extinguishing
your inner critic,
Welcome what you
so desire and deserve.*

MALIBU – PRESENT DAY

I WAS HOPING THAT LUCINDA would stick to the subject of singing, then I could tell her some of my great stories about recording in New York and the interesting people I met there. But she curved back around to the previous topic. "So, what was that about, with you and Howie?"

"Nothing really," I replied quickly.

"Nothing! You could've cut the tension with a knife."

"Just a feeling, but I'm sure I'm mistaken."

"A feeling," she reveled. "What kind of feeling?"

Thomas interrupted to show us his handful of findings. I was grateful for the diversion as I didn't want to get into a discussion with Lucinda about Maddie and Howie. I became captivated by one particular stone Thomas gave me that was shaped like a heart.

I also took advantage of the natural pause and excused myself. I walked over to our blanket, sat down and sipped on a bottle of cold water while taking in all the hellos. I felt Lucinda staring at me. She winked and nodded her head as if she knew something. *There's definitely more to this girl than meets the eye!*

Thomas joined me under the umbrella. He opened a box of crackers and shared them with some seagulls. As I watched him play with the birds, I thought about all the human energy flying around. The wise old owl in me recalled the first hits I felt with these new friends. Lucinda felt genuine, Ricky sentimental, Howie secretive and Maddie caged.

Not wanting to get too involved, I made a conscious decision to stop analyzing and to settle into the healing atmosphere of the beach instead.

MADDIE'S PAST

MADDIE'S TRAIN RIDE WITH THE AMERICAN kept rolling full-steam down the tracks even after she found out he was fifteen years her senior. Their age difference didn't seem to bother either one of them or her family although it did give the gossipers more fuel, but this only kept Maddie laughing.

After a month of wining and dinning, they were rarely apart. For the first time in years she cut back her hours at Belvidere's and the rush to find an architect job was no longer at the forefront of her future plans. The newly stated couple divided their time between Manila and the Village. One evening they would sparkle on the ballroom dance floor, the next they would attend political functions, then buy food for the village kids. Yet with all their different disguises they still had the energy and enthusiasm to work on projects for the family farm. On so many levels Maddie was now unbound. *Or was she?*

In the privacy of their condo love nest, she was having the best sex of her life with her movie star healer-man. She was in complete ecstasy, experiencing all the perks of being with a manly man, like being spooned by a long lean body or feeling safe and nurtured. In the past she was typically the strong one, the comforter, the alpha dog. But this time she was able to receive another's strength. It felt damn good, *so good* that all thoughts of Sonya vanished into thin air.

One night after dinner, Howie planned an exciting evening. "Mad, come in the bedroom, I want to show you something."

His request sounded casual so she left the dishes in the sink and moseyed into the room.

"Holy Toledo!"

Howie stood on the bed, sporting a pair of white bikini underwear. "I'm all ready for you," he grinned, running his hands through his wavy hair.

Maddie wasn't sure what to do. Howie jumped off the bed and grabbed her, dipping her over as if it were the finale of an intricate dance performance.

His hard body pressed against hers. "Wooo-hoo!" She giggled.

He jolted her back up and ravenously stripped off her clothes. Enjoying the ride, she grinned wholeheartedly.

"I will make you feel like you have never felt before," Howie whispered, lifting Maddie onto the bed. She was now taller than him.

In one swift motion, he withdrew a can of whipping cream from under a pillow. Maddie bit her lip with anticipation as Howie squirted the foamy delight all over her body. Then he slowly devoured the trail of cream, treating her like the best dessert he'd ever tasted.

The following morning Maddie had the condo all to herself. She lay in bed thinking about the fun she had last night with her great lover and all their similar interests. They also had strong convictions about staying fit, natural food remedies, self-healing, the importance of being independent, and being honest. She suddenly thought of Sonya for the first time in months. Maddie felt a tad guilty for not talking to her since meeting Howie, and definitely guilty for neglecting to mention Sonya to Howie. But as quickly as these thoughts flooded in, she shut them down and headed to the shower to drown them out.

On the bathroom mirror, she found a note etched in soap: *"Mad, I Love You. See you tonight. Have a great day."*

In the shower, more thoughts of her man danced in her mind. They lasted until her body cleanse was done and she wiped the steam off the medicine cabinet, blurring her reflection along with the soapy message.

Suddenly, she spotted a shadow just outside the corner of her eye, and wondered, *Is that you, Aunt Etana?*

The door creaked, closing an inch. Maddie quickly put down the toilet seat lid, sat down and prayed. A childhood memory about visitations from deceased loved ones flashed through her mind. She laughed, hoping to turn the fear into a gift of insight.

Just after she arrived at Belvidere's later, Maddie made a long-distance call, "Mom, I feel that Aunt Etana is watching over me."

"That is wonderful. And you are not scared?"

"Well, a little, but I'm gettin' better at this spirit-thing."

"Everything has its time. Trust your senses. You will know if it is a loved-one guiding you."

"Thanks, Mom."

"Heaven is here, Madaline, and *they* are just inches away. Always remember that, my lovely one."

MALIBU – PRESENT DAY

THE MEN WERE HAVING FUN throwing a football around. I thought us girls should get to know each other so I held up a bottle of water and shouted, "You want a cold drink?"

Lucinda and Maddie came over to the blanket. "Have either of you been to this beach before?" Maddie asked.

"No," we answered simultaneously.

"This is nothing like we have in the Philippines."

"Is that where you're from?"

"Yes. But I've been here for many years. I have two daughters. One's thirteen and the other is nine."

"Wow! You look great. You must have started young," Lucinda complimented.

"Uh, you might say that," Maddie chuckled in reply.

MADDIE'S PAST

FOR THE MOST PART, MADDIE wasn't easily impressed. But the American kept up his impeccable track record until the *big issues* started popping up.

"I don't know if I'm ready to leave my home," Maddie told Howie on the way to the dance studio.

"But I must return to the States. I have patients that need me and my cash-flow is dropping."

"I understand, but what about our future?" she asked with worried eyes.

Two months later, *dum dum du-dah, dum dum du-daaah.* Happiness prevailed at a small quaint wedding on the patio of Belvidere's. It was a celebration of new beginnings. No one asked questions. No one judged. There was only acceptance and the glow of love.

Maddie looked beautiful. She allowed her sister to make up her face with a light burst of peach. And since she wasn't the fancy-gown type of gal, she chose a striking white satin pantsuit that clung to her tanned body, giving her an indisputable air of sex appeal as well as grace.

While the cocktails and food were served indoors, Maddie's mom took her aside and hugged her tightly. She whispered into her daughter's ear, "Your life is forever changed." Then she placed her hands on her pregnant daughter's belly, closed her eyes and prayed.

Maddie smiled and took a step back so she could look into her mother's eyes. "Please don't worry, Mom. I'll come back home often," she promised. "And, Dad, I am always here for you," she said as he walked up to his women, arms open to embrace them.

The trio made their way toward Howie who looked dashing in a white tuxedo with a light blue bowtie. His wavy blonde hair had grown since Maddie first met him, making him look even sexier to his new wife and also a bit more feminine.

"Take good care of my daughter," Maddie's father gently admonished with a stern eye.

"You know I will, sir. I love your daughter very much." Howie bent down and hugged his father-in-law.

Although her parents' faces were smiling, Maddie saw sadness hiding in their eyes. As the day progressed, embraces and kisses from relatives and close friends drew her into the thick reality of farewell and change. For a split second she wondered if there was anyone—just anyone—out there who didn't support her decision. Out of the blue, Sonya suddenly ran up to her and hugged her tightly.

"I'll miss you, Madaline. You were my first love."

Maddie patted Sonya. "I will never forget you. I'll keep in touch."

"*I'll keep in touch*, that's all I get?"

"I, I don't know what else to say." Maddie led her away from the others.

"You never called me despite all the times I called you, all these months. I know you were avoiding me when I saw you in Manila."

"I was wrong. I should have told you what was happening. But in my heart I didn't feel that I owed you an explanation."

"Oh really! We were lovers on and off for a year—you owed me a conversation."

"You're right, you're right. I screwed up. But I'm so happy and I'm having a baby."

"I can't believe you're having a baby! Does he know about us?"

"N-no," Maddie stammered.

"Is everything alright?" Howie asked, surprising them with his sudden presence.

"Y-yes. This is Sonya. She's a friend from college and a great masseuse. She just stopped by to congratulate us."

"Nice to meet you," he said, smiling.

"You're a lucky man," Sonya responded with a flirtatious grin.

"Yes I am. I'll let you girls finish up, but we should be going soon, Mad." He kissed his bride and walked away.

"He was flirting with me," Sonya insisted.

"You're crazy, he was not."

"I know men like him, he was giving me the eye."

"I'm not listening to this."

"Do you really *know* him, Madaline?"

"Yes I do," she insisted. But then she wondered, *do I really?* Assuring Sonya, Maddie continued: "I'll write you and keep in touch."

"Sure you will."

"I promise, okay?" Maddie walked away and did not look back.

At sunset, the newlyweds said their final good-byes to Maddie's family. Several hours later, *Mrs. Maddie* was boarding a 747 Jet airliner to the United States, California to be exact with her Jewish-American husband.

Oh, and what happens in the Philippines doesn't always stay there!

MALIBU – PRESENT DAY

"DO YOU HAVE ANY CHILDREN?" Maddie asked me.

"I have three dogs and two cats. They're my kids."

"Really?"

"Yup! We love four-legged critters. Thomas and I also have many Godchildren, and we love to spoil them too."

"I bet you do. It's wonderful that people trust you both as Godparents," Lucinda said.

"Thanks—and we take the word to heart."

"What about you, any kids?" Maddie wondered, looking at Lucinda.

"I'm in the same boat as Marlo. I have three little dogs. Ricky and I are too focused on our careers to be ready for kids."

"I don't know why, but I thought Howie said you and Ricky had a kid."

"I'm sure we will one day. But right now you could say I'm just a mom to four-legged kids."

"I like your thinking! But one day soon you'll have a two-legged as well," I shared, having an intuitive hit.

"Soon? Well, my biological clock *is* ticking!" Lucinda pursed her lips, "But I don't think it will happen soon." I just grinned. She glared back at me.

"Anyway, I'd like to be engaged first, plan a beautiful church wedding with an outside reception, take an exotic honeymoon and do some traveling before having kids," Lucinda continued as if she were reading a "to do" list from her day planner.

"Nice plan, but that's just when life throws you a baseball," Maddie commented, bobbing her head up and down.

"You mean a curve ball?" Lucinda crinkled her blonde brows.

"Uh, I guess. Some kind of ball." Maddie laughed hard.

"What do you think, Marlo?" Lucinda challenged playfully. "You're sure quiet all of a sudden."

"I think engagements or too much planning can be overrated. If you love each other, that's all that matters."

"Really? Too much planning, engagements overrated?"

I was about to reply when Maddie switched gears and interjected, "So what do you do for a living, Lucinda?"

LUCINDA'S PAST

LUCINDA DIDN'T LIKE TO AVOID an issue. But she knew in her heart that at that particular moment she and Ricky weren't going anywhere with her commitment concerns until she calmed her heels. The best way she knew to do that was to go for an invigorating run.

When she got back to the house, sweaty and rejuvenated, she checked her phone for messages in case a friend or possibly an agent had called. There was one message, from an agent! The man's accent was strong but she understood every word. She hit replay to confirm her excitement.

"Heydo, Miss Lucinda. My name's Hugo. I'd want to sign you with my agency. You send me your resume and p'oto. I have many jobs for you with your good looks and talent."

Lucinda snapped the phone shut and smiled wide. She shouted to Ricky to share the news. He didn't answer, then she realized his car wasn't in the driveway.

He's already left for his job in San Diego, she remembered. That meant he would be away for the night. She felt sad that they had left each other in a huff, it was their first official fight. But she quickly snapped out of the slump by thinking about the call from the agent.

"Mommy's got an interview!" She shared her good news with her doggies while doing a celebration dance.

The following day offered many unexpected events. Lucinda woke at five a.m. and started a pot of coffee. While it percolated she phoned Ricky but got his voicemail, "Hi Ricky, it's me Lucinda. I'm sorry. I don't like this strained feeling between us, but I have wonderful news. I'm meeting with a talent agent today in Hardey Canyon. He seems very motivated. Please call to let me know you're okay. I love you."

She slid open the glass doors in the kitchen and stepped outside. A refreshing breeze swirled around, stimulating her senses. It felt weird to be at the house without Ricky and even weirder that they hadn't spoken since yesterday.

Lucinda looked around the yard feeling detached from her being when it dawned on her that a shift had occurred. She had definitely changed. She was not the same woman who had moved into the house.

The cooing of a dove brought her back to this dimension. Then the coffee maker chimed and faintly in the distance she heard a train whistle. *Huh!* she sighed, pouring the hazelnut blend into a mug. *It's a funny feeling. But why does the sound of a train whistle affect me so much?*

While sipping her morning java, she concluded that she needed to stop thinking about train whistles, her boyfriend, or anything other than her acting career. Lucinda placed her mug on a table and stepped onto the treadmill, punching the keypad for a vigorous uphill climb.

Four hundred calories later she hopped off the heated machine and poured another cup of rocket-fuel into her mug as she headed to the bedroom. She noticed that she had missed a call. It was Ricky, "Hey Babe, it's me. I understand your point about me being so friendly with my ex-girlfriends. If I were you I would be pissed off too. I'm an old dog, learning new tricks, well, not an old dog, but definitely learning new tricks." He laughed. "Um, hey, I'm happy for you and your meeting today. Be careful and leave me the exact address so I'll know where you're going. I'll be home tonight, early evening. We'll talk more then."

She smiled, feeling the confusion and stress melt from her shoulders. Lucinda went to the closet, picked out a low-cut shirt, her favorite tight jeans and a pair of four-inch black-strapped shoes. No water bra today, just a standard push-up. She stepped into the shower and washed her long blonde locks. Minutes later she was sipping the cooled coffee and applying makeup. While stroking on her eyeliner, she realized the caffeine was hindering her ability to get ready. So she jogged around the bedroom, took a few deep breaths and, just like a powerful locomotive, blew off some steam so she could finish prepping for her big-time Hollywood appointment.

This was her first time driving through the canyon. Inspired and mimicking Mario Andretti, Lucinda weaved through the curves, smiling and laughing at her precise maneuvering. Dropping the Mustang into low gear, she gunned it up the hill, ready to wrangle up an agent. Lost in her driving, she didn't notice the street sign until she was right upon it. Sharply she swerved, tires screeching, and turned onto a small side street. She slowed, checking addresses. At the end of the cul-de-sac was the house she was seeking, but she couldn't see it from the street. Tons of foliage surrounded the residence.

She pulled into a brick driveway and pressed a buzzer on the intercom at the gate. The tall black gate opened slowly. *Hmmm, a bit eerie and eccentric,* she thought, spotting several cameras around the entrance. Slowly she proceeded up the steep incline. The landscaping was beautiful, right out of a home-and-garden magazine. Large palm trees, bamboo, and flowers overwhelmed the lawn in an organized yet flamboyant style. The driveway was filled with classic cars and modern limos.

Lucinda had a good feeling about this. She quickly touched up her makeup and stepped out of the car. A large security guard greeted her and asked her to step over to his booth to check in. Inside the house moments later, Lucinda paused in the foyer feeling a bit nervous. The floor was marble, the artwork mesmerizing, and the crystal chandelier hanging overhead was monstrously exquisite. If she didn't know better, it felt as if she had just landed in *Hugh Humps-her's* playgirl mansion. Off to one side was an elegantly carved mahogany desk in the shape of the letter 'S.' No one was sitting at the desk, though a mug of something steaming rested by a telephone and computer. *Someone's got to be here,* Lucinda thought with trepidation.

The next instant, a middle-aged well dressed man, reeking of cologne, stepped into the room. Hugo greeted her, "Excuse my assistant for step'n out, she d'ust went to the powder room."

"No problem."

They exchanged a cordial introduction. Then Hugo raised his brows and escorted her into his office, his eyes devilishly scanning the whole package. The male 'oink-oink' sat on a black leather couch. He patted it, signaling for her to sit next to him. Lucinda smiled and slowly sat at the opposite end, placing her handbag between them.

A knock on the door made her jump. A big-breasted red-haired woman entered the room. "Would you like a cup of coffee?" she wanted to know, looking at Lucinda.

"No, no thank you."

"You okay, boss?"

"Yes. T'ank you."

The sexy assistant winked and jutted her hip in Lucinda's direction as she exited.

Hugo smiled, "She likes you."

Lucinda raised her brows.

"So, lets get 'down' to business. No pun intended." He laughed loudly.

Lucinda looked puzzled, not getting the pun.

"I have a project I feel you'd be perfect for." She listened intently to Hugo's spiel. He told her the script had good drama and suspense and she would be one of the stars. While talking, he reached into a cigar box sitting on the cocktail table. He never lit the cigar, just rambled on about filming in an exotic location and how he could launch her into a lucrative career.

The telephone rang. Hugo's secretary patched the call through. He excused himself, leaving Lucinda to her thoughts and giving her time to digest the long hook lodged in her throat. She was excited but at the same time had a bad feeling in the pit of her stomach. Something just wasn't adding up.

Hugo stepped back in, and returned to the couch, "So ad' I was about to say, I only p'oduce the finest high-end po'nography in da' market today and only book da' hottest women in Hollywood."

Lucinda pursed her lips and wrinkled her nose. She sighed heavily, raised her brows, then sighed even more heavily. She shook her head and started to open her mouth to speak. He chimed in at last, breaking the stale feeling in the air. "Lucy, if this isn't whadju had in mind, then you can do dis' type of work until you land a 'G' rating film."

"A 'G' rating film!" She stood and swung her bag over her shoulder. "No thank you! And my name is Lucinda."

In a blink, she fled the office and headed out of the canyon in the Mustang. Once she was miles away from Hugo's, she pulled onto a side street, turned off the car and cried. What she needed now was to look a friend in the eye for comfort and reassurance. The emptiness made her miss her Texas girlfriends more than ever. But she didn't dare call them and reveal her Hollywood drama. She wanted to stay strong.

"What've I done?" she screamed, looking at her mascara-smeared eyes in the rear view mirror. The more she tried to fight her emotions, the greater the surge inside her was building. Her stomach turned and the 'EFS' reared its head, working its way through her body, mind and spirit. *I'm a mess!*

She flopped her head over, accidentally banging her forehead on the steering wheel. The horn blared. Lucinda jerked up and looked around. No one was in sight.

She rolled down the window for some fresh air as she rubbed her banged-up forehead. It was quiet outside, serene and still. A feeling of comfort allowed her to breathe and compose herself, snapping her out of her misery. Then in the far distance, she faintly heard a train whistle.

No way, not again! What do you want from me?

MALIBU – PRESENT DAY

BY MADDIE'S QUICK INTERCEPTION, I surmised she was used to being a peacemaker. Rather than pursuing the subject of engagements and plan-making any further, I sat back and watched the two women engage in a conversation.

"So what do you do for a living?" Maddie asked Lucinda.

As I listened, I felt the presence of a spirit behind Maddie. It was the energy of an older woman. She was Filipino, petite, a bit chunky. She had a fiery personality and was letting me know she had been watching over her niece since Maddie met Howie. She told me she'd be back, and at that time I could tell Maddie that she was watching over her. I telepathically asked her why I couldn't let Maddie know now. She said there would be a better time, when Maddie would feel safer amongst us women. For now I was to remain quiet about my spirit-sighting.

This was a first for me, usually spirits want to be heard, especially here in California. In New Jersey they spoke to me in old houses or quiet rooms, in California they seem to be at the grocery store, post office and any other place where people are waiting in line. *If the people I stood next to only knew there were spirits beside them yearning to be heard!* I've learned to manage their communications to me. But as I snapped back into listening to the two gals chat, I was surprised that this particular spirit didn't want her presence revealed.

"I'm an actress," Lucinda replied. "But I also make a living as a makeup and hair artist."

"Good for you. It sounds like you have a lot of creative talent up your sleeves."

"One sleeve for sure, but I don't know about both." This made us laugh.

"Hey! I know a lot of actors and actresses who say that unless you have a good agent it's hard getting work."

"That's for sure," I agreed, applying more sunscreen to my face and shoulders.

"I just thought of something," Lucinda snort laughed.

"What?" Maddie and I asked at the same time.

"When I first moved here from Texas, I had one of those Hollywood nightmares you hear about when it comes to finding a good agent."

"Really?" we mused.

"Curious minds would love to hear your story," I said.

"Really? You want to?"

"Heck yeah," Maddie chimed in.

LUCINDA'S PAST

LUCINDA FINALLY REACHED HOME. She needed to get her mind off Hugo and the disappointment of not landing an agent. It had been a long grueling day but nothing a hot shower and a glass of wine couldn't fix. After the steaming cleanse and two glasses of wine, Lucinda felt calmer and cleaner even after her dirty experience.

With no girlfriend to confide in, she settled for the next best thing, comfort food. She stood at the stove flipping steamy buttermilk pancakes, wearing only a matching leopard print bra and thong panty with a towel around her head. Ricky walked in with a Hollywood trade paper under his arm. The dogs slid along the floor trying to get enough traction to greet him.

"Hey, babies," he said, tossing the paper onto the kitchen table.

Holding the spatula, Lucinda turned and smiled. "Hi."

"Hi, babe. It's good to be home. Man, that was a long drive." He kissed her on the lips. "I've missed you. It felt strange to be away from you all night."

"It did feel strange and I really missed you too."

"You okay? You look like you've been crying."

"A little," she admitted with sad eyes.

"Sorry I've been such a bonehead about my ex-girlfriends."

"So you understand how I feel?" She put down the spatula and tore apart strips of bacon before placing them into a hot pan.

"Yeah, I get it and I sure don't want to make you cry," he answered, sitting at the table.

"It's not just that it's other things too. Let's just say I had an interesting morning."

"Oh yeah! How did your interview go with the agent?"

"Not as planned. I'll tell you about it later."

"Okay, babe. So what's with the breakfast food for dinner? You got your period?"

"No. I just needed something buttery and sweet."

"Well, I can give you both and without the calories."

"Really, how so?" She unwrapped the towel from her head, then shook her long hair. It was wet and messy.

Ricky stood, tossed his paper to the floor and lifted her onto the glass tabletop. He unlatched her bra as he gently laid her down and slid off her panties with his teeth. Pressing his large pillowy hands between her inner thighs, he slowly massaged her as he made his way up to her belly button ring. With her eyes closed, she surrendered as he creatively brought her to a place of intense delight.

Meanwhile the pancakes bubbled and the bacon sizzled as the smell of burning butter and pork floated in the air. 'Beeeeaaaaaa,' the smoke alarm blared, jolting them out of the moment. Wobbly and tingly, Lucinda sprang to her feet and waved a dishtowel frantically over the alarm. Once the smoke cleared, she served her man and herself a stack of well-done flapjacks and extra-crispy bacon.

Over the meal, Lucinda filled Ricky in on her Hugo experience. But as with all storms, a peaceful feeling came in the aftermath. Yes, Lucinda was about to see a rainbow. Her prayers had been answered. Ricky signed off on the old girlfriends and she signed on with a successful female talent agent. She felt blessed and, since the train was rolling smoothly down the tracks, it was time for her to reach out to her Texan friends to share the good news. *Amen*!

MALIBU – PRESENT DAY

MADDIE AND I LISTENED intently to Lucinda. Her wide-eyed expressions and thin white muscular arms went along for the ride as she theatrically told her story about Hugo the talent agent. She was quite funny in an 'I Love Lucy' kind of way, though I don't think she really knew just how funny she was.

Lucinda spoke fast so I had to really stay focused as she continued, "Days later, when I researched more about him and found out he even does some of the filming in his house, it made perfect sense."

"Why? Where does he live?"

"In one of the canyons where a lot of unique artists and hippies live."

"Really, in the canyon?" Maddie asked, not so surprised.

MADDIE'S PAST

THE HEALER'S HOUSE, NOW MADDIE'S HOME, was a darling Hansel and Gretel cottage tucked neatly in the middle of a famous canyon in the San Fernando Valley. It was an enchanting area with gigantic ancient trees that shaded masses of boulders overlooking a creek leading to the Pacific Ocean. Brilliantly colored butterflies, dragonflies, songbirds, and red-tailed hawks took shelter in the canyon as well. It was green, dreamy, and magical. The new bride had never felt so in tune with Nature.

Inside the house, wall-to-wall bookcases containing hundreds of books lined the main room. "Have you read all of these?" Maddie asked Howie while she was getting acquainted with her new house.

"Most of them," he answered.

"It's so clean and organized," she said in awe.

"Yeah, I'm a neatnick."

"I thought you were just being kind when you would tidy up the condo, but now I see this is just how you are."

"Yup! Pretty much what you saw in the Philippines is how I am here too," he said, kissing her on the lips.

The house was warm and relaxing. It had two bedrooms plus one-and a-half bathrooms in a modest twelve-hundred square feet, but each foot was efficiently planned.

The kitchen was crafty. The countertops were white marble, the appliances black and white. The walls were a light-charcoal with a dash of sponge whitewash creatively accenting unique inlaid artifacts. Stainless steel pots and pans hung from a rack attached to the ceiling. Underneath was a small butcher-block table with years of wear and tear. But even that looked neat and authentic.

"Did you have a designer do this room?" Maddie wondered.

"No. I did it all," Howie grinned.

"Wow! Now I'm even more impressed. I guess there's many things I have yet to learn about you."

Howie treated his patients in what was originally intended to be a bedroom. Buddhist statues and a small array of Asian and Jewish symbolic memorabilia adorned the space.

"I love it here," Maddie said.

"Great. I'm glad you feel comfortable."

"I do, I do." She rubbed her pregnant belly and smiled.

"In the morning, I'll make an appointment with a doctor friend of mine. I wanna make sure all is coming along nicely with the baby."

"Sounds good. And thank you for taking such good care of me, I mean us," Maddie chuckled.

Over the following week, she adjusted to the big move. Maddie was grateful for this new life and spent time each day meditating by breathing slowly and purposefully. She always ended her ritual by giving thanks to a particular saint.

'Doc' is what Howie's patients called him. In California he was well-known as an energy mover, working with the body on a spiritual level as well as physical. Famous actors, glamorous models, and a melting pot of who's who in Hollywood came into the office for treatments. Maddie quickly noticed that calmness, patient confidentiality, and good chi were key factors to the energy flow in the house. She loved the quiet and felt more at peace then she had in many years.

Cooking also became a ritual and sacred time for her. "I'm making tofu with cheese, potatoes and fresh vegetables tonight," she told Howie.

"Sounds interesting. I've had tofu a few times but I bet your creation will exceed any I've had before, Mad. Everything you make has real yummyness."

"I don't know about that, but thank you. Hey, is yummyness a real American word?"

"It may not be in the dictionary, but we can pretend."

"Sure, why not," she laughed, "it goes with the other words I make up or say wrong."

"Don't be concerned with your dialogue, half the American people speak poorly."

The fragrant aroma of vegetables cooking in the kitchen smelled delicious. "Should we add some fresh lemons to your meal?" Howie asked.

"Sure. I love having fresh lemons from the backyard," Maddie said, sautéing the greens.

"Can you make lemonade again too?"

"Yes and I'm putting a new twist to it," she grinned.

"What might that be, my adventurous wife?"

"A little tequila!" She danced around the kitchen singing.

"What about for you? No alcohol, Mad."

"Of course not. I'll take the lemonade straight up."

Howie gently grabbed her arms, twirling her into him. They danced closely and slowly to the music playing in both of their hearts.

MALIBU – PRESENT DAY

"I USED TO LIVE IN A CANYON," Maddie said.

"Oh! Really?" Lucinda blushed. "There are a few canyons scattered throughout the Valley, so it could be any one of them," she diplomatically implied.

"That's true," I agreed.

"Hmf, I don't care," Maddie sighed. "I don't take it personally and we don't live there any more."

"Oooohh," Lucinda smiled, guzzling down some water.

I chuckled. Though we women had just met, it was evident we felt comfortable enough to be ourselves and speak our truths.

Maddie unzipped a backpack and pulled out a ball of aluminum foil. She carefully unwrapped it. "Anyone want one? I made them this morning."

A sweet smell blew in my direction. "What is it?"

"Buttered rolls."

"Oh my gosh, I love butter," Lucinda said, leaning closer to the treat.

"It doesn't look like you eat anything with butter," Maddie teased. "You're so skinny."

I cringed. This could be the end to the beginning of what I thought would be a nice friendship.

Lucinda put her hand out. "I'd like one, please."

Maddie smiled and handed her the smallest roll.

"Thank you," Lucinda bit into it. "Yummmmm."

"Would you like one?" Maddie offered another to me.

"They do smell scrumptious, but no thank you. Thomas and I made homemade pizza last night, so I'm just having protein and salad for lunch today."

"Okay." Maddie resealed the foil and sank her teeth into a buttery roll.

"Thomas would love one though." I continued

"Oh, of course."

I waved at Thomas to come over. He signaled back with the 'I'm talking with boys' sign. "Never mind," I mumbled to Maddie.

"That was delicious, Maddie. Thank you," Lucinda said as she wiped her lips free of the butter shine.

"Oh my gosh, all this talk of buttered rolls just reminded me of something funny. Kinda like your story," I looked at Lucinda, "but it involves food, not porn."

"Tell us," they said eagerly.

"I was working as a cocktail waitress at an Italian restaurant in New Jersey. One busy night, my boss asked me to cover the food section as well as the cocktail bar. I didn't want to, but they were in a jam, so I reluctantly agreed. It was my first time serving food. Within a short time I had several tables. I didn't like taking down the finicky orders and I wasn't able to balance the tray of food on my shoulder like the pros do, so I used a cart. The boss didn't like my delivery method, but she was desperate, so she didn't complain. At one of my tables, a customer sat alone. He seemed lonely and sad so I engaged him in conversation. He turned out to be a chatter bug. We got onto the subject of nutrition. He was quite overweight but seemed open to my feedback, so I felt comfortable enough to make a suggestion."

"What did you say?" Lucinda wondered, eyes widening.

"Well," I continued, "I said, 'Maybe you should slow down on the butter and bread. That could be what's making you feel sluggish.' I was on a roll, no pun intended!"

"That's not too bad," Maddie said.

"That's what I thought. Anyway, I continued blabbering about his eating habits until finally he shot up from the table.

"Where did he go? "Lucinda was eager to know.

"I couldn't tell so I stood at the table for a second thinking about what happened. I wasn't sure if I was standing in my power or in muck. But something in my gut told me to brace myself."

"You are crazy!" Maddie exclaimed. "You were going to be hammered."

"What, now I'm crazy? A second ago, you said what I said wasn't so bad."

"I changed my mind. If you had been working for me, I would have fired you because the customer is always right."

"Let her finish, let her finish," Lucinda interrupted. "So what happened next?"

"The hotheaded owner raced over to me. I stood my ground and put out my angel wings. 'Marlo, Marlo, Marlo, whatcha doing?' she said in her heavy Italian accent. The man stood next to her, smirking with a piece of bread dangling from his chin."

"What did you tell her?" Maddie asked.

"I told her exactly what I said to him."

"And you got fired, right!" Lucinda asked, surprised

"Yup! I was fired for speaking my truth. I mean, gee whiz, how was I supposed to know he was a critic for a food magazine!"

"Oh, my gosh!" Maddie laughed, "that was a good one, Marlo."

"Yeah, it's evident you weren't cut out to be a food waitress," Lucinda surmised.

"Guess not. I can cook the food but you'll have to get it yourself," I twanged. We all laughed at this.

"So, Lucinda, where do you live?" Maddie now wanted to know.

LUCINDA'S PAST

LITTLE BY LITTLE LUCINDA settled into her new home. It hadn't been easy to move into Ricky's place knowing that it was a smaller version of the Playboy Mansion. But each month she added a bit more goddess flare to it so the male and female energy was more balanced.

After much contemplation, she phoned her friend in Texas who would help put her house on the market. "If anyone offers the asking price, just sell it. And thanks for shipping out the rest of my furniture. I can't wait to sit on my comfy ole couch." Lucinda patted Ricky's stiff white couch and wrinkled her brows.

On the other side of the wall, Ricky was eavesdropping. He waited until she hung up, then asked, "Did I hear you say you're selling your house?" as he casually walked into the living room.

"Oooh, you startled me! Yes, and I feel good about it."

"Sure you don't want to hold onto it for a while?" He sat down next to her.

"Uh, no I told you a while ago about what I was thinking of doing. You seemed supportive."

"I am—it's just that it's your house and you love that house," he responded, fumbling with his fingers.

"I did, especially when I was happily married. But that was years ago and things have changed. It has a different meaning for me now."

"Uh-huh," he pondered.

Thick silence floated in the air between them. "What's your real concern?" Lucinda demanded, her tone changing from happy to serious.

"I'm just making sure you're one hundred percent sure about selling it. Property is always a good investment."

"Thank you for wanting to protect me, but it's the smart thing to do. The market is hot and it's way overpriced so if it's meant to sell it will. Then I'll put the money into a high yielding money market." She took a quick breath. "Besides, I'm here with you now and I'm thinking about our future."

"Ggg-ood move then." He paled while shaking his head in agreement, then wiped his forehead.

"Why are you sweating?" Lucinda wondered.

"It's sympathy sweat, for you making such a big, brave decision," he said in a deep caricature voice.

"You are too funny," she casually said, but inside her the 'EFS,' was beginning to awaken.

"Oh, and did I hear you say you're having some furniture shipped out?"

"Yeah, the big couch you said was so comfy and some other things I thought we could use here."

"Yeah, I recall that." He hesitated and twisted his lips in an annoying way.

"Okay, what's the deeper deal?" she asked, abruptly standing.

"I … I guess I'm territorial."

"Territorial!"

"Yeah, you know, alpha dominant with my house and stuff."

Lucinda bobbed her head back and forth. "Tell ya what, cowboy," her lips pursed. "You can be alpha dog all the time with your house and your stuff." She dramatized 'your' to the extreme, then stomped out of the living room and into the bedroom.

Ricky followed cautiously. "Cowboy?" he mumbled. "She's quick!"

"I'd like to be alone." She started folding clothes from a laundry basket.

He listened to his instincts which told him to leave in a hurry.

When Lucinda heard the front door shut, she flopped onto the bed and cried.

"What the freak is it, with guys and commitment, guys and change, guys wanting to be the boss! Father, please give us both strength and guide me," she prayed.

What a difference a day makes and of course praying helps. Lucinda and Ricky worked through the furniture drama in much the same way as they had over his ex-girlfriends—they talked. And when he thought about the big cozy great-for-sex couch, he was eager to toss his old one into his office.

Over the following year, their relationship strengthened. As with all couples, and other elements in Nature, the tides of ebb and flow are constant in their mystery. But Lucinda and Ricky were two of the blessed ones. They learned to take a breath and look at their situation from a higher perspective. Even though they uncomfortably muddled through the muck, once through it they received the gift of learning from each other.

Speaking of strength, Miss Texas' acting resume was also building and filling up with guest star roles on sitcoms and even a movie of the week. She scored a big touchdown when she landed a national commercial where she plugged tampons 'figuratively speaking, of course'!

When the commercial aired, her family and friends teased her, laughing at how properly dressed and clean-cut she looked. Lucinda laughed all the way to the bank—finally feeling that she was living her dream. *Ka-ching!* And this transaction was not 'EFS' deposit.

The house in Texas went into escrow and sold above her asking price. Lucinda was delighted. She was also busy even when she wasn't working at the studios, working part-time at the chic salon on the Boulevard where she had built a long list of clients.

The only thing she still longed for and had a hard time finding was girlfriends—or even one girlfriend. She wanted more than just a casual friend. She needed someone she could share intimate stuff with, have a glass of wine with. Someone to shop, laugh and also cry with. Her faith re-assured her all of this would come to her when it was time.

MALIBU – PRESENT DAY

"I LIVE IN CORALBASAS," Lucinda said in reply to Maddie's question.

"Oh, it's nice there. They have a great Native American museum that we frequent with the kids."

"Oh, yeah. I've never been but I hear it's pretty amazing."

"I love it there," I added. "And to think that area was one of the main homes to the Chumash Indians."

"I'm part Cherokee," Lucinda announced proudly.

"Really?" Maddie asked.

"Yes. Why?"

"Well, you're so pale, that's all."

I cringed again at Maddie's frankness. *And I thought I was blunt!*

"I'm so fair because my dad was German and his genes were more stubborn than my mother's," Lucinda responded.

"German and Cherokee? Well, you don't want to mess with that!" I laughed.

LUCINDA'S PAST

THE WEATHER WAS BEAUTIFUL in LA in June. Summer was getting into full swing. Lucinda and Ricky slept in, then leisurely had their morning joe.

"Wanna hang out by the pool and catch some rays?" Ricky reminded her about the Malibu beach party coming up on the weekend, thinking they should work on a layer of tan before hitting the sun-drenched beach.

"Sure. I better, look at my white legs."

"Yeah, babe, they are pretty white." He shielded his eyes.

"Ha, ha, ha." Lucinda rolled up a few napkins and tossed them at him.

"This will be the first big hangout with all the stunt guys. I can't wait for you to get to know Thomas and Marlo," Ricky said, sipping on his coffee.

She nibbled on a protein bar. "Oh, yeah, the stuntman you've told me so much about."

"He's not just a stuntman, he's my high school buddy from New Jersey. He's the one who got me started in the business."

"Of course, I remember."

"His wife is from Jersey too. I think you two will hit it off. Hey, wait a minute, you guys met briefly already. I introduced you at a softball game last year."

"Oh. Well, I look forward to getting to know Marlo. But if you guys are such good friends, why haven't we gotten together sooner?"

Ricky brought Lucinda up to speed about when Thomas pulled out of the movie business and was missing in action. It all made sense to Lucinda, but also made her more curious and excited about meeting two people who had gone through such a life-changing event.

"Let me tell a funny story about what happened with Tommy and me during the Thanksgiving football game our senior year," Ricky laughed.

"Wait a second! Is his name Thomas or Tommy?" Lucinda demanded to know.

"Ah, come on, you're messing with my rhythm."

"You know how I feel about addressing people with their correct names."

"His name is Thomas, but in school I called him Tommy. So every now and then I still call him by that name."

"What does he prefer?"

"My story, babe, my story! Geez, he likes to be called Thomas."

"Thank you. Thomas it is."

"Okay, Lucy, can I continue now?" Ricky teased.

She head-locked him and made him beg for mercy. Then they headed to the backyard to begin their tanning. The birds' chirping and cooing was music to their ears.

Ricky finally told his football story as they settled on cushy lounge chairs covered with thick terrycloth beach towels. After his brag moment was over, something else popped into his mind, "Why don't you sunbathe in the nude?" he suggested.

"Can't the neighbors see us from their windows?" Lucinda pointed to a second story house on the left.

"Naaaaah. No one can see us down here."

"Okay, I'm game." She slid off her tiny zebra-print bikini and placed a pair of sunglasses over her girlie-girl area, then applied sunscreen to her breasts.

"That looks really cute," he said staring. "What's her name?"

"Heeeey!"

"Wait! Let me help you with the sunscreen." Grinning, Ricky shimmied off his chair.

"Why thank you and how considerate of you. Say, why don't you take off your shorts too?"

"In a minute."

"Why not now?"

"Cause I'm not ready."

"Ready for what?" she teased back.

"Hey! Give a guy a break here."

She smiled, handing him the bottle of sunscreen. "Here you go."

He stood and danced around, shaking the bottle up and down. "At the Copa, Copa Cabana, the hottest spot east of Tarzana," he sang off-key.

Lucinda laughed until tears flowed down her cheeks. Finally, he applied the cream to her white flaxen skin. She soaked in the relaxing massage while he became aroused. Just as she was about to drift off, he blurted something, bringing her focus back into the backyard.

"I'm ready to take off my shorts!"

Lucinda grinned, quickly snapping alert. She repositioned herself onto her knees. He moved in closer. She looked up and winked. "Really?" he pleaded.

He placed his hands firmly on his hips and looked down at her.

"Close your eyes, big boy," she teased. He obeyed. He knew what was coming.

Splash!!! Ricky's eyes popped open.

"Come and get me," Lucinda shouted from the swimming pool.

"You're killing me!" he laughed. Then he dove in.

They wiggled onto a large floater and passionately played. Worn out, Ricky crawled out of the pool and slowly made his way back to the lounge chair while Lucinda swam forty laps.

Hours later and a few shades darker, the happy couple got dressed and headed out to run errands. But first they stopped at a café for a cup of coffee and snack. Ricky ordered a double espresso. Lucinda ordered a fat-free latte. They shared a fat-free blueberry muffin as they sat at a table for two by the window and watched people.

"Oh my gosh, it's Hugo the porn producer and his big boobed assistant." Lucinda pointed them out to Ricky as they entered the café.

"They should have been there to film us in the pool," he boasted.

She kicked him under the table and shielded her face with her hand. The high fragranced hard to miss couple ordered three pounds of coffee and two cups for the road.

On his way out, Hugo stopped by a table where a pretty woman was sitting alone. He handed his business card to her. She smiled, shaking her head as she accepted his card. Once the two were out of the café, she tossed the card into the trashcan.

"That was funny!" Lucinda admitted.

"That's Hollywood," Ricky replied.

They started chatting again about the upcoming Malibu beach party. "You know, the more I think about meeting your friends, the more excited I'm becoming. I really feel I'm going to make some new friends at last."

The words had no sooner left her lips before a whistle echoed in the distance. She froze and listened intently. The rhythm of the train on the tracks beat with the pulse of her heart. *Or was the caffeine already kicking in?*

Lucinda raised a brow. "Is there a train station around here?"

"Yeah, the Metro connection is nearby."

"Just checking," she said wide eyed as she took a swig of her coffee.

Malibu – Present Day

AFTER LUCINDA GAVE MADDIE and me a brief history of her unusual ancestry, we laughed at each other's horrific tanning stories. It's always interesting to hear how adventurous we were as teenagers in the quest to be christened with a golden tan.

The storytelling halted and the three of us relaxed into the ambience of the beach as we turned our focus to the boys who were still yakking away. *It's funny how when guys get together and chat it's just chatting, and when women get together and chat it becomes gossiping.... hmmm.*

Maddie leaned back in her chair and closed her eyes. Lucinda got up and strolled along the sand. I stared at the horizon, focusing beyond the waves and catching a glimpse of boats far out in the ocean. It gave me a sense of how big and spacious the world is—yet how quaint and tightly intertwined we all are especially with the people we meet on a personal level.

Moments later, Maddie sat up, letting out a loud yawn while stretching her arms over her head.

"Did you get some rest?" I asked her.

"Yes. It felt good too."

"Good for you. There's nothing like a good old cat nap to refresh the engine."

"Yeah. Ever since I had my kids, I don't sleep as deeply as I used to. Up until just a minute ago, that is. That sounds funny, doesn't it?" She looked over at me, puzzled.

"No it doesn't sound funny. It sounds like you might have found something you lost."

"It could be that I'm just overworked. This day is just what I needed."

"Just what the doctor ordered, right?"

"Uh, he didn't order it."

"Oh, no it's an expression, 'the doctor ordered it.'"

"Yeah, yeah, I know that," she said firmly, closing her eyes again.

As much as I like to help people, I've learned not to interfere unless someone reaches out. That's one of the difficult things about being so sensitive to others' feelings—knowing when to hush up and disconnect from the vibe, keeping things on a surface level. But there was something definitely brewing in Maddie's psyche that wanted healing. I thought about her aunt, and what she said about her needing to feel safe.

MADDIE'S PAST

BY MADDIE'S THIRD TRIMESTER, things had changed drastically. Her romance with Howie wasn't the same as it was overseas, or even last month. She was on his turf now and the grass was a new shade of green as well as pale and dry. She was catering to the needs of her loving man, but the tone in his voice and his actions were different than before.

Out of left field, Howie became whiny and bossy, pleading with Maddie to become his office assistant. He said the paperwork was overwhelming and weighing down his healing abilities. Of course she did not refuse his plea. She wanted to please him, and she felt a tad guilty that he stayed in the Philippines longer then originally planned because of her.

Maddie's new 'sexretary' job was like nothing she'd done before. But as usual, Maddie gave it all of her attention as well as her heart and soul. Using two beautiful Asian partition fans, she created a small office area in the dining room with a small desk and chair.

The months flew by. One Wednesday she noticed on the office's busy schedule that Jackelynn, one of the many female patients who had a romantic eye for the healer, was coming in. Maddie cringed. Howie seemed to enjoy the attention and flirtatious teasing of his female patients, but it was annoying for her to watch. She suddenly thought of what Sonya had said about him eyeing her on the day of their wedding.

But Maddie's recollection was short-lived. "I'm here!" Jackelynn blurted loudly as she entered the house with a snotty attitude.

"Good morning," Maddie replied, taking a deep breath to stay calm and professional.

The princess sat on a chair and re-applied a thick layer of lipstick to her artificially puffy fish lips.

"It's a beautiful day," Maddie smiled, facing Jackelynn.

"Ah, it's kind of smoggy." She flipped her hair off her shoulders.

The fumes from her sweet perfume ran right up Maddie's nose. She sneezed. Jackelynn cringed, fanning the air to avoid flying germs. Fortunately, Howie came in and greeted the patient, who declared, "Doc, boy do I need your hands today. My lower back is killing me."

"Okay, my secretary will get the room ready." He smiled and patted Jackelynn on the shoulder, then handed his wife some papers for the file of his previous patient. "Send this copy to the Pension Guild and please have him come back in two weeks."

"Sure." Maddie took the papers and grabbed a pen as Howie headed for the kitchen.

A male patient came out of the treatment room smiling and glowing. He sat at the desk to write a check as the high maintenance gal glared at Maddie and blinked nervously.

"Are you okay? Do you need something?" Maddie wondered.

"NO! I'll be better as soon as I have my healing from Doc." She hugged her purse and turned away.

The guy looked at Maddie and winked. "Breathe," he suggested. "See you in two weeks."

"Yes, yes," she grinned at him, then scurried off to get the treatment room ready.

It took all of Maddie's meditative skills not to knock out Jackelynn's lights. For months she had been dealing with this needy, flirty, snobbish actress who thought she had the right to be mean just because she was on television. Enough was enough.

When Howie stepped back into the room, he could see that his wife's patience was being tested. "I'm ready for you, dear," he signaled to Jackelynn.

"I'm always ready for you, Doc," she replied with a wink.

Maddie growled under her breath and stormed into the kitchen for a drink of water. As she drank it and gazed out the window to calm down, she drifted into a daydream. Suddenly she was face to face with the celebrity woman in a military setting back home in the Philippines. Her gun was drawn and she motioned to the civilian to move forward. The woman refused and reached for her over priced handbag. Maddie warned her not to make any sudden moves. When her prisoner did not comply and continued to reach into her bag, Maddie cocked the gun loudly and gave another warning. As her finger started to press the trigger, the woman pulled out a tube of lipstick and smirked.

The phone rang suddenly, snapping Maddie out of her dark fantasy seconds before she might have pulled the trigger. In her kitchen, she rubbed her pregnant belly and pulled herself together instead. Then she tapped on the treatment room door and walked in unannounced. Howie had both hands placed on the woman's upper buttocks or lower back, depending on one's perception. His eyes were closed.

"So sorry to interrupt, but you're needed on the phone right away. It's an overseas call," Maddie said softly but firmly.

Howie sincerely excused himself and left the room. Before she could exit, the patient sat up and barked at Maddie: "Was that really necessary?"

Maddie just smiled and left. At her desk, Howie was finishing up with the telephone call.

"Mad, next time let the phone call wait, no matter who it is and what they tell you. The disruption breaks the energy flow."

"Sure, sure." She fumbled with some papers until he left the room. Then she growled like a caged tiger.

Over the following weeks, during lunches and late night dinners in trendy Hollywood restaurants, Maddie observed that some of her husband's friendships seemed based only on what people could do for each other to help them achieve a goal. She wondered, *doesn't anyone just want to be friends, for the sake of being friends?* California people were another breed of animal and she felt like a turtle slowly coming out of its shell.

She was clearly learning a lot about the man she married. The man she had loved in the Philippines was not the man she was living with now. Many nights he worked on a Hollywood movie set or did a house call to heal one of his actor patients. When he got home, he was short-tempered and egoistical. Yet, being a considerate wife, she would heat up the evening's dinner and dine with her man, most nights in silence.

Finally, after one too many quiet meals, she spoke up. "What is wrong?"

"Nothing," he mumbled, with his face dropped over his plate.

"You seem so angry and uninterested in me."

"I'm not."

"Not interested or not angry?" she joked.

"I'm not angry."

"Good. But it seems as though I am in your way except for when I'm working for you."

"I'm sorry you feel that way, I just have a lot things on my mind."

"Can I help?" she asked, putting her hand on his hand.

"I'll let you know." Howie slid his hand from hers and finished his meal, then left the table without another word.

Maddie did the dishes, then retired to their bedroom, alone. Sadness overwhelmed her. For the first time since she had left the Philippines she cried.

Most days Maddie was on a short leash at her desk, which was always knee-high in paperwork. She missed running, dancing and having sex with her husband. It could have been the hormones, homesickness or the one-eighty-degree change in her husband. Whatever it was, she was an emotional wreck. She slept very little, her concentration skills were weak and a sense of isolation was creeping into her body.

Maddie was discovering that once you live in the canyon, you usually hang there. It was an environment best known for attracting hippies. She tried her best to make friends with her neighbors, but they were quiet folks who made conversation through smiles, eye contact, and peace gestures. For the most part she only found comfort and happiness when she spoke to her family on the telephone. When they asked for news about her new home, all she could say was, "It's good, it's beautiful and good!"

One warm evening, while Howie was out on a work call, Maddie longed to just sit and talk with him over a glass of lemonade. Feeling alone and lonely, she got anxious. *This house is too quiet.* Like a caged tiger at the zoo, she paced. *Come on! I don't know what to do!* She stood in the living room rubbing her big belly. *I'll clean, that's what I'll do, I'll clean!*

She ran a polishing cloth over some woodwork in the house as she prayed. *Saint Anthony, I'm lonely. I miss my old friends, especially Sonya. But I can't let them know how sad I am. What will they think? I wish I had a friend to sit with, share a beer, and sing some karaoke.* She sighed heavily. *Will I ever make any friends in California? Please hear my prayers and help me find ways to honor God's blessings.*

Maddie opened a window in the living room and shook the dust out of the rag. The slight breeze was calming. It assured her this feeling would pass. *Or was it Saint Anthony's presence?*

By the wee hours of the morning, the house had become sparkling clean and smelled fresh, just like her condo had after a good cleaning. Restless and tired, Maddie opened the front door for some fresh air and sat on a porch chair.

My life has taken a turn down a path that wasn't even on my conscious map, she marveled. *I don't even know what happened to my architecture career.*

She recalled meeting Howie, signs from Aunt Etana, the trepidation in her core, the love-struck feeling, the train ticket in her pocket, and her disconnection with Sonya. *Was it all real?* she wondered. *I need you, Saint Valentine. Can you guide me?* She again prayed and waited for a sign.

Minutes later, Maddie was just dozing off when the wind blew, stirring up an odd sensation. She flinched and touched her big belly, feeling the life-force pulsating inside. Maddie looked at the darkened sky where one bright star stood out amongst the many, twinkling as if it was speaking just to her. She said a prayer, asking for peace and contentment.

The baby kicked. *Oh my gosh!* A tear fell down her cheek. More tears, sad and happy, followed.

"*Connection*"

*I shall grasp this
pleasure,
this pivotal moment
in our relationship,
and embrace it
with all my heart.*

MALIBU – PRESENT DAY

THE WAVES WERE HYPNOTIC, rolling in and rolling out. Seagulls flew close to our blanket hoping to snag any leftover crumbs from the buttered rolls Maddie had made. But there were none – by now we'd devoured every morsel.

"Hi girls," Lucinda cheered as she joined us again. "That was a wonderful walk."

"Did you find any treasures, like Thomas did?" I wondered.

"Yes, take a look at these." Lucinda knelt on the blanket and gently dropped her findings beside us.

"Boot-a-full," I marveled, picking up a shell that contained a fossil.

Maddie moaned and opened her eyes, only half-awake. "Wh-what's going on?"

"We're admiring some seashells," Lucinda said.

Maddie sat up. "Oooh, let me see."

The intimate moment was interrupted by a long-haired guy shouting as he trucked down the beach with a guitar strapped to his back. An attractive blonde woman was with him. As they got closer, he shouted again: "The party can get started now!"

"Slow down, would you?" the blonde ordered, holding the brim of her big-rimmed hat to keep the wind from blowing it off her head.

"Sorry, babe." The long-haired guy pranced back to her.

The six of us stopped what we were doing to watch the pair waddle toward us, hand in hand. At first glance they appeared as opposite as opposites can be. She looked like a modern day Scarlet O'Hara while he was clearly a rock'n'roller.

Thomas was first up to greet them. "Hey Andy, good to see you again."

From there, all the men hugged and hoorayed and back-slapped like four young boys. Lucinda suggested we go over and save the damsel before she wound up in distress. As we mosey towards the blonde, I waved at her and smiled. She smiled back and wiggled two fingers in a semi-wave, but she seemed out-of-sorts.

"Hello. I'm Marlo, Thomas's wife." I said when we finally stood face to face.

"Thomas is the stuntman who's helping my Andy with his music, isn't he?" she asked, a bit winded.

"Yup, that's the one."

The blonde cleared her throat and said, "Well, it's a pleasure to meet you, Marlo. I'm Bea."

I chuckled to myself, not only did she look the part but her southern belle accent was strong and endearing.

"Phew, that was a long walk," Bea sighed. She finally dropped the beach bags in front of her, then fanned her face with her hand.

"I'm Lucinda, Ricky's girlfriend."

"Ah-ha, nice to meet you. Ricky's a stuntman too, right?" Bea wondered.

"Yes, and an actor once in a while," Lucinda boasted.

"Oh, an actor too. Are you an actress?"

"Yes I am, and I also do make-up and hair."

"Goodness gracious, I'm surrounded with Hollywood people." Bea looked over at Maddie and smiled.

"I'm Maddie, the doctor's wife. He treats the Hollywood people," she laughed.

"I'm speechless," Bea chuckled. "Actually, I'm rather breathless from the long haul. I guess it's time to get back to my exercise routine."

The four of us agreed, patting the parts of our own bodies we thought needed some T.L.C.

"Hey, Andy, get over here and meet these lovely gals," Bea sweetly demanded.

Andy lovingly obeyed and ran over to introduce himself. Then he scooted back to the boys. My take on Andy was that he was a very genuine and trusting person. But as open as Bea seemed at that moment, I sensed she was rather guarded. I wondered why…

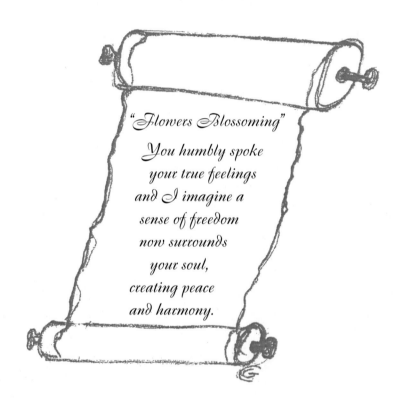

"Flowers Blossoming"

You humbly spoke
your true feelings
and I imagine a
sense of freedom
now surrounds
your soul,
creating peace
and harmony.

BEA'S PAST

BORN AND RAISED IN THE SUGARY STATE of Alabama, Bea was a confident woman who moved slowly and methodically. In 1995, Bea was single again and residing in New Jersey. She had a son in his twenties who lived on his own. Because of her smarts and work-driven energy, she was one of the few women making big bucks in the highly competitive field of office design. She had just landed a great job at a major banking corporation and was also one of the first female ergonomic teachers in the state.

Bea's sweet and sexy personality clearly knocked the socks off all the men in her path, though it could have been the high-heeled stilettos she liked to wear. You know, the expensive toe-pinching ones that look so good but hurt so much, the ones men fantasize about along with the whip and the blindfold. This damsel could work both business and personal rooms with class and pizzazz. Her southern belle persona gained attention, but she was a lady and expected to be treated as one. She carried a cross-stitched handkerchief in her purse and if a man was in her car she expected the door to be opened and closed by his hand.

When she wasn't in a full-time relationship (which wasn't often), she would mingle with 'the boys' at a local bar after work. She'd have a few rounds of beer and a couple of shots. The boys constantly teased Bea about her love life and nicknamed her 'ghost friend' as she'd disappear when she began dating someone, then reappear without a word after the inevitable break-up. But they loved her without judgments or expectations.

Typically as the evening progressed and the liquor gave her a nice buzz, Bea's good manners would go down the drain as she socked it back to the boys as quickly as they dished it out. She also loved to talk about sports and was up to date on all the major players. The boys loved how she talked like one of them, so they constantly challenged her and egged her on just to watch her feathers ruffle.

The boys' women as well as the gals in the office liked Bea too. But she kept a safe distance and didn't get too friendly with them. She had trust issues with women that stemmed from her mother. The roots of their relationship were twisted and deep. As a young girl, Bea's mom had rarely been around. Empty half-pint bottles of promises and uncaptured memories lived in a sad place within her core, so Bea believed she didn't need women in her life.

"Women spend too much time yapping about petty dramas and trying to look like celebrities. They backstab each other as often as they get their hair done," she said many times to the boys. "Heck, having girlfriends should be a physical sport where mouthpieces and heartguards must be worn."

But as much as the southern belle wants people to think she's all business and tough as nails, there were also delicate layers guarding her spirit. She was an avid dog lover and a gentle nurturer, patient and generous with all her heart. She loved her daddy deeply and her relationship with her stepmother was uniquely wonderful. But mostly, she loved men. She loved to be with them, take care of them, and play with them.

Bea believed she's here to meet her long-lost soulmate and receive the truest love that has ever existed. But how many men does she have to sample? Does she really need a man to make her feel complete? And does she need to experience the same lesson a hundred times? When will Bea be enough for Bea?

For the first time in her life, Bea wasn't living with a dog or husband. Her typical routine at the end of a long day was to retire to her bedroom in her townhouse. It was a large master upstairs with a queen-size brass framed bed facing an octagon window overlooking a garden. The walls were papered with a tulip design, and ceramic figurines of dogs and angels adorned the room.

A huge walk-in closet took up one wall. Inside it, nine-to-five business clothes hung neatly on silk hangers and high heeled-shoes lined the carpeted floor. Expensive logo handbags sat on the shelving. Faux fur coats, cashmere sweaters, and plastic-covered items were color-coded based on the four seasons.

On the other side hung a slim selection of casual clothes, including pink polo shirts, cardigan sweaters, bloomers, and name brand white sneakers that looked like they were rarely worn. Half-hidden in a corner underneath lacy negligees and black garter stockings was a silver box marked "toys".

Tonight Bea slipped into a comfy pair of flannel pajamas. She washed the make-up off her face, clipped up her hair, and lit a few candles. Then she mixed a cocktail at her unique bedroom mini-bar. With martini in hand, she slid under the luxurious quilt adorning her pillow-top bed and relaxed. Her mind began to wander as she couldn't help thinking it had been months since she was with a man and even longer since her last serious relationship.

Lonely and frustrated, she downed the drink and buried her head in the pillow. Minutes later she finally calmed down by shifting into a prayer. *"Lord, I pray for some time off from work so I can see what I'm doing and where I'm going with my life. I sure do miss the company of a man, taking care of his emotional needs, the feel of his skin, his earthy smell, his bulging body and his strong appetite for my flesh and my love."*

Her words became weary and slow as her body relaxed more deeply. She floated into a deep slumber. Little did Bea know her prayers were being heard. And they would be answered, maybe not in the way she had intended, but the Lord gives us what we need, not always what we want. This heart-felt prayer invoked the beginnings of Bea's life-changing events.

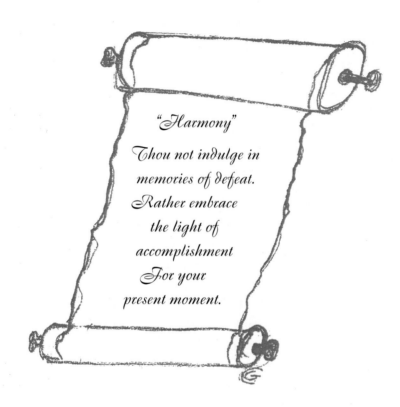

"Harmony"

Thou not indulge in
memories of defeat.
Rather embrace
the light of
accomplishment
For your
present moment.

MALIBU – PRESENT DAY

AS MUCH AS I SENSED that Bea was guarded, I also felt she was approachable and even a bit vulnerable around women. It was obvious the intros were done, as there was a long pause. We smiled and sighed, not quite sure what to do next while the boys stood around laughing and reminiscing.

As if on cue, the four of us casually excused ourselves and broke away to our blankets. *That's one of the grand things about being in your forties, you come to realize how important gaps in life are.*

Lucinda helped Bea set up fort. Maddie lay on her stomach, quite content. I watched Maddie roll up her khakis to get more sun on the back of her legs. She was obviously a modest woman, wearing a dark tank-top and shorts as a bathing suit. Lucinda on the other hand wore a leopard bikini that accented her thriving body parts. Bea was frilly, she seemed at home in her pink and white linen sundress with a matching two-piece underneath. I wore a black and white halter-top bathing suit with boxer-cut bottoms.

We were as different as individuals can be. Yet something in my gut told me the four of us had more in common than what met the eye. I knew I would have to explore this later as it was not what I'd expected to be feeling from a casual day at the beach.

MADDIE'S PAST

IT WAS A BRILLIANT DAY, a real blessing. A day that was Heaven-made. Maddie rocked in a chair cradling her newborn daughter. The front porch creaked with the back and forth motion. The chirping of the birds provided Nature's music to serenade the infant. Yes, the twinkling star Maddie had wished upon that lonely, windy night had granted her a healthy baby girl. And her struggling relationship with her husband had evolved into one of joy and unity. Finally, the personal interaction she'd missed from her Filipino family had been birthed in America. *The 440 Train had again switched tracks. Amen.*

"Look at this outfit I got today," Howie cheered as he charged up the porch steps.

"It's so cute!" Maddie cooed, reading the logo. 'I Love My Daddy' was printed across the front.

"It's not too much?" the proud father asked gleefully.

"No, it's perfect."

"And look at this!" He pulled out a stuffed giraffe that rattled.

"That's sweet. You're sweet. Thank you," Maddie smiled as happy tears came to her eyes.

"I also got something for you."

She placed a hand on her chest. "For me?"

"Yes, for you." Howie handed Maddie a small black velvet box. "I never gave you anything really personal before." His eyes sparkled with sincerity.

"You gave me this lovely little girl." Maddie gazed at her daughter and adjusted the blanket around the baby's precious head.

"I love you, Mad. I'm sorry that I've been shutting you out."

"It's okay. I was just being overly sensitive. I love you too, Howie."

Finally she opened the box. Inside was a carved turquoise cross. "It's beautiful!"

"It reminded me of when we first met and you were digging through your pockets."

"Oh yeah, you asked me if I would need the cross for protection," she remembered with a raised brow.

"Yeah, that was funny. Anyway, I thought this would look stunning against your bronze skin."

"I love it," Maddie assured him. "Thank you."

Howie clasped it around her neck, then kissed her long and tenderly.

The everyday office duties Maddie was typically engulfed in took a back seat after the baby arrived. She heard no complaints from da' boss-man who temporarily took over the paperwork for his patients. Evenings were relaxing for the threesome as the baby slept soundly while Mommy and Daddy rekindled the creamy passion they had known in the Philippines. Since breastfeeding came naturally for the former tomboy, Howie enjoyed the perks of his wife's bounty-filled breasts.

As promised, Maddie kept the bloodline ties strong. She sent photos, videos, and letters overseas monthly to Gramma and Grandpa as the next best thing to being there. Most afternoons the new mom would saddle up her papoose to her chest and venture out for a walk. Little by little, as her pregnancy pounds dropped off, Maddie picked up her pace to a quick stride, remembering the marathons she used to run. The chirping birds, running water in the stream, and other natural elements elevated her mood to a new level of contentment.

When she reached the final marker of her walk, Maddie would rest on a huge rock. A broken section of the boulder was perfectly shaped for her buttocks. She would lean against the earthly chair, stretch her shoulders and relax to the soothing heartbeat of her baby girl. This quiet outdoor place became her 'Private Idaho,' where she could speak to the saints, give thanks, and receive blessings.

Hours later, the girls would head home so Maddie could prepare dinner. This particular meal was a spread suitable for a queen, featuring sautéed portobello mushrooms smothered with pan-glazed bok choy, leeks, Swiss chard, potatoes, and oozing melted Monterey Jack cheese on a pile of steamed buttery rice. Along with it went Maddie's traditional lemonade.

At the table, Howie seemed preoccupied. "Is everything alright?" Maddie wanted to know.

"My father called. He wants to see his first-born grandchild," he murmured.

"Of course, this is wonderful," she said gleaming. Howie just grinned.

Without hesitation, Maddie cleared Howie's appointment book and the three flew to the Big Apple to meet Grandpa. From the airport they took a cab to his predominately Jewish neighborhood. Grandpa's house was quaint, older but freshly painted. The shrubs in the front yard were hedged evenly and meticulously. They also blocked a large-paned window, allowing only a birds-eye view from the inside. A ceramic statue of a feeding deer stood in the center of the well-kept lawn. The property was organized, yet homey, and the triple-lock on the front door was typical for a senior living alone in New York.

Howie's father opened the front door, before they rang the bell. "Hello, hello," he said excitedly. "Come in, come in."

Maddie's father-in-law was short in height but large in stance. He was frail in bone mass yet coherent in mind and wise as an old barn owl.

The four settled in the living room. Maddie sat on the couch next to her father-in-law and placed the baby on his lap. Tears welled in his eyes as he studied his granddaughter's angelic face. As they got to know one another, he would look directly into Maddie's eyes as he was talking and listening. She always felt that was a sign of someone who respected others and was confident.

"She's a gift from God," he said.

"Yes, she is."

"I wish your mother was here, Howard."

"I know, Dad, me too," Howie said, looking around the all too familiar room.

"Sweetheart, you see our grandchild." Howie's father looked up and stared for a moment, addressing his wife's spirit which he swore was floating around the house since her passing. Maddie looked at Howie who was looking at a photo of his mother and himself.

Soon, she went upstairs and put the baby to bed, giving the two men some time alone. Once the baby was asleep, Maddie unpacked, showered, and changed into her sweat pants. She headed downstairs for a warm cup of milk to help her sleep.

As she walked into the kitchen, it was evident the men were having an important conversation. "Sorry to interrupt. I can come back," she insisted.

"No … stay my dear," her father-in-law pleaded.

Maddie looked at Howie. He nodded his head okay.

"You've got a winner, Howard! Didn't think you had it in ya," the old man continued.

"You're a real piece of work, Dad."

Maddie chuckled, admiring the cute bantering between father and son. But Howie was not amused.

While sipping on the steamy milk, the elder leaned close to her ear. "My dear, better keep your eye on that one." He gestured to his son who was preparing a cheese sandwich.

The comment was spoken softly in volume but loud to her heart. This time she did not laugh. The more she watched the two men, it was apparent that the energy in the house had shifted and things weren't as cozy-wozy as she had thought.

"Come with me, I want to give you something," Howie's father said.

Maddie looked at her husband. He shrugged his shoulders and took a bite of his sandwich, a hunk of mayonnaise dropping onto his shirt.

"Come, dear." She was escorted into the dinning room to an old front-slant wood desk. Howie's father opened a tiny drawer with a key, then clutched something in the palm of his hand. She couldn't see what it was.

"This is for you," he reached for Maddie's hand as his hands trembled slightly. "Don't ever let Howard take these from you." He placed two rings with rubies and diamonds into her palm. "If anything ever happens and you need money, sell them."

Maddie's eyes widened. The largest gems she had ever seen sparkled in the rings. "Oh my gosh! I can't accept these, sir."

"You can and you will." He looked sternly into her eyes. "My beloved wife and I want you and the baby to have them. We had these made fifty years ago. They're a symbol of our deep love and friendship. And they're very rare and valuable."

"Their beautiful. I-I do not know what to say. I am humbled by your generosity."

"Just take care of my granddaughter and yourself. This is my wish."

"I will." She gently hugged him and kissed his cheek as Howie walked into the room.

"Don't you ever take these from Madaline. They're a gift for her and the baby," the old man harshly told his son.

Howie waved his hands in the air. "Some things don't change," he muttered.

"I don't want to cause a problem," Maddie said defensively.

"There is no problem here dear, is there, son?"

"Nope, no problem, Dad!"

The following morning, Maddie got up early to feed the baby, then prepared a delicious homemade breakfast of fried eggs, paper-thin lox and bagels with cream cheese. The smell of freshly brewed coffee finally woke the men.

"Hey! How about we all go for a walk. It's a beautiful day and the baby would love to be outdoors," Maddie pointedly suggested while everyone was happily eating.

The four took a stroll through the neighborhood, leaving behind any ill feelings from the night before. The remainder of the week was spent enjoying Maddie's fabulous home-cooked meals, conversing about politics and the world, and joyfully reminiscing about the old days when Howie's mom was alive, topped off with a smorgasbord of emotions.

"Connection"

Who are we really?
Different days,
a different face.
But inside,
who I am is
rather simple—
I love you.

MALIBU – PRESENT DAY

AS MUCH AS I WANTED to keep this get-together simple, I sensed there was something much deeper going on. I continued watching the women I had just met and then shifted my focus to the four men. They were clearly the catalyst that had brought us together, but something inside told me there was a spiritual meaning and more to be revealed.

I recalled my conversation with Mom about dreams and trains, her exact words were "That is yet to be revealed." *Was she right?*

After all these years, the recurring dream I still have has to do with finding a certain type of relationship. Might these women be the answer?

There was definitely something big brewing, something that wouldn't back down. This feeling was just as strong as when someone from Heaven is talking to me, trying to get their words across. When unseen energy is diligently making itself seen, the only way to hear what is really being said is to become silent. So I did…

BEA'S PAST

BEA TURNED OVER. The now-empty martini glass lay on the pillow next to her. From habit, she reached over and placed it on a nightstand without opening her eyes. A beat later, she squinted one eye open. The glow from her alarm clock revealed it was 4:44 a.m.

Bea fluffed her pillow, trying to fall back asleep. But her mind raced. She turned over again, roughly scrunching her pillow. *Lord, I'm lonely. I need a change, a new love, a new beginning and dang, I need some fun. Did I mention love?*

Reaching for her nightstand again, Bea pulled the string on a stained glass lamp and the light came on. She sat up, grabbed a pen and paper, and started making a shopping list: a bunch of bananas, a new pair of shoes, a pound of coffee, toilet paper, batteries, *and a new man.*

Bea thought about all the men in her life and wondered why she never went after what she truly craved. The tight collar man just wasn't working for her anymore. Miss Bea was really attracted to long-haired, rugged rock-n-roll type guys but always ended up with stiff business tycoons in designer boxers and expensive suits.

I know what those guys were missing, grit and soul, she concluded. *I know I've been a busy little girl, walking down the aisle three times, but each time having a strong feeling I should have fled the scene instead of saying I do. So why didn't I listen to my inner voice?*

Bea was having a pity party. Three marriages said and done by her mid-forties just might make her worthy of self-pity. But regrets get us nowhere and keep us from the "now-here."

It was time for Bea to set her love-life goals with her heart's desires rather than her business-brain mentality. But before going out on the hunt, she needed to learn how to avoid repeating the same pattern again. She needed to reflect. To do this, she needed a personal solstice.

That morning, Bea went into work as usual but did something brand new, she put her personal needs first. With coffee mug in hand, she knocked on her boss' door.

"Come in," a woman's voice replied.

Bea sat down in a large green leather chair and got right to the point. "I'm sorry about the short notice but I need to handle some personal matters. I'll need some time off."

"For you to ask, Bea, it must be important. Is everything okay? Are you ill?" her boss asked, concerned.

"No, no, I'm well, but I need to recharge my batteries. I'm just not packing the punch I normally have and something is telling me to chill out."

"How courageous of you to admit this and honor your health needs."

"Really? I wasn't sure how you would react."

"You won't do anyone any good, especially yourself, if you're not rested and feeling your best."

"Bless you," Bea said graciously.

"We'll manage without you, for how long did you say?"

"Well, I didn't yet. But I could use a week sabbatical."

"A week!"

"Yes, ma'am, a week. My assistant can handle anything that comes along."

"Dear, you take a month. I insist."

"A month!"

"Yes, a month. I was worried you were ready to give your notice."

"Oh heavens, no."

"Since you're an independent contractor, I thought, well, let's just say we're grateful to have you here and I would hate to lose you. This office has never run so smoothly."

"Oh my word, I'm blushing. And I'm just as grateful to be here. Thank you, thank you so much. If you need me for anything, you feel free to call me, okay?"

"You got it," her boss said, shooing Bea out of the office with a smile.

Already Bea felt freer. A shift occurred as she walked to the parking structure. Her body relaxed as if a weight had been lifted off her shoulders. She quickened her step, getting excited about her new beginning.

On the way home Bea stopped at the grocery to pick up some items on her shopping list. Over the next few days, she read self-help books, exercised for hours, ate healthier foods, and spent more time in prayer and contemplation than ever before. And every now and then the box in her closet marked 'toys' was put to good use.

Taking advice from several books, she began writing in a journal. Bea had a section for gratitude, such as thanking the Lord for hearing her prayers and thanking her 'boy' friends from work for all the fun they had together. Another section dedicated to venting old wounds was where she revisited her experiences with men. She looked for clues so she could break her old patterns. At times she drifted to the far away past where her mother issues were rooted. But she kept pushing them down, not ready for those buried feelings to surface. Bea believed the issue at hand had nothing to do with good ole' Momma and was strictly about men.

I thought this time off was going to relax me, but I'm more on edge than ever. Her highly stimulated mind winding and unwinding. *The school of self-reflection is quite frankly exhausting. Maybe there are uncomfortable times in our past worth visiting, but Lord knows right now I'm not in the mood!*

She moaned and turned on the television set, hoping to stop the commotion in her head. Then from across the room she heard something 'clink-clank.' Bea hopped off the bed to check out the situation. Looking around, she noticed one of the angel figurines from her collection was lying on the floor. She froze. It was Archangel Michael.

Suddenly, the volume on television turned up on its own, *"This is the time to dig up the dirt that lives deep down and get rid of the stale smell that has been hindering you from enjoying the freshness of life."*

Wide-eyed, Bea stayed locked into the voice on the tube as she picked up the angel. Surprisingly, it wasn't broken. *"Order this gallon of Nature's Powder now and receive a long-handled brush to work the cleaner into your carpet."*

Carpet cleaner? Bea thought. *That was freaky! For a minute I thought it was a message from Archangel Michael.* She placed the figurine back in its place and shut off the television. *Hmm, maybe it was a message.*

Feeling more confident with the angel's message, she sat on a frilly velvet stool that matched an antique vanity and had a sudden urge to pluck her eyebrows. She was tugging on a stubborn piece of hair when she heard a high pitch sound in the distance that startled her. *Ouch! That hurt. What is that noise?* She rubbed her brow, soothing the pinch. An overwhelming feeling in her heart told her something was coming. *Shoot, the sound is coming closer. I feel so strange and I haven't even been drinking tonight.*

Bea put down the tweezers. Looking at her reflection in the vanity mirror and feeling out of sorts, she unscrewed a jar of face cream and scooped a bit onto her fingers. She began smoothing it onto her skin. The disturbing sound was getting closer, making her even more anxious. She rubbed the lotion faster, blending it into her skin. *Now that's really strange. It sounds like a choo-choo!*

Bea picked up a sterling silver-handled brush and began stroking her golden locks. Twenty or so strokes later, the brush slipped out of her oily hand. A chill rippled across her body as she bent down to retrieve it. *For the life of me, I don't recall ever being bothered by a train whistle, but it's driving me batty. It sounds like it's coming from the kitchen.*

Restless, she flung on her floral print robe, tightened the belt and ran down the carpeted stairs in search of the sound. But as she flicked on the kitchen lights, nothing was there—just the ticking of the kitchen clock and a haunting feeling she couldn't shake.

The following morning while having a cup of coffee, she concluded that all the weird stuff last night was her imagination working overtime. Yet, as troubled as she was, she felt like something was leading the way, pulling her forward with her soul searching.

Over the following days, more books, inspirational tapes, and a new stationery bicycle helped heal Beatrice's frustrated psyche and energize her body. Basking in the hot summer sun and soaking up Vitamin D along with plenty of rest and healthy eats finally brought a calm resolution to her being. She realized her businesswoman role had bled into her personal relationships and her desire to be with a man with street spunk was not happening due to her illusionary expectations.

It's a simple fix! I'm ready to go after what I always wanted and be authentic. First stop the mall. A new playful wardrobe would clearly be necessary for this transformation.

Bea's usual shopping spree at a high-end sophisticated store was bypassed. For the first time, she visited a lower-end sexy, sporty boutique. With the help of an over ambitious sales clerk, Miss Alabama quickly found herself in a dressing room trying on low-cut tee shirts and ripped pre-washed jeans.

"How about this hot new bra?" the young sales clerk asked, reaching through the dressing room curtain to hand it over.

"Oh my! What's in this that makes it so heavy?" Bea peeked her head out of the curtain.

"Water."

"Water!"

"Yeah, it's incredible. When someone hugs you, they think it's the real thing." The woman grabbed her own breasts and giggled.

Bea swiped the drapery closed. She looked into the mirror and snapped the bra, then cupped her breasts with the palms of her hands, adjusting it. "Hmmm, they do feel soft."

"See, I told ya," the sales clerk whispered back.

"But water, I just don't know. What if I get a hole in it?" She looked at her profile and stood straighter, admiring her highly-alert chest.

"Not to sweat, they improved the design since the incident when a guy bit his girlfriend's cups and it leaked," the clerk rattled on.

Bea unsnapped the bra and quickly handed it back to the clerk, "Not for me, honey! Who in their right mind would wear this contraption?"

But the visit to the store wasn't a complete bust, no pun intended. Bea walked out with four shopping bags full of trendy clothing. As for a new pair of shoes, she stuck with a high-end shop and chose a pair of red, five-inch, Jimmy Choo, lace and leather high heels.

Next stop, the beauty parlor. "I want blonder highlights and more layers," she told her stylist.

Once Bea's hair was done, she moved into the nail salon for a manicure and pedicure. She chose a hot pink polish and a stencil with flowers and rhinestones. By the time Bea left the salon, she had a new bounce to her hair, lightness in her step, and an extra wiggle on her hour-glass bottom.

"When I get home, I'll go for a nice walk and take an afternoon nap. Then look out, boys, 'cause I'm coming out to play," she chuckled, gazing at her reflection in a storefront window while catching the eyes of many men passing by.

Though the sun had set, the night didn't cool down. It was hot and humid but it was also Friday, the best night to go clubbin' and meet someone on Route 35 in New Jersey. So nothing was going to keep Beatrice from finding Mr. Right and crossing off the last item on her shopping list, 'new man.'

She put on a new peek-a-boobs shirt, bootie-huggin' jeans, and the hot red pumps. She spritzed some flowery perfume all over her body. Then she put on the finishing touch, teasing and spraying her hair till it stood tall. The look: *high-class sleazy.*

Feeling confident, Bea skedaddled to her car and turned on the ignition. She dialed the air conditioner to full throttle, hoping to save her hair from flopping and make-up from melting. When she arrived at the nightclub, the parking lot was packed. She drove around the building several times before succumbing to the valet service.

"Well, well, pretty lady, you have fun tonight," the parking attendant grinned, handing her a claim receipt.

"That's just what I have planned," she replied.

Inside the nightclub, Bea adjusted her breasts with a twist of her shoulders, then pranced the 'I am single' march. The band had just left the stage. The DJ announced a special drink offer, then spun a dance medley.

Bea glided along the upper level of the bar, casually excusing her way through the crowd and working her pizzazz. Several men approached this beautiful damsel from Alabama but no sparks flew. So she politely acknowledged them with a brief smile and kept walking.

Bea promised herself to be patient and this was one promise she was going to keep. As quickly as the words ran through her mind, however, they changed. At the far end of the bar, she spotted a young broad shouldered man watching her. She curved to the left and slowed her stride to make sure he kept watching. He did.

He got off the stool and approached her. She kept her eyes on his. He was a young Clint Eastwood type, rugged and extremely handsome. They stopped in front of each other and smiled.

"You meeting someone?" he asked.

"I think I just have," she smiled widely.

His voice even sounded like Clint in 'Dirty Harry'. The guy was hot, hot and hot!

"Can I buy ya a drink?" he asked, moving in closer.

"Make my day!" she teased.

He laughed, "You're a lively one."

"I do feel very much alive tonight, thank you. I'll take a slow gin fizz, with two cherries," she said in a dramatized flirtatious tone.

He guided her very gently onto a stool and ordered the drinks, then stood next to her. She could smell his aftershave. It was alluring.

"It's nice to meet you. My name is Billie."

"Well hello, Billie. My name is Bea."

They smiled and sipped their drinks. She watched his body language. Although he had approached her, she felt he was shy and trying too hard to impress her.

As fine as this young man is, there's just something about him, she thought. *Plus he's young enough to be my son.*

"Is this your first time here?" he wondered.

"Oh, no, but it's been awhile."

They made small talk that revealed little tidbits about each other. He told her he modeled men's underwear for catalogs.

"Wow! Well, you sure have a body for modeling. May I ask what brand?"

"Calvin Klein."

"Oh, I know a few men who wear it," she chuckled. "Look here our first round of drinks are already down the hatch."

Billie ordered another round, while Bea showed the young stud how she could tie a knot in the cherry stem with her tongue. She lost his attention when a pretty boy in tight plaid pants, square red-framed sunglasses and a pink shirt approached the bar. He stood next to them, ordered a drink, drank it through a straw, and fussed with his hair while gazing at the underwear-model.

Billie became fidgety. "You okay?" Bea asked.

"Yeah, I'm great."

"Do you know him?" she wondered, tilting her head.

"Yes. But I'd rather hang with you."

She whispered to Billie, "I think he's gay."

"You do? Why? Is it his wardrobe?"

"No, not really. Although…" She raised her brows. "He looks feminine and I sense a woman-to-woman commonality. "

"Really. Do you think all men who are gay have that commonality with women?"

"Good question." She paused. "No, I think there are layers of beauty and complexity in our genes and emotions that influence who we are, how we feel and how we act."

"Interesting theory." A long pause lingered between them.

Finally she spoke: "He keeps staring at you. I'm convinced he likes you."

"You are?" He half-grinned.

Bea's mind raced. It was starting to make sense now, what she had been feeling about Billie. "You know, if you want my opinion, it's fine with me if a man likes another man, I give the guy credit for strutting around being true to how he really feels."

"Really, you do?"

"Why sure. That's what I'm working on, being honest about what I really want in life and brave enough to go after it."

"I like your attitude. You're a good person. I wish everyone felt the way you did," he replied.

"Thank you, but truth be told, I'm a work-in-progress."

"Me too," he smiled, relaxing his macho persona.

"Just be true to yourself and don't worry about what other people say."

"Easy to say, but not as easy to do," he said.

"You're right. I've been reading a lot of self-discovery books. They say things like 'treat yourself the way you would like others to treat you.' Evidently we set the pace to how we want to be treated by the way we take care of ourselves and treat others."

"I believe that too."

"What really matters is how you feel about you! Cause Lord knows everyone has a belly button."

"A belly button?" he crinkled his brows.

"You know, an opinion. Everyone has something to say."

"True, really true."

"I wanted to say everyone has a butthole," she confessed. "But I was being proper."

"You're funny."

"Kinda," she agreed, realizing the alcohol had hit her fine southern manners. "I am so sorry for my rude tongue."

"No harm. We're just having fun."

"I still better switch to tonic water for awhile." She smiled and hugged him, then wrote her name and number on a napkin.

"I'm going to stroll the club. If you ever need to talk, call me."

"I will. And thank you."

"You are quite welcome, and thank you, Billie, for reflecting to me what I needed to be reminded of, staying true to myself."

Bea walked towards the restroom, then sidetracked back around. She watched Billie and the stylish man talking. Their body language and grins said it all.

She continued to the bathroom. Inside, a group of women were smoking a joint by an open steel-barred window. She held her breath, entered a stall and lined the seat cover with toilet paper. *Might not be my night for a man!*

Suddenly a loud train whistle blew. The bathroom floor vibrated, jiggling the toilet. With the strength of good kegel control, Bea stopped her urine midstream. *What the darn tootin' is it with these trains? Can't a girl have a pee in private!*

MALIBU – PRESENT DAY

I WAS HAVING A HARD TIME CONNECTING to silence. As much as I wanted to figure out the core connections between us women, I really just wanted to have fun and play.

A flock of seagulls ripping open a bag of potato chips above my head brought me back to the outside elements, reminding me to surrender to the moment and not to push. I enjoyed talking with the women and thought maybe it was time we did some more socializing. But Bea was fussing with her hair and hat, and Maddie was still sleeping. Fortunately, Lucinda must have been thinking the same as me. When I looked her way she was already heading toward my blanket.

"I didn't want to disturb you but I thought it would be nice to get more acquainted," Lucinda said.

"You're not disturbing me. I was just thinking the same thing."

"Great minds think alike," she said, kneeling down. "What are those?" She pointed at a deck of cards on my blanket.

"These are Animal Totem cards."

"Animal Totems!" Lucinda queried. "Is that like Goddess and Angel cards?"

"Yeah." I was pleasantly surprised she knew what they were. "You wanna pick a card and see what message it has for you?"

"Sure." She sat down next to me.

This caught Bea's attention. I smiled and waved, signaling for her to join us.

I said a prayer asking for God's divine guidance to be with us as Lucinda shuffled the cards. She browsed the painted pictures, then paused at one, the Dolphin card.

"I love dolphins. Wouldn't it be great to see a few today?"

"It would be amazing."

"Hey, look!" Bea shouted suddenly, pointing toward the ocean. "There's a pod of dolphins."

I sprang up and winked at Lucinda. "You're good!"

She held the cards and stood, eyes wide open. "Holy horse tails! I better not tell you my other favorite animal 'cause it's really big and if it shows up I may faint!"

Her funny personality was beginning to shine through her beauty-pageant looks.

A sleepy-eyed Maddie ran towards our blanket. "How cool. Look! There's more coming."

We jumped and did the "happy dolphin dance" as we watched them ride the waves. Their sleek bodies slipped in and out of the water, graceful and *porpoise-ful!* I wanted to run into the water and ride the waves beside them.

The men looked up a few times but weren't as engaged by the mammal swimmers as we girls were. Thomas was strumming Andy's guitar while the boys improvised a song. It was a happy scene. The guys were out of their cave, laughing and talking about the Lakers and probably giggling about a few hotties in their skimpy bikinis down the beach.

"Whadya girls doing?" Bea wanted to know.

"We're playing with Animal Cards. Join us."

Maddie looked at us but did not sit. She stood stiffly, like a statue. "What exactly are you doing?"

"I'm shuffling the cards and connecting to their energy while thinking of a question," Lucinda said.

"Is this a Native American thing?" Bea asked, spraying a mist of water over her lily-white body.

"These particular cards are created by an Indian woman. They're in tune with Nature and the old ways, but very contemporary."

"I'm part Choctaw," the southern beauty twanged.

"Neat, and I'm part Cherokee," Lucinda added.

I smiled. "That's funny, we were talking about this earlier."

"You too! Who would believe that two chalk-white girls have Indian in their blood," Maddie teased.

"Hey now! Don't let the color of folks deceive you about where they come from and who their relatives are," Bea said.

"I don't mean anything bad. I love all kinds of folks," Maddie replied, contrite.

"No harm done. But it's pretty obvious you're the raw comedian of the group."

"That's a great observation," Lucinda agreed, grinning at Maddie. "Did you ever consider doing stand-up?"

"Who, me?" Maddie asked bashfully.

"Yeah, you," Lucinda chided.

"No, I couldn't do that," Maddie admitted. Then she abruptly changed the subject with a raised brow. "So, this is Tarot stuff you're playing with, right?"

"They're oracle cards. They offer divine guidance through the energy and wisdom of animals and nature."

"Oh, same thing though."

"Don't fret, Maddie. This is white-light stuff. The intention of the cards is to assist us in pausing and connecting within so we can feel the love in our hearts. These cards helped me through some major life transformations. They're a great tool to strengthen self-healing abilities."

"That was a mouthful," Lucinda said. "A good mouthful, though."

I grinned at her, then showed Maddie my diamond cross necklace and winked. "Iz'a believer," I said in slang.

"I, I feel it's good," Maddie stammered.

"That's fine and dandy, Marlo, but preaching that you believe in white-light stuff and living it are two different bowls of cherries. Don't you agree?" Bea blotted the 'no sweat' from her brows with an embroidered handkerchief.

"I agree," Maddie said, her face relaxing with curiosity as she squatted onto the blanket to look at the cards.

"I totally agree," Bea replied. "That's a truth for all of us, in some way or another, practicing what we preach, walking our talk."

"Taking it one step further," Lucinda construed, "are we really who we portray we are, or are we simply acting?"

I could only listen, pondering the truth of Lucinda's comment.

MADDIE'S PAST

THE TRIP TO SEE GRANDPA was great, or at least Maddie thought it was. Back in California, her husband became distant and short-tempered again.

During breakfast one morning, Maddie confronted him, "What's wrong, Howie?"

"I'm thinking about my father and his wisenheimer comments."

"It seemed like you both pick on each other, but still there is love."

"He's a trickster. He makes it sound like he's joking but he's seriously mean."

"He was just teasing you, as you were teasing him."

"No! He always does that. He doesn't think I've succeeded with my life. He thinks because I'm not a 'white-coat doctor' like my brother that I've failed in some way."

"I'm sorry you think that. But I really feel he loves you and is proud of you."

"Hogwash!"

"What about how loving and attentive he was to our daughter."

"Yeah, I'll give him that much. But I lived with the man for years. Trust me, I know him. He always expected more from me."

"I'm sorry. I don't want to make you angry or upset."

"I'll be fine, I just need to decompress. And on top of it he gave you some family jewels and treated me like I was the enemy."

Maddie didn't know how to respond so she let it go. She realized there were emotional issues that were best left alone.

Over the following days she swung back into helping Howie as much as she could. She didn't mind juggling motherhood and 'sexretary.' The baby was so good that she could have her by her side while she greeted patients, filled out insurance forms, and politely answered the phone.

A few months later, however, the train switched tracks. The effort of multi-tasking was becoming way too much for Maddie to handle. And the snooty, flirty, high-paying patients were wearing Maddie's patience down. One day before starting work, she and the baby went to their 'Private Idaho.' She sat on her favorite boulder, taking some time for reflection. *If my husband, the Doc was more appreciative, I could deal with the busyness and even ignore the Hollywood drama. But his mental abuse is getting the best of me.*

A red-tailed hawk flew near Maddie, startling the baby. Maddie kept her eyes on the hawk as he perched high on a treetop. An odd sensation came over her, this time it was not fear. *Aunt Etana, is that you?* The hawk cawed loudly. Maddie looked up. *Really, it's you?* The bird swooshed down from the tree, flying in front of her and the baby, then landing on a rock opposite them. *What are you trying to tell me?*

The hawk just stared. Its beady eyes locked into Maddie's. *Okay, now you're scaring me. If you're Aunt Etana, then stop staring at me.*

The bird turned away. *You heard me!* Maddie thought. It dove off the rock and picked up a tiny mouse that was scrambling across the ground. The bird hovered in front of her with the mouse squirming and squealing. Maddie yelled at the hawk to let it go.

The next moment, the mouse dropped to the ground and scurried safely into the brush. The hawk flew to the rock again. For an hour, the three sat together. It was one of the most profound connections Maddie had ever experienced.

Finally the bird of prey flew away, leaving behind a red feather. Totally in the moment, Maddie had lost all track of time. *Oh my gosh, Howie will be expecting lunch, then it's back to my cage to run the office.*

She stuck the soft feather in her backpack, and hurried home with the baby.

Once Maddie got the baby settled, she re-heated a pot of vegetable soup, then shaved and layered mild cheddar cheese on rye bread for grilled cheese sandwiches. Moments later, Howie and Maddie sat at the kitchen table enjoying lunch. Between bites, she fed the baby. Throughout the meal, no words were spoken. She allowed the silence and didn't force a conversation, in part because she was still enthralled by the hawk experience. She refused to let Howie burst her bubble. After lunch she rocked the baby to sleep, then got through a busy afternoon with back-to-back patients.

Maddie was on the phone when she was rudely interrupted by Howie shuffling papers around on her desk. "Didn't you get these deposits into the bank yet?" As a patient walked in, he barked: "Do I have to do everything around here?"

Embarrassed, Maddie greeted the patient and continued with the phone call. When the call was finished, she casually excused herself and retired to the kitchen with the baby carrier. *I hate being in this mood*, she thought. *The man changes like the wind. I can't let him get the best of me.*

For the rest of the day, Maddie fought tears of frustration and confusion. But she held her ground of professionalism, greeting each patient with warmth and a smile. She and Howie didn't speak to each other about anything but business affairs.

That evening, once the two were in bed, she couldn't stand the friction any longer. She tried to break the tension. "Would you like to go to the Farmers Market tomorrow? It's supposed to be a beautiful day."

"Maybe, I'll let you know in the morning."

"Okay," she said lovingly.

Both lay in bed reading, but the staleness between them was almost visible. Then out of the blue, Howie mumbled, "I'm planning a trip to Japan."

"Japan! Why?" Maddie dropped her book onto her chest.

"The center where I trained at many years ago is suffering. They need me."

"What about your daughter? She needs you too."

"And she has me. I won't be away for long."

"Hmph."

"Mad, you're a strong woman. You'll be able to take care of our girl, won't you?"

"Sure. Sure I can, but I thought we were in this together."

"We are. But when we first met you knew that I traveled a lot." Howie laughed, "In fact, we met because I was traveling."

"I guess I didn't expect you to travel so soon after our baby was born."

"Really?"

"You're leaving us for work at a time when we should be a family."

"I think I'm doing pretty darn good with the family thing."

Maddie took a deep breath. "Yes, you are. I guess I would like it if you just stayed with us. I'm still getting used to everything here in California, and the people."

"Buck up! You're a independent woman, that's one of the reasons I fell in love with you."

Maddie had a mental list of things that yearned to roll off her tongue. But instead she swallowed her feelings and surrendered to his comment. She began reading again.

But Howie wasn't done, "Mad, I need to do this for me! I'm a healer and I teach people my technique. It's who I am," he said, now taking a calmer tone.

"That's not who you are, Howie… it's what you <u>do</u>," she said firmly.

"What, are you my shrink now?"

"No. I am your wife."

Howie looked at her blankly. She returned the look. Simultaneously they switched off their reading lamps and huffed onto their sides. Back to back, with blood boiling, they each eventually fell asleep.

The following morning, Howie told Maddie to clear his work schedule. She didn't ask why and just did what she was told. Mid-evening a towncar pulled up in front of the house. Maddie watched her husband walk out the front door with two suitcases in hand. She rushed to the window. He walked back into the house and put down the suitcases. Surprised, she smiled.

"I'll be back in two weeks. There's money in the bank," he said, giving her a peck on the cheek. He went out again. The front door closed behind him this time.

Maddie stood at the window watching the car pull away and thought about her experience with the Hawk, or *was it Aunt Etana?* She now understood what the bird was trying to tell her, that she was strong enough to handle even this.

MALIBU – PRESENT DAY

I WAS ASTONISHED by our conversation, and loving every deep, mindful minute.

"Are we really who we portray we are, or are we simply acting? Now that's an interesting question coming from an actress," Bea teased.

"Hey!" Lucinda protested, still shuffling through the cards.

"I'm just playing with you, girl. That's how the boys and I got along, we always had fun with each other—no hurt feelings." Bea took off her hat and fluffed her hair, then put her hat on again.

"It looks like we have two comedians in the group. You didn't offend me," Lucinda assured her.

I released the breath I was unintentionally holding, thinking, *these chicks are funny!*

Lucinda continued, "I believe in speaking your truth. It's the foundation of a strong friendship."

"Or the end of one," Maddie laughed heartily. She was obviously used to being the biggest fan of her own jokes which made us laugh even harder.

I love belly laughs, it's like doing a bunch of sit-ups without the funky face contorting or the pain. How wonderful it was to be in the company of three, expressive, confident, yet humble women. I was glad Thomas had arranged this.

"How you girls doing?" Thomas suddenly asked, surprising us.

"It's like we've known each other for years."

"Really? That's great. Do you need anything?"

"Aren't you the handsome gentleman!" Bea flirted. "No, but thank you. Is Andy behaving?"

"Oh yeah, he's a good boy," Andy said, running up behind Bea and hugging her.

"Hush now, you snuck up on me!"

"Am I missing anything juicy?" he asked, rubbing his hands together.

"With four women talking, it's all juicy," Lucinda responded.

"What's juicy? You talkin'about me? What am I missing?" Ricky blurted, as he walked up to us, swaggering his big-bad self.

"Easy, cowboy," she warned.

"Cowboy! Nice, cowboy!" Howie teased, shoving Ricky aside.

"What's so funny over here anyway?" Ricky asked.

"Just girl stuff," Lucinda replied. "Nothing you'd be interested in."

"Actually, guys do like the gossipy stuff too," Bea said, looking at Andy. "Don't they?"

Andy threw up his hands. "What! Not me! She means the guys she works with, right?"

"If you say so, darlin'."

"So, do you girls need any food or drinks?" Thomas asked again.

"No, thank you," Maddie said. "Howie, you okay? Do you want a sandwich?"

"No. I'm super Mad, having a blast. How 'bout you?"

"I'm having lots of fun, these girls are funny."

We all shrugged and insisted, "She's the funny one!"

"Well, alrighty then, carry on." Thomas bent down and kissed me. "Come on, guys, I think they want to be left alone."

The three men followed his cue and kissed their woman. As they walked away, they were whispering and laughing as if some type of plan had worked. I squinted my eyes in concentration or was I only seeing what I wanted to believe?

BEA'S PAST

BEA CONTINUED WITH HER BUSINESS in the ladies room and shook off the haunting train sensation. Over the intercom, she heard the DJ announce the band was back onstage. *I love this song!* She zipped up the fly on her jeans, quickly washed her hands and scooted out the door singing along with the band.

With confidence she forced her way through the hand-clapping, foot-stomping crowd to get a closer look. The lead guitarist leaned into his riff with passion, swallowing his notes as he strummed his instrument. *That man plays his guitar like he's fondling a woman. How sensual!* But as captivated as she was with the guitar player, it was the lead singer who was raising Bea's temperature. She watched him as he bent down to sing to a group of man hungry women who were also feeling what she was. When he stood up, Bea finally had a bird's-eye view. The singer was tall and thin, but through his tight clothes she could tell his arms and legs were well-defined with strong muscles. *Sublime*, she silently sighed, *truly sublime.*

The singer turned towards her. Their eyes met. She stood on her tip-toes and smiled. He smiled back and winked. Blushing, she two finger waved. She was awestruck at his looks, talent, and presence.

Bea reached into her designer purse and pulled out a compact mirror, checking her lipstick. As she went to shut it, she noticed something sticking out of the inside compartment. *What's this?* With wide eyes, she peered closely and read: "The 440 Train—*First-class seating to the next chapter of your life.*"

How the heck did this ticket get in here? Bea looked at the singer, then back at the ticket. *All aboard, now that's one caboose who's not sporting a suit and tie.* She gazed at his honey-colored long hair, blazing blue eyes, and cute rock-n-roll wiggle. *But hold on just one minute, last night and again tonight I heard a train, and now I find a train ticket in my purse. I'm looking at this fine man and starting to think there's some kind of external influence making all this happen, or it could be the slow gin fizz? Regardless, I'm pretty sure my prayers have been heard and, Lord, I'm grateful you're fulfilling my shopping list!*

Bea tuned back into the music. The lead singer's voice was as good as anyone she had ever heard on the radio. His musical abilities stretched to the stars. Andy, like so many other musicians, was seeking his big break to stardom. For the rest of the set, Bea continued to make eye contact with Andy. She teased him by moving around the club, watching him hunt her down wherever she moved. When he spotted her, he smiled and dipped his microphone stand or gyrated provocatively, letting her know his performance tonight was for her.

After the final set of the evening, Andy approached Bea. "Hi. Can you hang around a few minutes? I'd like to talk with you!"

She calmly held in her excitement. "Ah, sure," she replied.

Up-close, his eyes were light blue, like crystals. His hair was slightly wet from stage sweat. As soon as Andy stepped away, several women swarmed him with compliments and questions. Bea wondered if he was too good to be true or if he was really who she felt he was. Minutes later, the DJ flashed on the lights signaling the bar was closing. Couples who had been making out gathered themselves and lazily shuffled to the door.

"Goodnight, Bea," Billie shouted walking towards the exit with his male friend.

She smiled and cheerfully waved. Slowly but surely, the bouncers herded almost everyone out of the club except for a few groupies who were trying to get backstage to meet the musicians. Bea stood near the entrance watching the roadies clear the stage.

"Did you like the tunes?" Andy asked, surprising her from behind.

She flinched. "Oph! You startled me."

"Sorry."

"That's okay. Did I like the tunes? Yes indeed. You know, I've never heard of you or your band until tonight."

"That's because I just moved here from Boston."

"Oh, that would explain it."

"Actually, we're not a band. I'm a soloist and they're studio musicians I hired so I can get my name out in the club scene while I work on my original songs."

"How exciting, but why did you chose New Jersey?"

"I used to come here during the summer and work with my Uncle Barney at the shore."

"Hmm."

"I helped run his burger stand, Hayberrie's Hamburgers, on the boardwalk at Seahike Park."

"Oh my gosh! I loved their cheeseburgers. It's a small world, huh?" Bea didn't let him answer. "Does your Uncle still own the stand?"

"No. He sold it and retired to Florida."

"Good for him. Life has some amazing twists and turns, doesn't it?"

"Yes, it sure does."

"But wait, how did working at your uncle's burger stand make you decide to come here to do music?"

"On my time off, I used to hang out on the beach with other musicians. I still keep in touch with two of the cats."

"That's great."

"Yeah, their names are Thomas and Ricky. But they decided to go to Hollywood to become stuntmen."

"Stuntmen! How exciting," Bea said wide-eyed.

"I'm planning to visit them soon. I even considered going there to do my music, but I chose Jersey for now."

"California, hmm, that would be fun."

"Yes it would. Anyway, the hum is that Jersey is one of the best places to land a record deal if you have good original songs."

"Wouldn't surprise me, look what happened to Bruce Springsteen in Asbury Park."

A man approached Andy and handed him an envelope. "Great night, man. You wanna work more, call me tomorrow after two o'clock."

"Thanks, I will." Andy grinned.

"Good deal," Bea said.

"Yup, I feel I'm where I'm supposed to be and timing is everything."

"I like your philosophy," she said, smiling. "How long are you here for?"

"For as long as it takes to make an album." He paused and looked directly into her eyes.

She was taken back. His self-assurance and gentle presence was invigorating. "Are you for real?" she wondered.

"Yes, I'm real."

"Are you married?"

"No."

"Have a fiancé?"

"No."

"Girlfriend?"

"Not yet."

"Boyfriend?"

"Boyfriend!"

"Sorry, it's just, well never mind."

"You're a babe," he said, kissing her on the forehead. "Would you like to have a really late dinner?"

"How late, all night long and breakfast too?" she replied.

"I know this sounds typical, but I assure you I'm not usually this up-front other than on stage."

Bea paused for effect as he waited with bated breath for her response.

Finally, "Yes indeed."

"Right on! I'd take you back to my place, but it's just an efficiency apartment and I have music stuff all around."

"Oh," Bea said, slightly disappointed. She wondered if he'd now suggest the cheesy motel next door.

"So let's go to the diner up the street," he suggested.

She relaxed. "I have a better idea. Why don't we go back to my place? I'll cook up a frozen pizza and open a few cold beers."

"Cute, frozen pizza and cold beer. Sounds great."

"Uh, by the way," Bea lowered her head shyly, "you look a lot younger up-close."

Andy laughed and brushed his long bangs off his forehead.

"Um. I hate to ask this," Bea continued, "but how old are you?"

"Does it matter?"

"Um, slightly, just please tell me you're over twenty-one."

"You're funny," he smiled.

"That seems to be the consensus tonight."

"Yes, I'm way over twenty-one, but thanks for the compliment."

"You're welcome, and thank goodness."

"Wait a second!" Andy blurted. "How old are you, pretty woman?"

"Why, Andy, don't you know it's impolite to ask a lady's age?"

He smiled wide, causing the skin to crease by his eyes and lips, revealing he wasn't as young as Miss Bea thought.

"Wait! Oh my gosh, I just realized I never asked your name." He blushed.

"Heavens to Betsy. And I didn't realize you didn't. My name is Beatrice but everyone calls me Bea."

"Pleasure to meet you, <u>Miss</u> Bea." She blushed slightly at the endearment.

"Likewise. Now let's go get that pizza in the oven." She took a step towards the door as Andy walked next to her with his hand on the center of her back.

"Howdya sleep," Bea asked the next morning, placing a tray of food over Andy's long legs.

He inched up to a sitting position in bed. "Great, I slept like a baby. Your bed is so comfortable."

"Thank you. It's five-star hotel quality."

"You're five stars too."

"Why, Andy, you're making me blush again."

"I hope I did more then make you blush last night?"

"Excuse me, but haven't you noticed a glow around me this morning?"

He smiled and pulled the tray closer to his body.

"Hope you like all the fixings," Bea boasted.

"Gee, fresh strawberries, eggs, homemade biscuits, and coffee. What's not to like?"

Bea fluttered her eyelashes like a lovesick puppy as Andy dipped a piece of biscuit into the sunny side-up eggs.

"I love the fixings, but I especially liked what I had for dessert." His tongue swiped along his lips.

"But we didn't have dessert!" she pouted.

He closed his eyes and slowly licked the butter off the biscuit.

"Oh, you mean that kind of dessert," she realized.

"Yes ma'am. And wow, are you a seductress! I never imagined one could do the things you did with high heels on."

"Thank you. Flattery will get you everything, sir." Bea slid onto the bed and cuddled up next to him. "You're quite the lover too, music man."

"Um, thanks, but I just took your lead. I'm not usually so, so."

"So permissive?"

"Uh-huh."

"Me either." She grinned and reached her hand between his legs. Aroused, he set the tray of food to the side and kissed her, pulling her on top of him. "You're utterly ferocious!" she moaned.

Their lovemaking lasted quite some time before Miss Alabama finally let out a howl that set off the dogs in the neighborhood. Moments later, a cell phone rang.

"Oh, that's mine," Andy said. "I should get it. It might be one of the musicians."

"You stay here." She shimmied off the bed. Her inner thighs were tight. Awkwardly, she bent down and lifted his pants off the floor.

The phone stopped ringing. She dug into a pocket and pulled it out. "Oops, it went to voicemail."

He waited a minute, then retrieved the message. His facial expression went from happy to troubled. Bea couldn't hear the conversation but she could tell the voice was a woman's.

"Is everything okay?" she wanted to know.

"Um, not really. I must apologize, but I have to get going. I have something to take care of."

"Drats. I was hoping we could go for a drive in the mountains. It's such a beautiful day."

"So sorry, babe." He got out of bed and kissed her softly on the lips. "This is really important."

"Okay," she twanged with an un-genuine smile.

"May I hop in the shower before I head out?"

"Of course. My casa your casa," she said with a lame Southern-Spanish accent.

Bea was overacting to cover up the fact that she was troubled by the call and his need to leave so quickly. Moments later, she heard the shower running and Andy started singing. A disturbing chill came over her. She felt as if she had just made another big mistake. Unable to move, she stood staring at his cell phone, debating what to do.

"What the hay." She grabbed the phone and hit the recent message button.

"Andy, it's me. We need to talk. I'm guessing you're still sleeping off a long night of music and women. I miss you so much. I can't seem to move ahead with my life. Can you meet me at the Twilight Diner at three?"

Bea put the phone back where she found it and ran downstairs to another bathroom. She hopped into the shower and quickly gussied up. In less than fifteen minutes, she emerged in a pink sundress.

"Wow! You look beautiful," Andy said, coming down the stairs.

"Why thank you, sir."

"Are you going out?"

"Yes. I'm going antique shopping."

"Sounds like fun. I would love to go with you one day."

"Really? It wouldn't conflict with anyone?"

"Anyone?"

"I mean anything."

"No," he said, oblivious to her insinuation.

"Okay then." She softened her tone, not wanting to sound like a jealous lover already.

"Thank you for the late dinner and the wonderful breakfast," Andy said.

"You're very welcome."

"Bea," Andy continued, standing in front of her, gazing straight into her eyes.

"Yes," she answered in a hypnotic voice.

"May I call you tomorrow?"

"Yyes, you can call me tomorrow," she said, snapping out of her lover's trance.

Together they walked out the door and got into their own cars. As Andy drove off in one direction, Bea smiled and waved excitedly. Once he was clear out of sight she turned off her car, went back into the house, picked up one of her self-help books and began reading.

"Miss You"

I am like a rose,
intertwined
amongst the ivy
Basking in the
sun-rays of
God's hands...
Waiting.

MALIBU – PRESENT DAY

AS THE MEN WALKED down the beach, laughing and grinning as if they'd just scored a touchdown, waves of memories washed over us women. We were each taken back to other places and times, seemingly swept up in a collective trance.

Lucinda was the first to break the spell, "Girls, snap out of it!"

"What the heck just happened?" Maddie asked, looking at Bea.

"I was thinking about when I first met Andy."

"And I was thinking about when I first met Howie."

"I was thinking about when I first met Thomas."

"And I was thinking about when I first met Ricky."

I had my confirmation. The men in our lives <u>were</u> the links that brought us women together. I thought about the new novel I was reading. It felt like the book was relevant to the four of us. It was all strategically connected.

I was excited, what I was thinking now was a stretch, yet my gut told me I was on to something. All I had to do was put the pieces together. I was about to ask my new friends a vital question to prove my theory when Maddie jumped ahead of me.

"Are you ever going to pick a card? Or are you just going to shuffle them?"

"Oh, yeah, of course." Lucinda took a deep breath and slid a card out from the pile.

MADDIE'S PAST

THE AIRPORT WAS LOUD. Thousands of people scurried about like busy little squirrels scampering for nuts. Keeping the pace with the fastest of the walkers, Maddie said a prayer: *Saint Christopher, thank you for keeping our family safe and healthy on our travels.* She ended her gratitude and shifted into what was before her.

"Excuse me, excuse me," she said, weaving the stroller in and out as best she could between all the quick-moving bodies.

Her daughter laughed and slapped her hands down on the stroller, enjoying the active ride. "Hold on, lovely one," Maddie warned as she quickened her stride even more. After a few more twists and turns down the corridor, she spotted a familiar face through the thick crowd. She raised an arm and waved.

"Mom! Mom!" she cheered. "It's so good to see you! It's really so good to see you."

The women united with a hug. "It's wonderful to see you too, daughter. Bless you. Oh my Lord, look at this angel," Grandma said, bending down to touch her grandchild.

"We've missed you, Madaline. You look well. Is everything fine?" her father wanted to know.

"All is great, Father. Howie sends his love and regrets that he can't be here, but he had to travel to Japan for work."

"Ah-ha," he replied looking her straight in the eye.

She kept a straight face and didn't let on that she was upset with her American husband.

"Well if you say so, but I can't help wondering...if."

Her mother chimed in. "We are grateful to have you and the baby with us," she said, breaking the inquisition.

The four stayed in Manila for the evening. In the morning they traveled to the village. Maddie's sisters and brothers had planned a fiesta with many friends gathered for the happy reunion. She was home, feeling safe and being the center of attention, just like the old days.

"Tell me about your life in the United States," a woman said softly.

Maddie turned around. "Sonya! Hi. M-my life is great. How are you, and how's the massage business?"

"I'm good, business is good. But I've missed you."

"I've missed you too."

"I thought you would have at least written. You promised you would."

"I've been busy. But I have thought of you, and I promise to keep more in touch."

"Please don't make promises you can't keep. So where is he?"

"Who?" Maddie asked, over-dramatizing the question.

"Who do you think? Your husband!"

"He's in Japan teaching."

"So tell me, does he please you in all the ways that... I." Sonya put a hand on her friend's shoulder. Her gentle touch sent a chill up Maddie's spine.

"Whoa! Sonya, I'm married now and have a daughter. Let's just be friends and leave the past to the past."

They looked into each other's eyes as Sonya moved in closer to Maddie who was frozen.

Suddenly, Maddie's sister appeared and yanked her away. "Sister, come quickly, we have the karaoke machine going and we need you to be the other half of Sonny and Cher." Maddie was grateful to have an excuse to leave.

The black-haired beauty sniveled, "I'm around if you need me!" She twirled a strand of long hair around a finger.

The fiesta lasted two nights and three days. On the fourth day, Maddie lazily strolled to the backyard of her village house. She was puffy-eyed, a few pounds heavier and quite a bit happier. She found her mother trimming a bougainvillea bush.

"Good morning, Mom."

"Good morning, lovely one."

"Your garden looks beautiful as usual."

"Thank you." She looked at her daughter while continuing to trim the flowers. "Did you finally get some rest?"

"Yes, I did. And it feels great to be home."

"It's wonderful to have you here." A long pause occurred before she spoke again. "Life is good for you, daughter?"

"Yes, Mom. Howie is a hard worker and he really loves our daughter."

"That is wonderful," she looked away and clipped some branches. "I sense something different about you."

"I'm a mother, and I live in America. Things have changed, but I am the same."

Maddie's mother studied her daughter's eyes. "Don't let anyone get into you, Madaline."

"You mean 'get to you'."

"No, I mean get in-to you."

Maddie's mind was beginning to awaken at the heartfelt questions and slow phrasing of her mother's wisdom.

"And does he take good care of you too?"

"Look at me. Do I look like I'm taken care of?"

"You always run in circles with questions you do not want to answer, Madaline."

Maddie laughed. Her mother didn't.

"Yes, you look like you're taken care of, but looks can be deceiving." The wise woman allowed another moment of silence and continued gardening.

"My life is different than when I was here," Maddie said softly, "but I am adjusting to the changes. Overall, I am happy."

There was another pause, then Maddie's mother turned around, facing her.

"I trust that you know what's best for you," she said as she cut a flower and placed it into a ceramic vase.

"I do." Maddie hugged her mother. "I have put away some money. Use this for what you and Daddy need or for the family." She handed her mother an envelope stuffed with cash.

"My goodness, daughter. This is a lot of money. You must be working hard." She slipped the envelope into her dress pocket.

"I still want to help my family, even if I'm living far away."

"You have always taken care of us. Now is the time for you to take care of yourself and your daughter."

"Yes, Mom. I am. It's funny, but those are the same words my father-in-law told me."

"He must be a smart man," her mother teased.

"Yes, I believe he is."

"Bless you, Saint Madaline, for the money, but mostly for coming home to us. It hasn't been the same around here since you left."

"Aw, you're welcome, Mom. And I'm not a saint."

"Close, very close. Let's pray together."

They sat under a tree that provided shade from the hot sun. Maddie quieted her thoughts and listened to the prayer. The noise throughout the village subsided, leaving only the beautiful voice of her loving mother. It was a moment of pure bliss and deep peace.

MALIBU – PRESENT DAY

THE THREE OF US WAITED ANXIOUSLY to see the card Lucinda picked. Slowly she turned it over: <u>The Butterfly.</u>

I decided to put my line of questioning on hold regarding the connection between us four and the new book I was reading. There was time to explore that later.

"How beautiful. I'm especially fond of butterflies. Read it out loud, would ya?" Bea requested.

"Out loud, really?" Lucinda gazed at the card.

"Great idea. It would be nice to hear the message from the winged one. I'm sure each of us will relate to it on some level," I said.

Lucinda read the message. When she was done, we smiled and made small movements with our bodies. I'm pretty sure we were each determining what stage of the butterfly's transformation we were at.

"Do you have anything to add, Marlo?" Lucinda asked, dangling a 'carrot' in front of me.

"Ah, sure, to reiterate, Butterfly has to do with change. First by retreating, taking the time to look within, enjoying some rest and silence, so you can connect with God and Nature. Then typically, an uncomfortable and eye-opening re-birth occurs, revealing changes that need to be made. Butterfly beckons a time to do something you enjoy doing. By getting in touch with your creativity, your fiery passion, a comforting and invigorating rhythm heightens, igniting a new awareness of your talents and self-love. Joy will naturally emanate from you, which will inspire others to re-birth as well. You will feel freedom in your soul and spirit. And from that place, balance will occur from the inside out, enriching your human experience with grace."

Lucinda closed the book and sighed heavily. "That was some reiteration. Heck, we should be reading your book."

"My book! You busting my chops?"

"No, I just have a feeling you have a book inside you aching to be published." Her face glowed with satisfaction.

She was gutsy. I admired her confidence. I grinned. "A feeling, aye?"

"Kind of like your feeling about me having a child soon."

"Ohhhh!"

"You're having a baby?" Bea asked, surprised.

"No-no-no."

Maddie filled Bea in on what we were referring to earlier while Lucinda and I taunted each other about *gut feelings*.

BEA'S PAST

IT WAS BEA'S FIRST DAY BACK TO WORK. She didn't get much accomplished all day as Andy lingered on her mind. She prayed he would call with an explanation for his quick and mysterious exit yesterday. The boys at the office could tell she had met a man during her sabbatical. And when she turned down their offer to go out for drinks after work, it confirmed their suspicions.

Hours later back at home, while she was preparing a meal, the phone rang. Her heart raced with anticipation.

"Good evening Bea, it's Andy. How are you?"

"I'm great, Andy, how are you?" She smiled wide and put dinner on hold.

"I'm well. Listen, I'd like to explain why I had to rush out yesterday."

She waved her hand in the air. "There's no need to explain. We just met and have no obligations to one another." She raised her eyes while nervously walking from room to room.

"No, I do owe you an explanation."

"Really? Well, if you must. I'm all ears." She sat on the couch.

"The telephone call I got was from someone I'm very close with."

"*Ah-ha,*" she thought, clenching her jaw, waiting for the big "I'm married" spiel.

He continued. "We've been through a lot together and we made a pact to always be there for each other."

Oh my Lord, she thought, nibbling on her long polished nails.

"Bea, it was my sister who called."

"Y-your sister?"

"Yeah, my older sister has had a very troubled marriage. She recently divorced and is having a difficult time without her husband. I've been helping her get through it."

"How kind of you to be there." Bea lip-synched "*it's his sister, it's his sister*" while swaying her bootie back and forth.

"It's another reason why I moved here, to be closer to her."

"Family is important," Bea said, with a fresh outlook on the situation.

"Yes, they are. I'm confident she'll be fine, but for now she needs some extra love and support around her."

"If there's anything I can do to help just let me know."

"That's very sweet of you. Thanks. I will."

They talked for hours, getting to know each other much better before finally saying goodnight. And later in bed while saying her prayers, Bea sent an extra thanks to the Angels for bringing Andy into her life.

The 440 Train Bea had boarded was no slow-moving choo-choo. It was a fast locomotive. In two shakes of a lamb's tail, Andy, his ten-year old parrot Jupiter and a truckload of music equipment moved into her townhouse.

Her new sweetheart's enthusiasm, rock'n'roll looks, creative energies, well-mannered personality, infectious love-making and genuine kindness was all she had hoped for. So how could she refuse or resist taking their romance to the next level?

Being a nurturer, Bea not only reached out her hand and her heart, she also became his talent agent and financial manager. Miss Alabama worked her gift of gab and landed her 'Bo' in some of the hottest night clubs on the East Coast.

Yet as busy as she was with helping Andy and his music career, she utilized the knowledge from all the self-help books she read and acted on the changes she needed to make. This time around she made time to have drinks with the boys and didn't cut herself off from her friends. She also occasionally met with Billie and his flamboyant partner for drinks. Andy didn't mind their separate friendships because he too kept his promise and spent a lot of time with his sister.

Life was sweet and Bea was determined not to let anyone or anything complicate her blossoming relationship with her rocker stud, her self included.

MALIBU – PRESENT DAY

WHILE THE MEN CONTINUED with their male bonding, the bond between us four women blossomed like a flower to the rays of the sunlight. The feeling of comfort and compatibility was almost abnormal. The more we talked, the more it felt as if a vortex had opened, quickening our connection.

I stayed grounded while it was happening, wondering if I was the only one sensing this streamlined energy. But then I remembered the weird silence we fell into a few minutes ago, each recalling how we had met the men in our lives. I was just about to ask the girls that important question when Thomas and the other men ran up, daring us to go boogie boarding. Fun was just what I needed to sidetrack me from all the feelings I was having.

"Let's do it!" Lucinda said standing.

"I'm game."

"Me too," Bea giggled.

"Really?" Lucinda contorted her face.

"Yeah, me too. And what about that surprises you?"

"I can see your point," Maddie laughed.

"What! Just because I'm a lady doesn't mean I can't keep up with the boys."

I smiled. Bea was a unique woman.

"It's always the quiet ones," Lucinda said laughing.

"Hush! I'm anything but quiet."

"You're right, modest would be the better word."

"I'm not that either." Bea took off her dress, revealing a sexy two-piece and a tattoo of a monarch butterfly that encompassed her lower back.

"Oh my gosh! Outstanding."

"Let me see," Lucinda ran her finger along the wings, tickling Bea.

"That's freaky." Maddie said. "A butterfly."

"Oh yeah!" we exclaimed. *Just another sign,* I thought proudly.

"Now which one of you gals is not hitting the waves?" Bea looked at Maddie.

"Uh, I'm coming too."

We bravely ran into the chilly ocean, latching onto our men and their boards, *boogie boards, that is,* and rode the waves with as much vigor and enjoyment as when we were teens.

MADDIE'S PAST

MADDIE AND THE BABY arrived home a day before Howie was expected to return. She laid her weary daughter in the crib for a nap and walked around the canyon house waiting to experience a feeling, either of being home or being out of place. The chirping of birds from the backyard brought a smile to her face. *This is my American home. I am home.*

She walked out to the backyard and picked a few lemons from the tree, then made herself a glass of lemonade. Since she wasn't breastfeeding any longer, Maddie splashed in a dollop of tequila. Then she ripped open a bag of tortilla chips and a container of sour cream and began nibbling. She didn't hear the front door open.

"Looks like I'm just in time for happy hour," Howie said, approaching her.

"Hi! You're home early."

"Yeah, I caught an earlier flight."

"How was your trip?"

"Long, but good. I never imaged it would turn into six weeks."

She poured him a glass of spiked lemonade and handed it over. He bent down and kissed her on the lips, grabbing the glass at the same time.

"You look beautiful. You're glowing." He smiled as if seeing her for the first time.

His stare ran goose bumps up and down her body. "Thank you. And you look handsome too. You cut your hair short again. I like it."

The time away prompted a strong sexual attraction between them. The tension they'd felt prior to their travels melted like ice on a hot summer's day. They quickly downed their drinks and headed to the bedroom where they made love for hours then fell asleep in each other's arms.

Jet-lagged and fatigued from their long journeys, the three slept in until late morning. Hours later, Mommy and baby played with some new toys Daddy had brought from Japan while he unpacked his suitcase. "So how was your trip with the family, Mad?"

"Great. Everyone asked about you."

"Whadya tell them?"

"I told them the truth, you went to Japan to teach."

"Good, that's good."

She smiled as she tickled the baby. Howie watched with admiration.

The house was as homey as a home could be. With the windows slightly cracked, a fragrant scent of flowers blew in and swooped around. Meanwhile the aroma of toasted bread and coffee highlighted the happy-family scene.

Then the telephone rang, interrupting the Norman Rockwell painting come to life. "Hello, brother," Howie replied into the receiver, then listened for several seconds. His silence and body language alerted Maddie. Something was wrong. "I'll be there as quickly as I can."

"What's happening?" she wanted to know.

"It's my father." Howie began re-packing his suitcase.

Maddie got on the phone and rescheduled his upcoming appointments. The memories of her one-time visit with her father-in-law would have to last a lifetime.

When Howie returned home his demeanor had altered drastically. The air around him was swarming with personal regrets. Maddie stayed clear of him as much as possible, giving him the needed space to process the passing of his father. It was a time of transition and transformation.

For Maddie, the months that followed passed quickly, the years even quicker. Not much changed other than chronological time. Her daughter turned seven and her relationship with Howie remained a rollercoaster. It was slow going up, fast coming down, whiplash on the turns and bumpy overall.

A second child, another beautiful baby girl, came along so Maddie had to step up her pace to juggle a few more hands, feet and clients. Multitasking had once been one of her strong points. *Was it still?*

The canyon house became too small for the foursome, so they packed their goods, moving out of the woods and into the suburbs known as The Valley. Taking care of her family was Maddie's new marathon. Although the train whistle continued to blow, signaling changes, she had learned to tune it out by putting everyone else first and being content with the scraps. *Or was she?*

Her new house, a recently built two-story home was ideal. It had a five hundred square foot office on the first floor with a large bathroom and a private entrance. In a matter of days she had Howie's business up and running. Her sense of humor and warm smile continued to set the stage, making his patients feel at ease with the new environment. And by now her dedication and hard work was as critical to the family practice as Howie's healing skills.

On a personal level, the winds shifted tremendously. Howie decided to see a doctor for his "misplaced energy", and he seemed happier and more considerate.

As promised, Maddie and the girls flew to the Philippines once a year while Howie traveled to various countries inspiring novice healers. On the most recent trip to her homeland, she attended Sonya's wedding. While the guests were busy dancing and drinking, the two women snuck off to a secluded spot and had the long-anticipated conversation. While saying good-bye to a story in their lives that no longer existed, they embraced in a hug.

"Gee, Sonya, your boobs sure got bigger."

"No silly, it's my new water bra."

"A water bra, what is that?"

"Here, feel." Sonya pulled down the neckline on her wedding gown. "It's really neat, they feel like the real thing."

Maddie backed up. "No thanks. I believe you. It's just that, well, who the heck would wear that thing, I mean other than you on your wedding day?"

"You should get back to your new husband." Maddie started to walk away.

Sonya grabbed her hand, "Wait, one more thing, we should have a proper good-bye."

They kissed each other on the cheek. And then the lips. And then they looked at each other with surprise, and kissed again with a burst of passion only true lovers know.

MALIBU – PRESENT DAY

AN HOUR OF BOOGIE BOARDING was quite enough for us women. Wearily and happily, we came out of the ocean, adjusting our water-saturated, sand-filled swimsuits. Our lips were purple, our skin rippled with goose bumps, and our bodies were renewed by the tight feel of salt.

"I haven't had that much fun in years," Bea said as she applied a fresh coat of sunscreen to her face and body.

"Me neither." Lucinda tilted her head to one side, shaking the water from her ear, then switched to the other side.

"I felt like a kid. It's so exciting to ride the waves."

"It was scary!' Maddie admitted. "That was my first time boogie boarding," she added with wide blood-shot eyes.

"What!" The three of us stopped what we were doing.

"Yeah, that was my very first time."

"You were great," I insisted.

"Is this one of your jokes?" Bea wanted to know.

"No. Really. I've seen people do it, but I never did it until today."

"You looked like a pro," Lucinda said, plopping down onto the sand.

Maddie shrugged. "I used to be a pretty good athlete, so I guess it helped."

"I'll say so," Bea agreed. "You're a born athlete, but me, I definitely need to join a gym, I feel worn out."

"You did great. We all did great. It's not like we do this every day, or every month, or even every year. We're fabulous!" Lucinda cheered.

"Yeah!" Maddie raised her clenched hand in the air.

"You bet! We all did great, and we swam in the same water where the dolphins swim. What more could we ask for?"

We laughed at each other and drank lots of water, munched on some snacks, and rested in the calm that comes after a workout.

BEA'S PAST

SOME TIME LATER, BEA'S TRAIN ride switched tracks. The shadow side of fast and ferocious was dark stagnation. Putting it bluntly, she was getting slam-dunked with a lot of lessons.

The fun nightlife she had been digging so much suddenly got old. She learned that burning the candle at both ends isn't as easy when you're in your early forties, as it is in your twenties. By the time she got home from work, she was too tired to re-vamp and go watch Andy perform till two in the morning, then re-vamp again by six a.m. for her day job.

Already she was bored with being the happy-go-lucky music manager. As icing on the cake, she was fed-up with the groupies who were notorious for offering her boyfriend sexual pleasures in the backseat of their cars.

The mood around Bea's sugarplum house wasn't sweet and edible any longer. One evening it all came to a face-off. Andy was at the kitchen table strumming his guitar, working on some lyrics. Bea walked in, poured a glass of wine, fed Jupiter a handful of sunflower seeds in his cage and sighed dramatically.

"Dahlin'…I don't understand why you don't work more on your original music than on the cover tunes," she said loud enough to mess up Andy's concentration.

He stopped strumming. "I work on my songs in the day when you're at work, but I gotta keep doing this until I make some decent money."

"Wasn't your intention in coming to New Jersey to get your original songs heard and produced?"

"It was. I mean it is."

"But don't you see, what you're doing is taking away from your true passion."

"Ouch. That hurts." He strummed a sad chord on his guitar.

"It hurts, darlin', because it's true."

"Ouch, ouch, ouch," Jupiter screeched. They couldn't help but laugh.

"Hush, Jupiter, and eat your seeds." Bea quickly moved on to her point. "If your dream is to create music, then you must concentrate one hundred percent on that goal."

"Man, those books you've been reading have sure come in handy." He strummed a triumphant lick.

Bea crinkled her nose. "Funny, smarty pants."

Andy reached for a beer from the refrigerator.

"So, about you playing the club scene..." she continued.

"Club scene, raaaaaaah," Jupiter screeched.

Andy laughed. Bea did not. He put down his beer, reached for her and gently patted her bottom. "Babe, let's forget all this nonsense and go spend a night at the shore. It'll be quiet and relaxing."

"As good as that sounds," she looked towards the window, "one of us has to bring in the money to pay the bills."

"Ouch." He frowned, releasing his hold on her.

"Ouch, ouch, ouch." Jupiter squawked again.

This time no one laughed. Andy tried to lighten the mood.

"Come on, babe, we can bring that box of 'toys' you hide in the closet and get wild in the hotel."

"Tempting, but no!" She stepped away from him.

"Why are you all businesslike tonight?"

"Businesslike! Ouch at you!" she mocked. "I need some air." She stormed out the door.

Bea sat on the bench in the garden that her bedroom overlooked. The sun was just setting. It was peaceful. *Angels, I thought this one would be different. Am I heading in the right direction? I love Andy, he is what I prayed for. Maybe I'm just not used to the musician's lifestyle.*

She sat in silence for quite a while, reflecting on some of the books she had read. This helped change her perspective on the situation and see that she was not allowing Andy to be the person she fell in love with. She was also not giving herself a fair chance in a relationship that was different from the ones she'd had before.

When she finally headed back into the house, Andy was sitting on the couch with the lights turned low. "Are you okay?" he wondered sincerely.

"I'm good. Are you?"

"Yes, I'm good."

"I guess that was our first tiff," she said, sitting next to him.

"Ah, that's nothing." He hugged her.

"You're a star, Andy. A bright, loving star." She lay across his body and looked up at him. "I love you, and your hair looks so good, I just want to get lost in all of you."

"Thanks," he said, stroking her lips. "I love you. Let's go upstairs, pretty lady."

She nipped at his finger. "Tame your microphone for a minute, big boy."

"My microphone!" He blushed.

"Yes sir, your long, hard..."

"You're wild!" He started to unbutton her pink cotton blouse.

She let him get to the bottom button, then sat up. "Wait a second! While I was outside, I came up with a great idea, tell me what you think."

"I'm hard, can hardly wait to hear your idea!" He wiggled a bit, repositioning.

She smiled. "I want to financially support you while you pursue your original music career."

"Whoa. Where'd that come from?" His voice was firm but everything else softened.

"My mind, silly!"

"Are you sure it's not coming from your heart?"

"Of course, my heart too."

"Thank you so much, but I can't accept, babe."

"Why not!" She stomped her foot.

"It's too much pressure on you."

"But I want to do it so you can focus on your music. You have a true gift that needs to be heard by others. I can help you get there."

"Can I think about it?"

"Sure, think all you want, but it's a great opportunity for both of us."

"How so for you, Bea?"

"I'll be your silent partner, so when you make it big you can pay me back. It'll be a great story to tell."

"Are you sure, because a few minutes ago you were upset about money and things."

"I told you, I thought about this and I'm sure."

"It's just that you made a complete one-eighty and that concerns me."

"What are you saying? I'm coco-loco?" She rolled her eyes around.

"No, no, but I'm not sure you really had enough time to think this through."

"How much time do I need then?" She looked concerned.

"Hmmm… I'm not doubting your good intentions, but I never want you to regret this or have it come between us."

"It will only come between us if we let it. I won't. I want to do this for you, and for me."

He paused. "I'm going to pay you back."

"Of course you will," she said, glowing with satisfaction.

"Then how could I refuse, so, I graciously accept."

The lovebirds danced up the stairs and wrestled passionately until Bea shorted out Andy's microphone. After the interlude, they snacked on cheese, crackers and wine, and made a life-changing decision, it was time for an addition to their family.

MADDIE'S PAST

THE KIDS WERE GROWING FASTER than the palm trees in the front yard and the full-time mom-sexretary was in full stride with all the action. One day while sitting at her desk going over the appointment book, Maddie asked Howie, "Why is this date marked off as Malibu Beach Party?"

"Because we're going to meet a few friends for lunch."

"What friends?" she asked.

"Thomas and Ricky, a few of the guys I used to work out with years ago at the gym. They're stuntmen. And Andy the musician, he's my client."

"Oh."

"I ran into Ricky on the movie set last week. He mentioned a few of the guys and their girls were getting together. So, I thought it'd be fun for us since our girls are going to sleepovers this weekend."

"Oh, yes, that's right."

"I thought we could have a date."

"A date?" she asked, truly surprised.

"Yes, a date. Wouldn't it be fun to have some adult time together?"

"I guess. But I love and cherish our family time."

"Of course, it's great, Mad, but don't you ever miss socializing with other women?"

"Well, sometimes I do think about having a girlfriend or two. Then I get busy with life and I forget."

"This will be fun. We can play Frisbee, swim, eat on the beach or just hang out and relax."

"Okay, it sounds like fun."

As the day progressed, Maddie thought about the beach party and meeting other women. She hadn't realized how much she missed interacting with a girlfriend. Strangely enough, a faint whistle sounded in the distance. *That's a train! Wow, I haven't heard that sound in such a long time.*

She greeted the next patient with a smile and showed him to the healing room. When she returned to her desk, she drifted again: *Why haven't I heard a train whistle in such a long time? And why am I aware of it now?*

Her brows rose. She flashed back to the experience at the condo the day before she met Howie. *Ohhh! Something or someone is coming. But this time I'm ready!* She laughed. *And this time I know it's not you, Aunt Etana.*

MALIBU – PRESENT DAY

"HEY LISTEN, GIRLS," BEA SAID. "I don't know about you all, but earlier while I was munching on my sandwich I was thinking how nice it is that we're meeting today."

"Uh-huh, umm, yeah," the three of us said in harmony.

"I'm not used to socializing with girls," she confessed.

"So all these years you've been socializing only with guys?"

"For the most part. I tried the girlie stuff a few times, it didn't go very well. There's usually so much petty drama."

"Sounds like you've lived an interesting life," Lucinda said.

"Interesting is a multi-defined word, and yes, girls, that would be me."

"No drama here," Maddie threw in with perfect comedic timing.

We talked about where we were from and our families, about hormones, current events, and a basketful of girlie-stuff. I started thinking again about my theory and our unique connection. Then an idea dawned on me and, once again, the synchronicity was lovely.

"I'm starting a book club on Wednesday night, twice a month meetings. Wanna come? It'll be a fun gathering with a few other women."

"Yeah. Sure. Sounds like fun," they replied.

"Do you have a book picked out?" Bea asked.

I was getting excited. "Matter of fact I do. Have you girls heard about the new book by Luna Lee?"

"The name sounds familiar." Bea recollected, then snapped her fingers. "Of course, I read her book about mysticism years ago."

"I never heard of her," Maddie said, "but I'm sure Howie has."

"What's the name of the book?" Lucinda asked.

I was just about to answer when Thomas came from behind, startling me. "Hey, Marlo! Sorry to interrupt you girls, but we should get going."

"Huh?" This caught me off-guard.

"We have to feed 'the kids.' And we didn't leave any lights on." He smiled at the girls. As much as I wanted to stay and chat, I agreed with Thomas that we should hit the road.

Once again I was cut off at the pass. But I found it funny, amusing in an elf-like way, like when you can't find your keys or you keep dropping things.

But again, surrendering and letting things flow is a daily work in progress. *Amen!*

"Connection"

It's as if I've
been here before—
A familiar face, some
similar smells,
Deeply poignant sounds.
Woven in my soul
is a memory –
Is it you again?

BEA'S PAST

WITHIN A FEW MONTHS, BEA had turned the guest bedroom into a music studio. She even went so far as padding the walls as a sound barrier. Andy retired from the club scene to work day and night on his music.

The new addition to their family had also arrived. Bea was a new Mommy. It was a girl. They named her Opal. She was a precious jewel with soft shiny black hair. Her sweet soulful eyes reminded the new parents that love would get them through any transition.

Now would be a good time to tell you Opal was a full-breed Dachshund. Since two-legged children were no longer an option for Bea, the next best thing was a puppy! And as cute as puppies are, they are also work. This little girl was no exception. The high heels on Momma's expensive shoes were nibbled down to flats. The screens on the sliding doors were chewed to smithereens and warm yellow land mines that blended into the Berber carpet were discovered by accident.

With all the newness came more changes and transitions. The southern belle's once-glowing face was becoming haggard. It could have been a result of her sitting in morning and evening rush-hour traffic on the Jersey Turnpike and dealing with severe back pain, or finding out from her doctor that she was peri-menopausal which was causing her mood-swings. Whatever it was, it felt alive and growing inside her, causing suffering.

One evening while driving home from work, a swarm of negative thoughts rambled through Bea's mind. Suddenly, an overwhelming feeling in her heart told her to take an alternate route. She took the next exit and wove through the side streets. The area was unfamiliar yet she had faith that her autopilot would lead her back home.

Miles later, she neared a busy intersection. A train whistle sounded in the distance. Her mind flew back to the day when she first heard the familiar sound and experienced a personal shift. Up ahead, the traffic signal quickly turned red. She hit the breaks, skidding to a stop. Bright red glaring lights flashed as railroad gates slammed down in front of the car.

Bea's heart raced. *What the hay!*

The speeding locomotive flashed by, shaking the car and pulsating her spirit. Chills rippled across her body. Her eyes fixed on the dully-lit windows in each car. She could see the passengers. The motion made her dizzy.

Suddenly, the train morphed into a huge butterfly. The center of its body was the train, and out of the windows sprung huge colorful wings. Then, as quickly as it had come, it disappeared into the night. The gates rose, the light turned green. All seemed peaceful and quiet, all but her emotions, which were shuffled about.

The rest of the ride home, Bea was solemn. She was also ungrounded so she relied on her autopilot to get her home safely. No radio blaring, just the sound of passing cars and the tires on the pavement.

When she arrived at her front door, she was as gooey as a hot biscuit just pulled from the oven. Bea breathed deeply and stood on the porch for a moment, trying to get present. She prayed for sanctuary and a healthy home-cooked meal. She hoped the good smells lingering outside were coming from some gourmet fixings her man was whipping up and not their neighbor's kitchen. She fantasized hearing the soothing sound of a harp playing on the stereo, then Andy handing her a lemon drop martini as he planted a passionate kiss on her lips. Bea had a 'take me away moment' like all women long for but have a hard time giving to themselves.

When she entered the house, Opal ran up to her, barking excitedly.

She snapped back into reality as she bent down and scooped up her precious baby while she received hundreds of tiny wet kisses on her face and ears.

Jupiter screeched, "Bea's home, Bea's home, raaaattttttt."

Her mood changed again when she saw Andy in front of the television, eating pizza, and drinking a beer without her.

"Hi, babe," he said, still planted on the couch.

"Helloooohhh." She cringed, ripped open a frozen food box in the kitchen and tossed it into the microwave. From there she continued walking straight up the stairs to the bedroom. Opal followed and, with the help of a doggie staircase resting against the mattress, jumped onto the bed.

Ten minutes later, Bea was soaking in a jasmine scented bubble bath, sipping a glass of white wine, and playing footsies with her pink polished toes while she reflected on her situation. *Shoe-fly, I'm going through the change of life! How should I tell my young lover? Should I even tell him?* she wondered.

She then started thinking about the train and how its appearance signified that change was coming. Or better yet, it was already here and it was a biggie. A few more sips of the wine helped keep her mind from ricocheting and also numbed her lower back pain. The relief was pure bliss.

The following weeks, however, were not so blissful. Miss Alabama had a break-through. One night after dinner, while clearing the table, she declared, "Andy, you gotta get a place of your own!"

"What? I don't understand. Where's this coming from? I thought this is what you wanted."

"It was. That's past tense." She lowered her eyes.

"But I'm so close to having a completed album to show producers. You and me, we're a team remember… silent partner?"

The truth stung. "It's not you, it's me," she said raising her teary eyes. "I'm mixed-up, sad, afraid, and I'm not a hundred percent sure why."

"I deserve more of an explanation!" he demanded gently.

"Well, I kinda know why, but knowing isn't helping me."

"What is it? Are you sick? Oh my word, are you okay?"

"No, not sick, just going through some changes."

"Thank goodness. I got scared. I love you, Bea. I thought we were doing well. I feel bad that I didn't see your pain."

"I'm not sure why, but I've been thinking a lot about my biological mom and I feel a setback."

"Really?"

"Yes. I'm good at covering up my resentment, frustration and insecurities. But lately I'm feeling resentful that you have this fun, leisure life. I guess what I'm saying is, I need some space."

"I'm sorry you're feeling mixed up. I don't want to cause you pain. I'll leave if it will help you."

"Really! Just like that?"

"Yes. I want what's best for you. And this is what you want, right?"

"Umm, yes. So, will you go live with your sister?"

"No, remember, she went back to her husband."

"Oh yeah. Umm, then where will you go?"

"I'm not sure. But I'm so close to finishing these songs. I want to make sure my next move will forge me ahead even more."

"I understand, and I'm sorry I'm so mixed up!"

"Relax, relax, everything will work itself out."

"Really? Just that easy?"

"Yes. If we have faith it will be easy, then it will."

"That sounds hauntingly familiar," she chided.

"Well, what about Opal?" he wanted to know.

"If it's okay, I'd like to keep her."

"She's happy here, so she should stay with you. I'll miss her though."

"I'll miss Jupiter too. You're a good man, Andy. I hope one day I will understand why I sabotaged this relationship." Bea ran out of the room, crying.

"Miss You"
Yesterday,
tomorrow, now—
Memories,
they're here in me.

MALIBU – PRESENT DAY

I NEVER DID ANSWER Lucinda's question about the title of the novel. I figured it would be a better surprise on the night of the book club. The four of us exchanged telephone numbers and e-mail addresses. I promised to contact everyone in a few days.

As we were saying good-bye, a thought popped in. I decided to ask one question about my theory to see if I was still on the right track about our meeting. It was just another tiny piece of the puzzle I needed to know.

"Do you girls mind if I ask your ages?"

"Tsk-tsk, Marlo, don't you know it's rude to ask a woman her age?" Bea snarled.

"I'm 43, and not afraid of aging," Maddie shouted.

"I'm 40," Lucinda said. "I'm not sure how I feel about it yet."

"Me, I'm 42 and proud of my earth-years," I added.

We all looked at Bea. "Well, shoot, I'm the oldest. I'm 44." She started to walk away, then turned. "But it also means I'm the wisest."

"Of course!" we agreed.

On the ride home, I thought more about the women. I was excited about the mystery that was unraveling in front of me. The 'biggie' question that would mystically tie us together would have to wait until we saw each other again. Whatever would be revealed would be a test of my gut instincts and proof that a higher power works at linking people together. I knew something phenomenal was happening.

Then my logical side came in: *Maybe, Marlo, it's nothing exceptional at all. It's simply sheer coincidence; our men are all buddies, we're all in our forties and we get along like we're longtime friends.* I cringed at that possibility, then knocked that left-brain theory out of my mind. *No way!* I laughed. *There's more to this than meets the eye. I just know it!*

I was driving. Thomas suddenly looked over at me. "Did you have a nice day?" he wondered.

"I did. I really like your friends and their wives and girlfriends are great!"

"It seemed like you were getting along really well for just meeting each other."

"Exactly! It's like we've known each other for years. I have a really good feeling about them."

Thomas was happy to hear this. I turned on the radio, 'No One', by Alicia Keyes was playing. I took this as a sign. My husband rested his head back on the headrest and grinned as we headed down Malibu Canyon, the early evening sun casting shadows on the rocks and trees.

BEA'S PAST

BEA AND ANDY'S BREAK-UP was amicable, a big-time first for Miss Alabama. No long drawn out saga, just a short and sweet good-bye. She even drove Andy and Jupiter to Newark Airport. Over the following days she played the good-bye scene over and over in her head, and realized she was actually baffled and hurt at how easily he had left.

After weeks of depression, re-bound dating, and too many nights out with the boys, she decided to stay home and start a new lease on life by having fun solo. It was finally time for Bea to be enough for Bea. Tonight she would un-strap the high-heeled, toe-pinching shoes and get acquainted with the little girl inside who used to chase butterflies, eat key lime pie, and trust that all would be okay just like Daddy always promised.

She picked up the telephone and dialed. "Hi, Daddy, I was thinking of you and Mom. I want to tell you how much I love you both."

"Why, bless you, child. How are you and Andrew doing?"

"Well, Daddy, Andy and I…"

It was a long phone call, but when she hung up she felt happier and more focused than she had in a longtime. Sporting a tranquil smile, Bea stepped into a cozy pair of pajamas and made a strong old-fash-ioned martini with lots of tart green olives. She then put a CD into the player and bee-bopped around the bedroom. Her audience, Opal, was impressed. She wagged her tail and barked, then chased her momma around the room, nibbling at her feet.

When the music stopped, the tipsy southern belle fell back onto the bed, balancing her drink in one hand. *Your momma has gone co-co-loco,* she laughed. Opal sighed and laid her head between her paws.

Bea set down the drink and reached into the nightstand. *Where the heck is that thing?* She shoved the contents around. *Oh, I'll need these too.* She ripped open a package of batteries. *Oh yeah, now I remember.* She went into the closet, grabbed something, then ran and flopped back onto the bed.

She inserted the batteries into the bottom of an odd-shaped thing. It was about nine inches long, curved at the middle and rounded on the top. She took a long sip of her drink and sighed heavily, like a dirty drunken man would sigh, then turned the thing on: *Bzzzzzzzzzzz.*

Opal made a dash and hid under the covers. *Holy Toledo, it's fast and it tickles. I hope I can do this 'cause I'm feeling kind of loopy.* She bent over and began buffing her right big toe nail. She moved the gadget up and down and around, trimming and smoothing the rest of her toenails. *There, that wasn't so hard!* Opal peeked her head out from the blanket and moaned. *What, girl! Whadya think I was gonna do? Oh … that…*

Many full moons came and went, causing an emotional stirring inside Bea that made her rethink her attitude towards her own sex. For the first time in her adult life, she wanted a girlfriend. She talked frequently on the phone with her gay friend Billie and found great comfort with their conversations. But still she felt something was missing.

Not ever having experienced a true female bond, she had a hard time wrapping her mind around the concept. What she knew for sure was that she was lonely. The boys at work had less and less time to have drinks. Babies were coming into their families, so their days of beer and nuts were replaced with formula, strained peas, and diapers.

Desperately driven to fill the void, she went on a search for girlfriends. After months of coffee clutches, tea parties, and book clubs, Bea realized that the girls she hooked up with had more issues than a magazine has in its archives. Thoughts of her mother began flooding her perception, so she went back to reading books, many, many books, fiction and non-fiction, hoping to find the answer she sought.

One very lonely, low estrogen deprived evening, Bea was watching television. The show featured up-and-coming Hollywood stars. She thought of Andy and wondered how he was doing, and how close he was to becoming one of those stars. By the time the show ended, her mind was engrossed with thoughts of her ex-lover. Unable to fight the temptation any longer, she picked up the phone and dialed his number. He wasn't home.

Bea hung up and did not leave a message. Instead, she made herself a strong apple martini, ran a bubble bath and lit a few candles. She clipped up her hair, undressed, and stepped into the water. It was perfectly warm. *Tomorrow will be a new day.*

She took a sip of the cocktail, then, holding it in mid-air, slid under the water, immersing her body. The underwater submerge was tranquil, until a disturbingly familiar sound made her spring up. She paused, water dripping off her face and breasts. It was a low-range hum, moving closer. Bea wiped the suds from her eyes. *Sweet Clementine, it's a bleepin' train whistle.*

Within minutes it was blowing louder. She splashed the water around her in the tub, like a spoiled child. *What do you want? What in heaven's name does it mean this time? Are you screaming at me 'cause I derailed with Andy or 'cause I phoned him?* She switched her tone: *Is another man coming into my life? Or maybe you want me to find my mother?*

Bea sighed and took a long sip on her martini. Her tummy became upset. It churned and gurgled. Then something tickled her shapely bottom. A few bubbles floated to the top. She laughed at her own drama. *Hush, I should have never eaten those beans!*

She laughed harder, trying to forget about the train and her mom, but she could not. The two rocked hard on her psyche. She cupped her martini glass tightly, like a child would hold onto a baby doll. She prayed. She laughed. She cried. Tears dropped into the bath water, making circle-swirls. She dropped her chin and prayed even harder.

Hours later, the phone woke her. "Hi Bea, it's Andy."

"Andy, wh-what time is it?"

"It's one in the morning here, so it's four your time."

She rubbed her eyes and rolled onto her back. "I was in a sound sleep, give me a minute and I'll be okay."

He paused. "I saw you called on the caller ID box."

"Um, yeah. I wanted to talk with you, but I hung up when your message came on. I feel like a sissy!"

"Bea, now, now. Be gentle with yourself. Tell me, how are you?"

"You always have my best interest. I'm good, well, okay. Well, not well. I don't know why I was so uptight back then. You were only doing what I offered you to do, and what I told you I wanted," she rambled nervously.

"It's okay, babe."

"No, it's not okay. Lord, I've missed you. You're the kindest man I've ever known, with the most sincere eyes—and I blew it."

"Nothing is blown, it just changed."

"I didn't realize how much I missed you and how good we were as a family. You, Jupiter, Opal and me."

"I've missed you too, babe, and Opal. It was hard not to call you but I knew in my heart you just needed space," he said softly. "I realized too that space was something I may have lacked in giving you."

"Not at all. You gave me plenty of space. But I had expectations, and after all those books I've read, expectation is not a friendly place to live."

"Water under the bridge," he assured her.

"Oh, and guess what?"

"What?"

"You'll be happy to hear I have my hormones in check."

"Great! So, are you officially menopausal?"

"Peri-menopausal. It's the quiet before the storm. Though that's not an accurate description. It's more like coming through the birth canal again... this time with my eyes wide open."

"You're funny. I remember when my mom went through it."

"Your mom!" she silently gulped.

"So you see, I understand. Us guys go through transitions too, you know. You girls aren't the only lucky ones."

"Ha, ha, ha." More awake now, Bea sat up in bed.

"For a thirty-three year old man you sure are enlightened."

"I'm old soul," he said in a bad Chinese accent.

"Good one! And you have big chopstick," she mimicked back.

"I see you haven't lost your sense of humor."

"It's still around."

"Seriously though, speaking of souls, Bea, I just have one question."

"Yes?"

"Did you do any soul searching with your childhood memories regarding your mother?"

"Hmm, a little."

"What did you discover?"

"She did the best she could at the time, based on what she knew and who she was. I forgive her for not being the kind of momma I dreamed of having, but I'm grateful to her for loving me the best way she knew how. I know deep down she does."

"Good for you. It's important to make peace with those old wounds. We can always talk with each other if things come up, okay?"

"Thank you, darlin'." She fluffed her hair as if he could see her through the phone line.

By now the sun had risen. They said good-bye several times before hanging up the phone. With a new skip in her step, Bea got out of bed and stood in front of her ceramic dog and angel collection. She said a prayer for guidance, then randomly opened a page in a book about angels and began reading. *Archangel Sandalphon! You again. You've helped me with integrity, now you're here to assist me in being able to receive good things in my life. I get it! Thank you for the confirmation.*

She put an instrumental piece on the stereo and lay back on the bed. The music and presence of the angels filled her heart and soul.

The stars aligned, the winds shifted and the train switched tracks. It didn't take long for Bea and Andy to rekindle their relationship long-distance. After several intimate and honest phone calls, they decided to get together again. This time Bea would do the moving.

She booked a one-way ticket to California for her and Opal, and gave two weeks' notice at work. Her understanding boss took her to lunch and handed her a cash bonus for being such a stand-up employee, along with a letter of recommendation. Without skipping a beat she sent out her resume to prospective companies in the Los Angeles area.

For financial reasons, she decided to sublease her townhouse. When Billie and his partner heard the news, they asked for first dibs. Although they had seen the house a few times, they wanted to stop by to discuss a few decorating ideas and finalize the deal.

"I do love the green-painted walls," Billie said.

"Yes, it's calming and it feels like a refreshing meadow," his partner delighted.

"It's dreamy. And the pink plantation shutters and blue crown molding are fab!" Billie delighted, "Who would have thought?"

"I had those specially painted," Bea said, walking into the room with a tray of martinis.

"Most of the furniture is from the Victorian era, so where exactly do the leather accents fit in?" Billie's partner wanted to know.

"She's very kinky underneath it all," Billie whispered loudly into his ear.

"Oooh, you mean she hasn't come out yet!" the partner teased.

"Not yet, boys. I still leave my toys in the closet," she chuckled. "Should I leave my handcuffs behind for you two?"

They squirmed and laughed, muffling their voices, then got down to business. Bea was excited about the move to California so she had very little trouble saying good-bye to her home and the Garden State. Packing wasn't so easy though, she knew Andy didn't have a big place and she could only take two suitcases of clothing, shoes and necessities. The rest went into storage.

Andy met Bea and Opal at LAX. Sparks flew when the two saw each other. And Opal whined with excitement as her daddy cuddled her in his strong gentle arms again. It was a thirty-minute drive to his apartment, without traffic, of course. With traffic it's a crapshoot.

Andy's apartment was a modest one-bedroom. It was even smaller than Bea had imagined. The walls were painted flat white. The beige carpeted floor was as hard as linoleum, or was it dirty white?

But for the sake of love, the spoiled southerner sucked it up. She was grateful to be starting over with her sexy boyfriend. Their surroundings were unimportant as long as they were together.

In the living room, Jupiter perched on a branch in his cage. "Hello, Jupiter."

"Awkkk, hello Bea, love ya baby." She laughed and rubbed his feathers through the cage.

"Let me show you to the bedroom," Andy said, towing her suitcases. They didn't have to walk far.

"See that six-drawer bureau?" he pointed. "You can have it for your clothes."

"Thanks, it's a beautiful antique." She knelt down and unzipped a suitcase.

"Yes, it's from the forties. I found it at a second-hand store."

She opened a drawer and noticed a film of dust. When Andy wasn't looking, she used an embroidered handkerchief from her purse to wipe the bottom of the wood drawers.

"Hey, babe, forget unpacking and come 'ere."

He flopped on the bed, patted the mattress and winked. "I missed you so much."

"Oh, darlin', did I miss you these past months!"

He pulled his shirt over his head and rubbed his hairy chest. "I missed your kinky massages."

She threw a shirt at him and jumped on the bed. "I'm so happy to be here."

He pulled her on top of him. They kissed. He moved his lips with heartfelt passion, his hands slowly caressing her bottom. She loved all the teasing, but wanted him totally.

"Make love to me," she breathlessly begged.

He rolled her over and slowly removed her clothes. She vibrated with anticipation. Their bodies sang their hearts into delirium.

After the passionate reunion, they ordered a pizza and relaxed in front of the television just like old times. Weary from the plane ride, Opal nestled alongside them. Then Andy freed Jupiter who jumped onto Opal's back. It was a priceless moment.

The following days, Bea caught up on much-needed rest as she enjoyed the simple life of hanging out by the pool and chilling. Her boyfriend worked diligently on a secretive project but promised to tell her about it soon. She learned not to press and allowed things to happen. This made her feel good about herself.

After a couple of weeks, she decided she'd had enough downtime and was ready to look for a job at last. So she followed up on her resume mailings. The next day she received a call from the president of a major corporation. Monday would be her first interview in Santa Monica. She joyfully shared the good news with Andy.

"Congratulations. I sure do admire your enthusiasm," he cheered.

"Well, babe, working in an office is what I do best."

"Don't sell yourself short, you're plenty good at many things."

"Um, are we talking about things I can do with my clothes on or off?"

"Both," he said, grinning, "I have good news too. Next weekend you're going to meet my two friends from the Jersey shore and their girls."

"The guys from the boardwalk that became stuntmen?"

"Yeah. And another cat named Howie who Ricky turned me on to. He's a healer. He's helped me with my vocal cords."

"That's great. A healer, how interesting. I think I'm going to like California and all its rare critters," she chuckled.

"But wait, there's more! The best news is, when Thomas and Andy heard my tunes, they turned me onto a connection for a feature film."

"And...?"

"And they love my stuff. They really love it. My music is going to be in the soundtrack for the movie."

"Oh, Andy, how wonderful! I'm so happy for you. It looks like things are going our way."

"I'll toast to that. Let's celebrate with a pizza and a six-pack."

"Sound yummy. I just knew you'd reach your star."

"I couldn't have done it without you."

She blushed. "By the way, darlin', where are we meeting your friends?"

"In Malibu."

"On the beach?"

"Yeah."

"Oh, no! I'm not in shape for the beach yet."

"What are you talking about? You look great."

"You are a charmer, music man." She fluttered her eyelashes. He grabbed his guitar and got on one knee, serenading her with an original song about her beautiful body.

The following day, at Bea's insistence, Andy took her to an upscale department store in the Valley where she bought a two-piece with a matching dress. On the way home he sidetracked, showing her around the Valley's west side. The palm trees, mountains, and tidiness of the Valley were breathtaking.

As they neared a popular California college, she noticed train tracks running parallel to the street. A few miles later, as they were nearing a busy intersection, a whistle sounded in the distance. The traffic signal turned red. Andy hit the breaks. Red lights flashed. The railroad gates dropped in front of the car. Loud and pulsing, the train's whistle blew. Bea's mind flew back to the time in New Jersey when she had a similar experience. The speeding locomotive flashed by as she recalled that day, blending it with this moment as if they were one. A chill rippled through her body...

BOOK CLUB – PRESENT DAY

"WELL, IT DOESN'T SURPRISE ME, girls! Since we met that's all that's been happenin', unexpected coincidences! I've read a lot of books about coincidences, synchronicity, and all that kinda woo-woo stuff. But setting that aside, I'd like to make one more toast," Bea declared, raising her wine glass.

I took a breath and held onto my patience, waiting for Bea's toast. We moved in closer and raised our glasses as she continued, "Thank you, Ricky, Howie, Thomas and my sweet baby Andy for bringing us four women together. I haven't felt this comfortable since I hung out with the boys in Jersey."

We chuckled and clanked our glasses. I started to speak, but Maddie jumped in next. "Okay, now I'd like to add something," she said. "Cheers to not only new friends but a new life!"

I clapped my hands to move things along. "So, girls, let's get back to the title of the book and why it sounds so familiar."

"I thought we already figured that out, it's because of the toast to the 440 thing," Maddie concluded.

"Well, I think there's more to it."

"Yeah, it's strange that we're four women in our forties and the book we're about to read is titled 'The 440 Train'," Lucinda said. I smirked.

Bea took a handkerchief out from her purse and blotted her brow. "Why do I feel all fluttery, like something is about to happen?"

"You okay?" I asked.

"I think so. I felt like this one other time. It was many years ago. You're going to think I'm coco-loco, but I kept hearing a train whistle, inside my house."

"Hey! Wait a minute, that happened to me too," Maddie shouted, "right before I met Howie. When I would hear a train whistle blow, it really bothered me, so I prayed extra hard to the saints to help me."

Every chakra in my body was glowing with energy. I waited with bated breath.

"And I was having visions of my Aunt Etana who has passed away," Maddie added theatrically.

"Holy cowboy, you're making me remember something too," Lucinda added. "I also heard a train in Texas, right before I met Ricky. I was running around the house trying to find the darn thing and my three little dogs were following me. It was hysterical."

"Sounds like a comedy," Maddie mocked. "Or a thriller," she whispered.

I jumped in, "Right before I met Thomas, I had an intense inner shift while a train whistle was blowing. It's as if the sound of the whistle was chipping at my soul, asking me to remember something."

"Like an awakening?" Bea exclaimed, fanning her face with the book.

"Exactly!" I insisted.

"Are we all losing our minds?" Bea wanted to know.

Lucinda jumped in. "No, on the contrary. I think we're witnessing a rare phenomenon."

"A phenomenon?" Maddie trembled.

"I also had peculiar dreams and strong feelings from deceased family members." Lucinda admitted. "But what do the train and the whistle signify?"

"I actually have a theory," I said. They all turned toward me. "I'm pretty sure it's about change."

"It's like The Butterfly card at the ocean. And the metamorphosing process," Bea concluded.

"Yeah, and like the big butterfly on your back," Maddie joked.

"Hush, girl, can't you see we're on to something? Tell us more about your theory, Marlo."

"It seems the train whistle cuts into us and gets our attention. I remember feeling like something was missing in my life. My gut kept telling me something was coming. Now I know it signified a life-altering change. I had no idea, though, that Thomas would be such a big part of the transformation. Does this make sense?"

"Yes." Lucinda stood. "I used to stuff my emotions to the point of physically being tied in knots. But by the time I moved here, I had begun changing. I set my ideals high and demanded respect from Ricky. I wasn't going to settle for anything less. It was rocky at times, but being with him actually made me stronger. Now I know how to express myself instead of holding things in." She sat back down.

The three of us just shook our heads until Bea spoke, "I wasn't true to myself in regards to the type of man I used to marry. I realized my heart and soul yearned for a man my southern peers probably wouldn't approve of. But I gave up caring what others think. I deserve to be happy and live with integrity." She held her chin high. "Andy helped me make that my reality."

"I was always doing for others," Maddie confessed. "When I met Howie, it was the only time I ever really thought about me first."

"Wow! Sounds like we all had huge shifts going on when we met our men. That must be the link between us," I said.

"Let's not forget the men and the changes in their lives that occurred when they met us," Lucinda suggested.

"That's an 'Amen.' But there's one more thing I'm curious about." I raised a brow.

"There's more?" Maddie sighed. "What about the book?"

"Be patient, we'll get there. Is there anything else you can recall, anything out of the ordinary that happened the day you met your man?"

They squinted their eyes. "Hmmm?" they echoed.

"Let me sidetrack for a minute, did you ever notice that the words listen and silent share the same letters?"

"That's deep," Bea said.

"I like deep stuff." I smirked cutely.

"I think we figured that out," Lucinda teased.

I grinned. "So, when we're silent we can listen to what is really being said from the person we're with and from the Unseen world."

"Unseen world?" Maddie shuddered.

"Yeah. Spirits who have crossed over to the good blue road of Heaven."

"Wait a minute, are we going to have a séance? 'Cause if we are I may check out." Maddie looked around nervously.

"No. Nothing like that."

"Well, you've piqued my curiosity. What are we going to do?" Bea rubbed her palms together.

"Let's try something. Please close your eyes, then breathe in and out through your nose deeply and slowly a few times. Don't force your breath, just become aware of it. When you feel calm, then just be. Are you are open to doing this?"

Three pairs of eyes suddenly closed. They were all willing. Several peaceful minutes eased by. When their faces were more relaxed, I asked them to think back to the day they each met their man and recall if anything tangible appeared out of the blue.

"The ticket!" Lucinda shouted. "I found a ticket in my skirt the day I met Ricky on the set. I thought it was a wardrobe ticket. It said something about The 440 Train. I remember thinking it was a sign."

I clapped my hands. "Yes!"

"I found the same ticket in my vest pocket the day I met Howie at the Asian games, and I also thought it was a sign."

"What the darn tootin' is goin' on here! 'Cause I found a ticket in my purse when I met Andy at the club in Jersey. It said something about The 440 Train. I knew it was a good sign."

I did the happy dance in my seat.

"Marlo! What about you? Did you find a ticket too?" Lucinda jumped up, excitedly.

I wanted to answer but couldn't. I was in total absorption of what had just taken place. I could feel the vortex of energy in the center of the room again. So I took a sip of water while silently looking at them.

"Well, come on, <u>did</u> you find a ticket?" Lucinda insisted, placing her hands on her hips.

"Yes, yes, YES!"

They sighed. Lucinda flopped down on the sofa. Maddie made the sign of the cross and Bea poured more wine into her glass.

"I found the ticket on the windshield of my car the night I met Thomas."

"So what in heaven's name is going on?" Bea asked, folding her handkerchief into a tiny square.

"Yeah, what is happening? I'm getting a little freaked out," Maddie said, pushing her glasses up the bridge of her nose.

"From what I've read so far, fourteen years ago Luna Lee began planting seeds for her first fiction novel. She had friends and hired hands from all the over the world pass out bookmarks that looked like train tickets. People who worked in bookstores, food stores, retail places, you get my drift, they all slipped the bookmarks into people's shopping bags."

I paused, took a breath, then continued, "Some of the messengers just passed out the tickets on the street and even at train stations. People would stick them into their pockets and purses, unaware of what it was or what it said until one day, when they least expected it, they would find the ticket." I uncrossed my legs and took a sip of wine, then repositioned my body.

"This is better than a television series," Lucinda chuckled.

"Wait a minute!" Bea chimed in. "So what you're saying is that the four of us all found a ticket?"

"Yes! Somewhere and sometime over a fourteen year span, we were given one."

"Unbelievable," Maddie said. "And we all found it when we met the men in our lives. This is too freaky! First the train whistle, now this!"

I couldn't help but laugh. "Exactly! What are the chances of the four of us, states and countries between us, finding a train ticket the day we meet the men we're all with now? And those men are all friends who ended up in California, then introduced us on a beach in Malibu. And here we are years later, in our forties, at a book club, about to read Luna Lee's 'The 440 Train,' the book responsible for the tickets." I let out a loud sigh. The girls were wide-eyed.

"It still doesn't explain the train whistle," Lucinda said.

"Yeah, there's not an explanation for that," Bea agreed.

"I agree. There is no explanation. But this is what I'm talking about. I mean, come on, isn't this profound proof of something much bigger than us? The Universe's Divine Plan which has brought us to this moment, NOW? And if anyone dares tell me this is merely coincidence, I'll flip them off their feet with my angel wings!"

"You go, girl!" Bea rooted.

"Is anyone else scared by this?" Maddie wanted to know.

"I'm not afraid. I have all my angels around me," Bea admitted.

"Not me either. I think it's wonderfully exciting," Lucinda said. "It takes a lot more than this to scare me. But I have to confess, this is the most mystifying thing that's ever happened to me other than the whistle and ticket. I really need to process all this."

"We all have some processing to do," Bea said.

After a few quiet moments, Lucinda finally asked, looking at me: "So what's it all mean?"

"I don't know for sure! But I think we're meant to become good friends and what will happen with this foursome is yet to be revealed. I have faith that all is on schedule."

"You mean 'The 440 Train' is on schedule?" Maddie joked.

We laughed with her, lightening the intensity of what we had just uncovered.

"It's truly remarkable that you figured out this scenario," Bea said.

I shrugged my shoulders and grinned.

"Yeah. Tell us exactly how you came to discover this," Lucinda requested.

"A hunch. Divine guidance. I just had a feeling about you gals from the way we get along so easily and our comfort level around each other. For having just met, we seemed a bit magical together. All I did was listen to my gut and ask some questions."

"Did you know something would happen like this before we met on the beach?"

"No, Lucinda. I didn't have a clue."

"I did. I told Ricky I felt that I would make some new friends. Now that I think about it I also heard a train whistle the day before the beach at a coffee shop, and many other times as well."

"Wow! See. You're in tune."

"Heavens to Betsy, me too. Andy and I had to stop for a train the day before the beach and I got a strange feeling. And there were other times when I heard a train whistle, I even think I hallucinated once when I saw butterfly wings come out of a train."

"Holy moley! And I thought I had a wild imagination."

"This is riveting," Lucinda said, wide-eyed. "The Butterfly again!"

"Yeah, the Butterfly again, what about you?" Bea dreamily pointed to Maddie.

"I did think it would be nice to make a friend," she said softly. "And I did hear a whistle when I was at my desk and when Howie and I were having some rough times. Oh my gosh! Now I'm really freaked out."

"And you, Miss Marlo?" Bea asked, looking at me.

"I heard a train whistle the night before we met," I laughed. "It made me think about whales and whistles and their sound frequency. But I didn't have a clue about the four of us, not until the day on the beach. Then I remembered something my mom said about a recurring dream I've had about a train."

"Hmm. Very interesting," Bea concluded. "Well, I think it's great that we're all in touch with our gut instincts, and it seems like we can learn from each other."

"We already are," Lucinda said.

"I never had friends like this in the Philippines."

While the women continued chatting, I remained stuck in my thoughts about the Universe's magic. And I was reminded that these mysteries are what makes life so enthralling.

"I'm really anxious to hear about my new girlfriends' hopes and dreams, and even more of our similarities. I mean, why else would we be together?" Bea projected.

"That's what Luna writes about. Happenstance. People who come into our lives, and what we can learn and teach each other."

"Heck with 'The Four-Forty Train' this is a book," Maddie said.

"Maybe one day it will be," Lucinda predicted, "since we have a writer among us!" She winked at me.

"I'm not sure if I'm ready for all this magic stuff. Just yesterday I was at the shooting range sharpening my target practice," Maddie admitted.

We silenced quickly, not quite sure what to say. Finally, Lucinda spoke, "Nothing wrong with that. Mixing it up keeps everything balanced."

Bea and I bobbed our heads in agreement. "Yeah, I wouldn't peg you for one who played with dollies when you were a little girl," Bea teased.

"You got me." Maddie put her hands up, surrendering. "Then let's start reading this book," she insisted.

"Before we start, who needs a pee break?" I wondered.

It was the quickest pee break I ever saw four women take. Since it was already nine o'clock, we decided we would only read the first chapter and then discuss it. We also thought it would be fun if Bea read aloud since her southern tone was a delight to hear.

Bea began: *"THE FOUR-FORTY TRAIN…"*

It was late evening. The fog rolled in. It was thick, warm and gooey. I could only see a few feet in front of me. It was an abnormally eerie night, but I didn't mind. I had to get out of town. The fog was less frightening than the person I was living with. I needed a break, had to escape from the hold my lover had on me.

The irony was pathetic. All my life I had been the one being chased. I'll be the first to admit that at times I've used my good looks to get what I wanted and I've had more one-night interludes than I care to count. I loved the attention, caressing and pampering. But then it changed.

Suddenly it was me who couldn't get enough. It was me doing the telephone calling, the following, and the pampering. It was me who only wanted one lover.

I became subservient and put twenty-five years of artwork on the back burner. I didn't care about making an impression as much as I just wanted to be loved. My agent was furious. He felt my recent paintings were not up to par. He said that when I fell in love I lost my creative passion and intuitive guidance.

In the beginning it felt good to love someone so much that I lost myself in them. But enough was enough, this time my lover had gone too far. I couldn't stand the lies any longer. I packed some art supplies, a suitcase full of clothes and some favorite things. I told my assistant to handle the gallery. I was fleeing for my sanity.

Following my instincts, I ended up at the train station. For hours, I sat on a bench near the tracks and watched the trains roll in and out. Then a train came thundering in. It was a beauty. I looked at the number on the locomotive. It read: 440.

I got the chills. This was the sign I was waiting for. I wasn't sure of its destination and quite frankly I didn't care, so I asked another traveler to look at the posted schedule and let me know when it was departing.

"Tomorrow at eight in the morning," she told me.

This would be the train I would take. That night I stayed at a sleazy motel, ordered a pizza with the works and uncorked a bottle of vintage wine I had packed. I polished off the bottle and the pizza and slept like a baby.

The following morning, I arrived at the ticket window well before eight. "A one-way ticket on the Four-Forty train please," I said to the ticket man. I was a bit nervous, breathing heavily, my hands trembling as I offered him the fare. He studied my face, then handed me the ticket. For the first time in a long time I was listening to my instincts and doing the best thing for me.

Moments later, the Conductor howled, "All aboard!"

I waited for the rush of people to board first. I could afford to be patient. When the conductor gave his last call, I headed to the train. I paused at the steep steel steps and adjusted my heavy bag higher on my shoulder.

Once on the train, I looked around. Many seats were occupied. Everyone seemed so solemn. I didn't like the vibe. It reminded me of my own feelings.

I walked to the back of the train, near the caboose, where there were less people. Three women sat in the car, each alone, a few rows from one another. Although they too looked quite solemn, I felt compelled to retire to this car.

All of a sudden, a wave of emotions washed over me. My prior experiences with empathic energy was a speck on the Richter scale in comparison. I could feel the three women's energy and their expressions told me we all had something in common. I felt queasy.

Slowly, I walked towards the first woman. She had black hair, cut in a short and sassy style. Her skin was as radiant as onyx. She was reading a book. She lifted her head and half-smiled at me. Her dark green eyes were like a lost puppy dog's. I blocked her emotions by focusing on my walking and my breathing. I felt as if I were moving in slow motion. Finally I passed her.

A few seats down I came to the second woman. She sat tall in her seat. Her copper penny colored hair was braided in pigtails. She was tan and looked like Pocahontas as she skimmed through a magazine. Without moving her head, her brown eyes lifted, suspiciously staring at me. I smiled. Her eyes dropped back to the magazine.

A few seats down was the third woman. She had straight blonde hair with even blonder streaks and a dash of freckles on her cheeks. Her lips were full and heart-shaped. She was naturally pretty. She fumbled with some trinkets set out on her lap. Still fumbling, she looked at me and nodded her head. I nodded back.

I sat on the right side of the train, two seats behind her. The other two women were on the left side. I suddenly realized I've always been looking for balance and for the first time in a long time I was aware of it. I was also aware that I would be saying 'for the first time in a long time' a lot from now on!

The train's whistle blew loudly, signaling that we would soon be leaving the station. By this point I was feeling more grounded and connected with my own space. I settled in my seat.

Moments later, the conductor trotted through the car. "All aboard the Four-Forty Train. Welcome to the next chapter of your life!" I thought it was a strange way to welcome us. What did he mean by 'the next chapter of your life'?

Bea snapped the book shut. "I love this. I feel like I'm reading about us."

"It could be us," Lucinda said.

"Yeah, it could be," Maddie agreed.

"It is us, and it's <u>everyone</u>," I said. "Every time we make a choice to do something new, step out of our comfort zone, tap into our courage and take a leap of faith, we experience new feelings and meet new people. Hypothetically speaking, it's like we've boarded a train, not knowing for sure where it will take us.

"That's what we all did when we met the guys," Lucinda said.

"It's truly remarkable. Shall I continue? Or does someone else want to read?" Bea asked.

"You read. You've got a great voice," Maddie ordered gently.

"Why thank you, Miss Maddie, then I shall read on." Bea over-dramatized clearing her throat and flipped open the book.

The conductor continued to make his way down the aisle. A frantic waiter ran up to him, babbling about something.

"I'll be back for your tickets once we get going." The conductor addressed the four of us.

I had all intentions of ordering a strong drink once I was checked in. The train started to slowly pull away from the station. I looked out the window and waved to no one, then took off my hat and placed it on the empty seat next to me. I was grateful the wave of emotions had finally subsided.

Little by little, the train picked up speed. The landscape looked different from inside the train car. I thought the scenery would make a great painting. It would be fun to paint from the perspective of a moving train.

Minutes later, the Conductor came back. I watched him punch each woman's ticket, then slip it in the seat pouch behind their heads. In a few moments we entered a tunnel. The lights in the car flickered, casting shadows everywhere. The life I had just left behind was my past. Where I was now was the present, and where I was going was still to be revealed.

"Ticket, please." I didn't hear his request so the Conductor tapped my shoulder. I looked up. "Sir, your ticket please."

I handed him my ticket. "When can I get a drink?"

"I'll send for the waiter, sir." He stuck the ticket behind me.

Bea again slapped shut the book. Lucinda stood. Maddie sprung up too.

I smiled wide.

"What the hay?" Bea shouted. "She's a <u>he</u>?"

"Why'd you think it was a woman?" I stood and stretched.

"I, I just assumed."

"Me too. I thought it was a chick!" Maddie exclaimed.

"Very tricky, but that's how we think. We label and assume things about people before we know all the facts," Lucinda said.

"When I first read this chapter, I also thought it was about a woman. But when I re-read it, it made sense that the person could just as easily be a man."

"Luna Lee is a clever writer," Bea said.

"She sure is. I once heard someone say a novel is a confession, and it's up to the reader to read between the lines."

"That's a good one, Marlo," Lucinda said.

Completely entertained, we decided to retire the book at that point and chat a bit about the first chapter. We also revisited the unique link we shared which had brought us together. It was refreshing how well we got along and felt free to be ourselves.

Moments later, we began cleaning up the dishes and went into the kitchen. Silence filled the space as we individually digested a bounty of food for thought. Once the cleaning-up was done, good-byes seemed timely.

But Bea suddenly said, "I have something I need to share."

We leaned against the granite island and gave her our full attention.

"I'm meeting my mom for lunch next week in Long Beach," she said softly.

"How wonderful."

"I'm not sure if it is wonderful."

"Oh?" we wondered.

"Girls, I haven't seen my blood-mom since I was twelve years old."

"Ah," we replied, even more curious now.

"It will be a good thing," Maddie reassured her.

"We shall see," she sighed.

"How did you connect after all these years?" Lucinda asked, intently staring at something on the kitchen chalkboard beside her.

"Andy located her. He's helping me make peace with old wounds. I just can't believe she lives here in California. I never knew she left Alabama."

"Wow! Well, if you need to talk after you meet with her, please call me," I offered.

"Me too," Maddie said.

"Me three," Lucinda added, turning towards us with an odd look on her face.

"I will. And thank you all so much." Bea's lips stayed together, sporting a quaint smile.

"Well, if we're sharing then I might as well tell you my news too," Maddie said as she doodled with her vest pockets.

"Yeeesssss," we wondered.

"Howie wants a divorce." Our jaws hung open. "It's okay, it's okay. Forget what I said," she stammered.

We allowed some quiet time to pass, giving Maddie space to talk more if she chose. Sure enough, she opened up again: "I don't want to talk about it too much, I just needed to get that off my chest 'cause it's been weighing heavy on me. So far, I've only been talking about it to the saints. It feels good to tell someone I can see."

I grinned at her childlike innocence.

"You did a good thing by venting." Lucinda placed a hand on Maddie's back.

"Really?"

"Really! I learned the hard way about holding on to emotions. It does more damage than good to keep them bottled-up. It's healthier to release them and move on," Lucinda said convincingly, then looked back to the chalkboard.

"I do feel better," Maddie said, releasing her shoulders.

"Maddie, I have a confession about the subject. I'm quite an expert in the field of divorce, so if you need any tips call me." Bea's revelation lightened the mood.

"Really? Okay."

"Bea, are you really an expert?" Lucinda teased.

"Hush. That's not something I admit every day. But yes, I am."

"More than once?" she pried.

"Yes, more than one time," Bea twitted.

"More than twice?" Lucinda asked, tweaking her lips.

"Yes, more than two times." She glared at Lucinda with an 'I dare you' look.

"More than three!" Maddie interjected.

"Bing, bing, bing! Three is the lucky number," Bea sang.

We bobbed our heads in the same fashion as when we found out Maddie shoots a gun for pleasure.

"What's your fascination with the chalkboard, Lucinda?" Bea asked, changing the subject.

Lucinda opened her mouth, sighed, shut it, then asked, "This photo, the guy in it looks like someone I know."

"Really?" I asked.

"Yeah, really. What's his name?"

"Um… Randal."

"Oh my gosh! I can't believe it," she removed the magnet holding the photo and brought the snapshot closer to her face. "He's my ex-husband!"

"Say what?" Bea ran up to Lucinda and grabbed the photo. "He's cute."

"Oh my gosh! This night, keeps getting better," I said.

"Now that's strange." Maddie sat on a stool and laughed.

"Marlo, how do you know Randal?" Lucinda wondered.

"I don't actually. I know his new wife, who used to be Thomas's ex-fiancé. Her name is Jada."

"Holy horsetails," Lucinda sat down. "The last time I heard from him he was moving back to England. He told me he'd met someone."

"Well, he probably met her on an airplane. She's a stewardess."

Bea giggled. "Get a pen out, someone get a pen out and start taking notes for this book we're living."

"Yeah, last we heard she was moving to England—and she was pregnant."

"So, this is their boy?"

I didn't hear her question. I was thinking back to the day Jada said good-bye to me and how I thought it strange that she needed to see me in person. But now it made sense. It was just another thread in the weaving of this magical pattern.

"Marlo, is this their son?" Lucinda asked, louder this time.

"Yes, yes," I answered, snapping back to the present moment.

"This is simply amazing. I mean, words can't describe what I'm feeling." Lucinda cupped her face in her hands.

"You okay, honey? You're not still carrying a torch for this hunk, are you?" Bea stroked her new friend's hair.

"NO! I'm elated for him. It's just the timing. Well, again amazing, now there's even more to process about our connections."

"Wait until Thomas hears about this he's going to be shocked. And Nina, wait until she hears, she'll never believe this one."

"Who the heck's Nina?" Bea raised her brows.

"She's my friend and sister-in-law. She lives on the east coast."

"Does anyone else know a Nina on the east coast?" Maddie shook her head around.

"No," Lucinda said.

"Not me," Bea replied.

"Me neither. Okay, no weird connections there," Maddie teased.

"You're a real jokester. Anyway, this is a lot to take in for one evening," I sighed.

"This night is full of surprises. So, Marlo, let's not stop here. It's your turn. What would you like to share before we say goodnight?" Lucinda asked in an exhausted but inquisitive tone.

"Me? Uh, I'm good. I had my fill. I think it's a wrap."

Just as the words left my lips, someone from the Spirit world stood behind Lucinda.

"Oh boy!" I exclaimed.

"What?" she wanted to know.

"Now?" I mumbled under my breath.

"Who are you talking to?" Lucinda demanded.

"Someone from the Spirit world."

"Really?" she asked, tilting her head.

"Really," I answered, nodding my head up and down.

"I don't believe this game. You're teasing us," Maddie said, hopefully.

"No, I'm not teasing." I was just about to relay Lucinda's message when another spirit came in. It was the woman from the beach, Maddie's Aunt.

"Give it to her, she can take it," Maddie cackled, having no idea what else I saw and what was about to happen.

I looked to Lucinda's guide, then Maddie's. I was told to talk to Lucinda first.

"Come on, what's happening, tell her," Maddie ordered nervously.

"Lucinda, I have a message from your brother."

Lucinda smiled. She picked up a glass and poured some water into it. "Okay. I'm ready."

"Wait! Where is he?" Maddie asked.

"Carl's in heaven," Lucinda stated earnestly. I smiled.

"He is what?" Maddie shuttered. "I thought you were twisting our leg. You mean you really can hear and see and…?"

"Yep. People who have passed away, they talk to me."

Lucinda threw her hands up as if genuinely saying *of course you can talk to people in heaven.*

"Holy Toledo!" Bea said excitedly. "I actually thought you were playing too."

"No, it's real. But I know how you feel. When I was a teenager I buried this gift because people ridiculed me. I lost friends and was even banned from some of their houses. It's taken years to overcome the stigma. I've learned to speak my truth because, in my heart, I always knew it was a gift from God."

"That's noteworthy," Bea said. "So what happens when you see the people?"

"They hover behind a loved one, then talk to me. Sometimes I can see them, but mostly I feel and hear them. All they want is for me to relay a message. It's a way for them to make contact, giving their loved-ones hope that they're still with them. Then they drift away."

Lucinda's brother was waiting for me to acknowledge him again. His clarity was getting stronger.

"I'm intrigued," Bea rattled on. "I've seen TV shows about this but have never personally known someone who can talk to the other side."

"Hey, guys, can you be quiet for a minute." Lucinda insisted as nicely as possible.

"Your brother Carl, he tells me that he and your father are together." Lucinda smiled. "Your father loves you very much. He's standing behind your brother."

"There are two?" Maddie cringed.

I raised my hand, holding off any more interruptions.

"Your father isn't going to talk to me, only Carl. I see your father holding a big fat orange and white cat. They've been watching over you for many years."

"Oh Lord, it's my childhood cat."

"Your brother tells me to remind you about how much fun you guys had playing Monopoly and how he always bought all the train stations."

She sighed heavily. "I felt him that day, on his birthday. I knew it!"

"He says yes. And you still have one of the cards from the game in a keepsake box. Carl wants you to begin writing your life story. He says it will be healing for you and also for many others who've had similar experiences."

I took a long slow breath and tightened my core muscles to stay strong and connected with 'me.' Then I continued: "He says his favorite candy is Snickers, and you and he used to save your allowances to buy a bar. He says not to worry so much about what other people think, but rather pay more attention to how you feel and stay true to your ideals."

Carl's spirit faded, followed by Lucinda's father and the cat, until they were no longer in the room. Lucinda's eyes smiled with tears. I took several calming breaths, and drank some water.

"I'm mesmerized." Bea blotted her sniffles with her handkerchief.

"That was so bizarre," Maddie said. "You sure they're not still here?"

"They aren't, but someone else is."

"Now who?"

"I was told you are ready," I said, looking at Maddie.

"Ready for what?" she turned pale.

"It's your aunt. She's here."

"Who-oo. Mm-my aunt?"

"Yes. Her name is Anna or Anita."

"Etana!" she said robotically.

"That's it," I confirmed. "She tells me that she loves you very much, and she's been watching over you since you and Howie hooked-up." Maddie gulped so loud we could hear her swallow. "She was the one with you at the condo, umm, in the bathroom. And in the woods with the hawk."

"Oh my gosh! I knew it!"

"No wait, she was a hawk, yeah, yeah, she was the hawk. Um, she hears your prayers, and helps you work through things or watches others guide you, like, um saints, yes, saints."

"You are hearing her say this?" Maddie asked, looking white as a ghost.

"Yes. Wait. Hold on. She knows you'll get through this transition with Howie, and asks you to remember your strength, your inner strength, and don't be afraid to be powerful."

I took a long breath and sighed. Aunt Etana left, echoing words of thanks to me and laughing, *I told you I'd be back when she felt safe.*

"She's gone," I said.

"She's gone?" Maddie asked.

"Yup. That's it."

Maddie became quiet.

"Thank you, Marlo," Lucinda said. "These tears are tears of joy. I feel my brother and my father around me a lot. You simply confirmed what I have suspected for years and I'm really happy to hear they're together with my furry friend. As far as the writing thing, that will take some consideration."

"You're welcome and thanks for being open to his message. I would feel sad to see our friendship end because of what I just revealed about myself."

"Silly girl, our friendship is just beginning."

"Or maybe it's a continuation from another lifetime," Bea declared.

"That would explain our speedy friendship," Maddie said, with more color in her face.

"This is a lot to digest in one evening," Lucinda said. "But God doesn't give us more than we can handle!"

We did the bobbing thing again with our heads. I thought about the cute little bobble-head toys you put in your car window. We were them!

"Girls, it's been rosy, but I need to get up early in the morning for work," Bea twanged.

"Wait! I also have some news!" Lucinda added.

"Of course! Beg my pardon."

"Give me a minute," Lucinda requested.

"I'm hanging on a chandelier here," the southern bell said sweetly, exaggerating her plea.

"Go easy, Bea," Maddie said firmly. "She just got some intense news from heaven."

"Thanks, Maddie. I'm fine. It's just that I really didn't have intentions of telling anyone yet," Lucinda paused and thought about something. "Okay, okay, I'm pregnant!"

She bounced up and down. We joined her, celebrating in what seemed like the game we played as kids, 'ring around the rosy.'

"The day at the beach you knew!" she whispered to me. I just shrugged my shoulders.

After we settled down from this great news, we set a date to meet again in two weeks. Then Lucinda, Bea, and Maddie grabbed their books and headed to the front door.

"What's this pretty book?" Bea asked, looking at my greeting card 'idea journal' laying on the table by the front door. She leafed through the pages of sketches I had been given by Castlemark's artist.

"That's my workbook for this month. I'm three-quarters of the way through. I write poems to go with these images for greeting cards. I don't usually let anyone see it until it's done."

"Well, now that we've established we're all sistahs, so to speak, you wouldn't mind if I took a little peek, would you?"

I was a little thrown by her interest, especially since she had said she was tired and ready to head home. "Oh, what the hey."

As Bea grinned in triumph, a sketch fell out of the journal. She turned it over. It was a beautiful monarch butterfly.

"Another freakin' butterfly!" Maddie declared. We all laughed.

Lucinda responded, "You know, this is another sign. Bea, I think you're supposed to write a poem to go with this picture."

Before I could protest, Bea grabbed a pen off the table and scribbled some lines on a blank page. Then she put the butterfly drawing back between the pages and firmly closed the book.

"Hope you like it!" Bea proclaimed, quickly opening the front door and rushing out. Maddie and Lucinda followed in her wake.

Before I could look at what Bea had written, mysteriously enough and ever so appropriately a train whistle blew in the distance.

It was rather comical to watch the trio turn on their heels and freeze. Maddie laughed nervously. Lucinda, Bea, and I just shrugged in surrender. Then we hugged and did the 'happy to have this time with you' dance before they got into the car and drove off.

It had been an extraordinary evening. I looked up to the crescent moon shining in the star-filled sky and gave thanks for so many blessings. I looked forward to journaling about the turn of events, sensing that our synchronous experience might even help me create a greeting card or two. *Maybe what Bea wrote will give me a clue!*

Inside, I checked on Thomas and our four-leggeds. They were snuggly bunnies, watching an old black-and-white flick on television. I kissed my husband good-night and told him I'd be coming to bed soon. He was too tired to talk, he just smiled and sighed.

I got into a pair of pajamas, moseyed into the kitchen and made a spot of tea. Brother and Sister followed me while Momma stayed with her daddy. Patchouli and Sirius came in, meowing for some food. I fed them in their favorite spot, the large walk-in pantry, free from canine food snatchers.

I grabbed my laptop and the tea and went out to the back yard. The solar lamps illuminated the area. I suddenly felt compelled to work on my novel.

While the two dogs anxiously sniffed around, I settled down on a white Adirondack chair with a swing-arm writing board and opened the computer to my book "Invisible Flowers."

I said a prayer to God and my writing team, asking for guidance, simplicity and continued direction for my highest health and the highest health of others. The words poured out. My typing speed couldn't keep pace with my creativity.

Finally, I took a break and gave my hands a rest. I ended my writing session by saying a prayer of thanks for the gift of pen. While massaging my fingers and looking up at the stars, I reflected that the way we women had met was very deep on many levels. But the reasoning was simple: four women can be mirrors to one another, reflecting truths of how we tick on this trek called human life.

As for my recurring dream, the one where I'm rushing down the train aisle looking for someone, well, my new friends indeed revealed who I was searching for, it was me. I was looking for my true authentic self. Mom will be happy to hear my revelation, which I'm sure she already knows.

Overall I was content with solving of the mystery of our connection. Then I thought about the train ticket and wondered if by chance any of them still had theirs. I would ask them at the next book club gathering. Not only would we be reading a new chapter in 'The 440 Train,' but it would also be a new chapter for each of us, four forty-something women who are obviously still learning some of life's greatest lessons with the men who connected us and now with each other.

As much as I proved the Universe does assist us on our journey, we also have the wonderful gift of Free Will, which is what connects us to all things. And the train whistle was definitely symbolic as a soulful sound that signifies change. It made me feel like a butterfly emerging from my cocoon.

Then it hit me, it isn't so much that I'm a passenger on a train moving through Life, but rather <u>I am the Train</u>. Where it takes me, or any of us, is always our choice and the destination is yet to be revealed.

All Aboard!

The End – or is it The Beginning?

ABOUT THE AUTHOR

Linda Colucci has been writing poetry and short stories for four decades. This is her debut novel. A second book in 'The 440 Train' series is in the works. She lives in California with her husband and four-legged kids.

To find out more visit: www.the440 train.com